ONE THING
LEADING TO ANOTHER

Sylvia Townsend Warner

ONE THING
LEADING TO ANOTHER
and Other Stories

SELECTED AND EDITED BY
SUSANNA PINNEY

VIKING

VIKING
Viking Penguin Inc.,
40 West 23rd Street,
New York, New York 10010, U.S.A.

First American Edition
Published in 1984

LIBRARY OF CONGRESS CATALOGING IN PUBLICATION DATA
Warner, Sylvia Townsend, 1893–1978
One thing leading to another.
I. Title.
PR6045.A812O5   1984   823′.912   84-40066
ISBN 0-670-74990-7

Printed in the United States of America
Set in Ehrhardt

CONTENTS

EDITOR'S NOTE
AND ACKNOWLEDGEMENTS

The stories in this volume, as in *Scenes of Childhood and Other Stories*, are a personal selection from ones not previously collected in book form. Some were originally published in magazines, but others have never appeared in print before.

I would like to acknowledge the magazines that originally published stories in this collection. *The New Yorker* (and its editor William Maxwell) for 'The Proper Circumstances' (1944), 'A View of Exmoor' (1948), 'Mr Mackenzie's Last Hour' (1949), 'One Thing Leading to Another' (1962), 'Some Effects of a Hat' (1963), 'The Three Cats' (1964), 'A Saint (Unknown) with Two Donors' (1965), 'A Pair of Duelling Pistols' (1968), 'Sopwith Hall' (1969), 'The Duke of Orkney's Leonardo' (1976), and 'A Widow's Quilt' (1977); *Lilliput* for 'A Breaking Wave' (1948); and *Housewife* for 'The Mother Tongue' (1948).

'Some Effects of a Hat' was directly inspired by an experience described in a letter written by Sylvia Townsend Warner to George Plank on 12 September 1962 and included in *Letters of Sylvia Townsend Warner*, edited by William Maxwell and published by Chatto & Windus and The Viking Press in 1982. The letter is quoted in full on pages 64–65, and precedes the story it inspired.

I would like to express my gratitude to Norah Smallwood, Carmen Callil and Jeremy Lewis for their generous help and advice.

Susanna Pinney

ONE THING
LEADING TO ANOTHER

A SAINT (UNKNOWN)
WITH TWO DONORS

Mr Edom, who kept the Abbey Antique Galleries, was a man of punctuality. He had other neat virtues, too, such as discretion and probity; but it was his punctuality he took pride in and found positively enjoyable. When Mr Collins came on trial as assistant, Mr Edom laid it down as law that when he said 'precisely' he meant 'precisely'. In the course of four years' growing affection Mr Collins observed that in his zeal not to be late Mr Edom was invariably too early, and that 'precisely' could be anything up to a quarter of an hour.

At eight-thirty precisely – that is to say, about eight-seventeen – Mr Edom would leave his lodgings, walk along St John Street, and let himself into the Galleries, where Mr Collins was expected to appear ten minutes later. This interval of solitude was a sort of matins to Mr Edom. He had a look round, recollected himself, and prepared his mind for the day. As for Mrs Knowles, the cleaner, being a family woman she could not be there reliable till five minutes to nine. On Saturdays she could not come in the morning at all but obliged for an hour in the evening, during which time Police Constable Davenport, who was her second cousin, made it a point to be within earshot, in case a burglar broke in and set off that bloodcurdling burglar alarm, the very sound of which made her ready to faint dead away.

The morning Mr Edom and Mr Collins were destined to remember as 'that morning' was a fine September morning, and St John Street was looking its best. The trim house fronts, the empty pavements, the spire of St John's Church – considered by many as even finer than the Abbey's – a blue sky, and one well-placed cumulus cloud made up a delightful picture. Mr Edom was looking at the spire, which, because it soared above rites classed as Low, and because incense made him sneeze and sneezing made him feel conspicuous, he had strong reason to prefer, when a jackdaw's swoop carried his sight downward to

3

observe that two men were standing in front of his shop door. Beside them was a handcart, and on the handcart was a bulky object, muffled in sacking.

As he approached, the larger of the two men looked round, saw him, and nudged the other.

'Are you Mr Edom?' inquired the smaller man.

'I am.'

The larger man said reproachfully, 'We thought you was never coming.'

Nettled by this imputation against his punctuality, Mr Edom took an instant dislike to them both, and said coldly, 'Well?'

'We've been here this last half hour,' said the smaller man.

'More,' said the other.

'Why?'

'We've brought something along.'

'What?' Mr Edom, chafing on his own threshold, could vouchsafe only monosyllables.

'Well, in a manner of speaking, it's a throwout. His Reverence—'

'Who?'

'Father Brady. He threw it out – because of it getting into his new kneelers. But seeing as it's what you might call an antique, we thought we'd begin by bringing it along to you. Here, Jim. You undo it. Handle it careful, though.'

Looking more attentively at the two men, Mr Edom thought he'd seen Jim before, unloading sacks of potatoes in the market.

'Careful round that elbow, Jim! Easy does it. It's not as young as it was.'

Neither were the sacks, which stank. Mr Edom stepped back. 'I don't want to see it, whatever it is.' But it was too late; the last wrapping was pulled away. Standing on the cart was a life-sized matronly lady in an ecstasy. At the same moment, Mr Collins, speaking from behind him, exclaimed, 'Good Lord! There's Baroque for you! High Baroque at that. Where would you say she came from? She looks Italian to me.'

'If you ask my opinion,' said the smaller man, 'she's an antique. That is, judging by the weight.'

Jim agreed, adding that those wormholes weren't made yesterday.

4

Mr Edom remarked that some of them were.

'But where did you find her? How did she get here?' asked the besotted Collins.

'We brought her along from St Philomena's. We delivered a load of kneelers there last night, and Father Brady said he was throwing her out and we was to come round early this morning to fetch her away.'

With uncalled-for initiative Mr Collins was now tapping the lady, and pronouncing that she wasn't past praying for and that it would be quite possible to do something about her nose. 'It's odd how noses go first,' he mused.

The men were folding up the sacks. Miss Larpent, leading her spaniel for its morning walk, came past. The spaniel shrank back and barked violently. Violently, Miss Larpent dragged it onward.

'It's wormed all through. It's out of the question,' said Mr Edom. 'I'm sorry, but you must take it somewhere else. Come, Collins.'

As though they were both called Collins, the men began to lift the lady off the handcart.

'Stop! I tell you, I don't want her. Kindly take her away.'

By now they were supporting her in midair, while Mr Collins, who had obligingly gone down on his knees in answer to Jim's request to give her a shove up, mate, appeared to be in the act of adoration. Miss Larpent, pausing, had been joined by Mrs Toller and old Miss Palk, out with their poodles. Three schoolboys stood gaping. So did the milkman. In another moment, a mob would gather.

'Have a heart!' exclaimed the larger man. The boys cheered the sentiment. The dogs barked. Mrs Knowles, coming briskly round the corner, cannonaded into Miss Larpent, said, 'Beg your pardon, I'm sure,' in a tone more befitting extortion with menaces, and rushed on to the defence of her employer – as nice a gentleman as ever trod, but too meekhearted for his own good. Mr Edom, barring the way into the Galleries, shouted, 'Take her round by the back! Collins! Show them where to go. Leave her in the yard, mind. I won't have her indoors.'

'What about paying?' mouthed Mr Collins, and was told to settle with them somehow. A less temperate employer might well have left Mr Collins to settle out of his own pocket, but when Mr Collins came back, furtively brushing his sleeves, Mr Edom asked how much it had taken, learned that they had gone for fifteen shillings apiece, and paid without comment. It had to be admitted that Collins kept a steady head for bargaining – if for nothing else.

But Mr Edom was still angry. Things had got out of hand. He had been rushed. Collins had taken too much on himself. It would be another Majolica Swan. The majolica swan, rescued by Mr Collins from a house of ill fame, had eventually been bought with enthusiasm by a doe-eyed lady from London, who featured it in an article in *Country Life*; but in the interim it had caused Mr Edom acute embarrassment – its eye was so horribly knowing and its plumage so pink. Meanwhile, it was already past nine o'clock and he had not even opened his letters. 'The whole morning gone!' he muttered to himself. This was overheard, as he had intended it to be, by Mr Collins. But it fell on deaf ears. Mr Collins could think of nothing but how soon he could get into the yard and have another look at his love, his nonpareil, his princess snatched from Saracens. Young men traditionally fall in love with mature women. Mr Collins was madly in love with his matron in ecstasy and believed she was a Bernini.

His wish was answered sooner than he dared expect. Though thirty shillings is not a great sum, one can't disburse it without feeling some degree of interest in what one has got in exchange. 'That figure,' said Mr Edom in a dispassionate voice, 'that image, that whatever you call her – I suppose we ought to have a look at her. Mrs Knowles will call us if anyone comes in.'

Secluded in the yard, the lady looked even more commandingly rapt and enskied. A fine figure of a woman, and further extended by her state of ecstasy, she was as tall as Mr Collins, and considerably taller than Mr Edom. She had been put down with a jolt. There were trickles of yellowish powder on the stones, and more lay in the folds of her draperies. 'When I was a youngster, I'd have been set to go into every one of those holes with a needle and paraffin wax,' said Mr Edom.

'You learned the hard way,' Mr Collins said.

'I did.'

They walked round her once more.

'They've let her go too far,' said Mr Edom. 'Mind you, it's not a style I'm in sympathy with. But when you think what a lot of work someone must have put into her, it seems a shame, I must say.'

'Do you know what the small man told me? He told me that Father Brady said if they would take her off his hands they were welcome to whatever they could get selling her for kindling.'

'She's too wormed to be any good as kindling.'

Once more they walked round the lady. Mr Edom gave her a smart tap on the bosom and said, 'T'cha!' There was reproach in his tone, but there was regret, too. 'Of course we could kill the worm. Any fool can kill worm nowadays – I'll say that for those scientific chaps. But suppose we stop it? What are we to do with her then?'

'Put her in the Galleries.'

'I thought you'd say that. But what about my good name, Collins? Haven't I made it a rule never to sell anything with a trace of worm? Only last month you saw me turn down those Trafalgar chairs. I could have sold them a dozen times over, but I wouldn't look at them. So what are people going to say when they come in and find this?'

'Religious art's different. People who won't stand two wormholes in a sideboard wouldn't look at a saint without them. Give them wormholes and you give them something for their imagination to play on.'

'People are fools enough for anything,' said Mr Edom. The condemnation, however, seemed to afford him a secret pleasure; it was as though he were about to burst into some after-dinner confidence. He repressed it, and glared stonily before him. 'There's one thing, and that's flat. Before you lay as much as a finger on her, Collins, I'm going to make sure Father Brady doesn't think I'm by way of buying his throwouts. No misunderstandings on that score. Yes, Mrs Knowles?'

'There's an old party picking up wineglasses. Name like Periscope.'

Identifying a familiar customer, Mr Edom re-entered the Galleries, saying, 'Good morning, Mrs Killigrew.' Mrs Killigrew, as usual, was finding it hard to make up her mind. Mr Edom, most unusually, found himself in the same predicament. Should he? Shouldn't he? And if he should, what was the right word? That acknowledgement of the victory of science over woodworm had tweaked his thoughts toward other fumigations. Had the lady in an ecstasy been, so to speak, dealt with before she was thrown out? The word wasn't likely to be 'excommunicated', and 'decontaminated' seemed needlessly injurious. But had she been dealt with? Did remnants of sanctity still lurk about her; was she still part of the Roman Catholic Church? He was not a superstitious

7

man.

Mrs Killigrew was still unable to decide whether a fitted workbox wasn't after all what she would rather buy than the six engraved wineglasses she really needed, when a dealer named Smollet, trading in London under the name of Roderick Random, came in for a look round. He was followed by Miss Larpent, who said, looking rather wild and hard-pressed, that she wanted – now, what was the name? Yes! An egg timer – one of those nice old-fashioned things where you stood the sand upside down; and consoled herself, when told there wasn't one, by helping Mrs Killigrew make up her mind. The pursuit of something Mrs Killigrew might want even more had got her into the back of the Galleries and poking behind a scrapwork screen, in case the morning's marvel was there, when a couple of Swedes came in, both enormously tall, magnificently muscular, and speaking perfect English. What they wanted was Art Nouveau hatpins. Mr Edom was prepared for this craze. Under the bulging eyes of Miss Larpent he unlocked a drawer and produced two Celtic bosses and a blister-pearl snail on an ivy leaf – and made a nice little profit on the transaction, having bought them off a white-elephant stall for eighteenpence apiece. The Swedes, their passion satisfied, marched out; presently Mrs Killigrew, the wineglasses, and Miss Larpent were gone, too. Mr Edom drew Smollet aside for a quiet cigarette. Smollet was a pleasant, conversable fellow, who took the vagaries of the antique trade with philosophy. Of late, he had specialized in paintings, so Mr Edom inquired, 'How are Landseers?' and heard that they were getting a bit too pricey but that Smollet had been uncommonly lucky with an Augustus Egg. Rosa Bonheur, too, was worth attention. And religious art, asked Mr Edom, how was that doing? 'Do you do much with fumed-oak suites?' replied Smollet. 'Mrs Salt says she's buying Overbecks. Well, she can afford to. A woman must have her whim. But I haven't heard that she's sold one. As for anything larger than you can keep in your pocket for a pet, it's doornails. You can't even sell it to churches now – not since that chap Picasso went off on chapels. That's what started the rot.' Mr Edom looked at Mr Collins, who was tidying up after Mrs Killigrew and not even needing to pretend he wasn't listening. Thinking of his wormy idol, he moved with a swelling port, and smirked.

Smollet, as politeness bid, was praising the unspeculative, irreproachable classicism of Mr Edom's stock, and assuring him he had chosen the better part, when the telephone rang. Mr Collins answered it. A high-pitched gusty yell surged into the Galleries. Mr Collins turned pale, said, 'It's Father Brady,' and handed the receiver, still gustily resounding, to Mr Edom, who, holding it away from his ear and speaking with exasperating calm, said, 'Indeed' and 'By all means' and 'Any time that suits Your Reverence' and finally, 'The sooner the better.' In the electric pause that followed, Smollet announced that he must be going, but would look in again next month, and was gone.

Mr Edom turned to his assistant. 'Collins, what exactly did you say to those men in the yard?'

'I'm afraid I called Father Brady a Vandal – because they didn't know what Goth meant. I also said he was an ignoramus, and didn't know a work of art from a boiled potato, and that I hoped his kneelers would choke him. I'm afraid I went too far.'

'Not at all, not at all.'

'If you want me to, I'll apologize.'

'No, no. But leave the rest to me. Let's see, now – which would be the best chair for him? I think we'll put him in the bergère.'

The bergère was squat. Father Brady, accustomed to using every inch of his commanding stature, was reduced to glaring out over his knees.

'Now then,' he demanded, 'what's all this hullabaloo about?'

Mr Edom looked at him inquiringly.

'I haven't come here to quarrel, mind you,' Father Brady went on. 'I'm a man of peace. But I've been hearing this, and I've been hearing that, till I'm perfectly bejingled. And I mean to stay till I've got to the bottom of it.'

'I'm always pleased to see people come in. No obligation to buy.'

Mr Collins started at hearing his Mr Edom, who spoke as an equal to Smollets and Roebecks, assume this grovelling, commercial tone. Father Brady started, too – apprehensively – and muttered something about looking in nearer Christmas. There followed a long pause, during which Christmas, though imperceptibly, drew nearer. 'There's being too much talk altogether,' Father Brady said. 'Odious, harmful talk.'

He spoke feelingly, because he spoke of his own sufferings. It had begun with the milkman, who while delivering milk at the presbytery told the housekeeper that he had witnessed Jim Ensor and Herb Lake offering to sell a statue to Mr Edom and boasting they had got it out of St Philomena's. Quelling this alarm ruined his breakfast. His ears were still ringing with his housekeeper's assurances that even if Jim Ensor and Herb Lake had not in this instance committed a larceny it was only natural to conclude that they had, since their characters were notorious, and everybody knew how Dorothy Ensor and – to her shame be it spoken – Mrs Patsy Wendover feasted on early peas and the first asparagus filched from the market under the noses of honest customers who couldn't afford such delicacies, so sacrilege would be nothing to that pair, when the pair in question were back with their handcart, offering to remove anything else His Reverence wanted to get rid of. It was from Lake, venting his spleen at being told there was nothing more for them, that he heard how the assistant had described him as a scandal, an ignoramus, and a boiled potato. Scandal was a thing to be avoided at all costs; but before he could see what avoiding action could be taken Miss Palk was upon him, roaring that the statue had been at St Philomena's even in her mother's day and had always been known to be immensely valuable; and that if nobody else would act with a vestige of Christian feeling she would drag it away from Mr Edom with her own hands, to teach him and his ruffianly hirelings they couldn't steal church property unresisted, even if they did get up before sunrise to do so. She was still declaiming, and the poodle was barking at the presbytery cat, and the housekeeper, who had arrived to defend the cat, was remaining to explain to Miss Palk how the whole affair was a plot to scandalize His Reverence's name – Herb Lake had out and out confessed it, and for Herb Lake to tell the truth was something so out of the common that you needs must believe him when he did – when the milkman's sister came rushing in with the news that the Jews were after it already; there were three of them in the Galleries smoking cigars with Mr Edom, and a Jaguar two doors farther down, with tiger-skin upholstery and a bloodhound on the back seat. Father Brady had flown for shelter to St Philomena's, where, secluding himself in a confessional, he had prayed violently to Our Lady Help of Christians to be kept in charity with all men. But when he crept out, his housekeeper was waiting for him, and rubbed so much salt and sympathy into his wounds that by the time he rang up the Abbey Antique Galleries he was as angry as anyone could wish.

Unfortunately, he had set out with such impetus that he had not arranged his anger under headings. So now he repeated that there had been too much talk.

Mr Edom nodded gravely, and contrived, Mr Collins noticed, to look as though he were Father Brady's bishop, who hoped to temper justice with mercy but at present couldn't see his way to.

'I'm a busy man,' Father Brady said. 'And the parish, praise God, is growing by leaps and bounds, without a whisper of a curate. So let me tell you in plain words, I've neither time nor patience for being scandalized and slandered.'

Mr Edom held up a hand for silence, and said in silvery tones, 'I was afraid this would happen. I and my assistant did our best. But we were too late. There were people about. The statue was on the handcart, exposed to public gaze. It was bound to create remark. And the language of the two porters was injudicious. They shouldn't have used the expression "thrown out by His Reverence".'

'And haven't I a perfect right to throw her out?'

'As to that, I can't say.'

'It was alive with the worm.'

'Shockingly so. It must have been neglected for years. But the expression "thrown out by His Reverence" should never have been used. As I said, we did all in our power to avert scandal. But it was too late. No one,' said the bishop feelingly, 'regrets the incident more than I. Mr Collins, my assistant, will bear me out.'

'It was the irreverence,' confirmed the chaplain, 'that was so awful. She might have been a carcass of beef, the way they hauled her about.'

The accents of truth often miscarry. These did. Father Brady said with a snort, 'Well, we're used to being blamed for worshipping images. Now it seems we're as bad if we don't. There's no pleasing you.' And feeling that he had got the last word, he scrambled out of the bergère. The interview had not gone as he had intended. He had been out-generalled, though he could not see how; but being in the main a sensible man, he admitted a defeat and sensibly went away to think about something else.

It was expected that the Helen of all this rumpus would figure in the window immediately. When she did not, it was taken as proof that the Jews had got her, that she had been bought for the nation, that Mr Edom, having stolen her, was afraid to exhibit her, that he was warming his toes at her on these chilly September evenings.

'Take your time,' Mr Edom had said to his assistant, fending off the horrid hour of her reappearance. Mr Collins obeyed. There was a disused privy in the yard, and this he converted into a fumigating chamber and gave his darling three separate doings. Then he aired her, to get some of the smell out. Then he brushed her. Then he restored her nose with plastic wood, and did a few small repairs to her draperies, and coloured the renovations to match the rest of her. Then he oiled her all over, and left the oil to sink in; and repeated the process. Then he wax-polished her. Even when all this was done, her complexion had a bleached, hungry look, so he went to the beauty shop in Abbey Circus and bought eyeshade of various tints, grease paints, dry rouge, and a *basané* face powder. His first attempts were too dramatic and had to be removed with cotton batting; but by delicately dabbing on, wiping off, and judging the effects from a distance he achieved his intention: which was to suggest that in her High Baroque youth she had been coloured, and retained traces of it. Mr Edom, disapproving but engaged, recommended a final application of selected grime and a faint streak of cobalt in a fold of her draperies, together with a judicious ageing of her profile by sandpapering.

The horrid hour had come. Somehow or other, he must reconcile himself to having her in the Galleries. At the last moment, he saw a chink of hope and generously suggested that Mr Collins might like to keep her in his lodgings, for private enjoyment. It didn't work. Mr Collins's first pure passion had been corrupted by the ostentation of the creator; he had done such a good job on her that he wanted to see it appreciated. Vowing that never again would he give Collins his head, Mr Edom helped to carry her into the Galleries. This was on a Friday evening, after closing hours. They moved her from place to place; they tried her in front of the scrapwork screen, behind the day bed, beside the harp. Wherever they tried her, she appeared aggressively human. 'The only thing to do,' said Mr Edom at length, 'is to sky her. Get the stepladder, and we'll hoist her on top of the court cupboard.' Skied, she seemed to settle down. Mr Collins admitted this, though he wished the court cupboard were not in a corner, and an ill-lit one at that.

'I suppose she'll be noticed, up there.'

'Bound to be.'

On Saturday evening Mr Edom was roused from his Madeira and walnuts by P.C. Davenport. P.C. Davenport had been proceeding down St John Street when his ear was caught by a loud scream coming from the Galleries. Making a forcible entry and thereby setting off the burglar alarm, he had found Mrs Knowles in a crouching position under a table, uninjured but hysterical. She had been tidying round as usual, she stated, when she looked up and saw something right over her, as large as a stuffed bear. P.C. Davenport put this down to imagination; he had not been able to see anything like a bear. But Mrs Knowles being so upset, he had thought it best to take her straight home before coming to report.

Even in panic flight, Mrs Knowles had broken nothing. Formally introduced to the matron in an ecstasy, and admitting that, on a steadier view, the likeness to a bear was fanciful, she continued to assert that if she were to come in on Saturdays she must bring Doris with her. Doris was as sensible as if she were a grown girl; she would finger nothing, provided she had a toffee apple to occupy her mind. But if Doris did not finger, she must have exhaled, for she left tidemarks of stickiness.

Doris was not all Mr Edom had to contend with. There was also Miss Palk. Miss Palk had constituted herself a sort of recording sacristan. Whenever she saw strangers in the Galleries (and as her flat was almost immediately opposite, she had every opportunity to do so), she would appear at their elbow and draw their attention to the immensely valuable and ancient statue from St Philomena's – though now, alas, it didn't look at all the same, her dear mother would have been hard put to it to recognize the object of her special devotion. This would not have helped sell the figure, even if anyone had shown signs of buying it; but no one had, except a lady from the north, in tweeds with diamonds, who said there ought to be a Fund for buying back what should never have been torn from its rightful church, and how willingly she would support it if there were. Why didn't Miss Palk insist on a collecting box being kept in the shop? It was the least the proprietor could do. Knowledgeable visitors commented on the unaccommodating particularity of baroque – it just didn't Mix. The more frivolous complained that somehow or other they had got sticky. Children asked who that lady was, and if she could be wound up to play tunes. But Mr Edom's familiar and valued customers said nothing and looked elsewhere, except for Mrs Otter, who with a flash of her old spirit said she loved Mr Edom's fallen Elizabeth Fry.

By now it was November. The mists from the Abbey water meadows crept through the town in a medieval way, as though they carried pestilence. Noises were loud and ungainly, for there was no resilience in the air. Shoes were plastered with dead leaves. A death sweat came out on anything French-polished. Mrs Knowles said it would be a green Christmas and we all knew what came of that. She glanced at Mr Edom as she spoke. Though deaths in general are enjoyable, she would be sorry to see Mr Edom fattening a churchyard; and it looked to her as though he were not what he was. To Mr Edom it looked as though his shop were not what it was. Apart from hauntings by Doris and Miss Palk, it had lost tone. The wrong people were coming in, and far too many of them. They bargained, they jostled, they damaged; they didn't appreciate what they bought, but said it would do for Christmas presents. Ever since the ecstatic lady's advent, the Galleries had been going down – as neighbourhoods do when the Irish get in. She was a false note, like disproportioned sin, like the Majolica Swan. He smiled grimly when he remembered debating with himself on that fatal morning whether she ought to be unfrocked – which wasn't the word either. A dozen exorcisms would have made no difference. He had no one but himself to blame. He should never have given way. He knew at the time he should have spurned her.

He was scrupulous not to say a word of reproach to Mr Collins. Mr Collins felt the scruples, and would have preferred reproaches, as he could have called them unjustified. It seemed to him that if Mr Edom could be got to take an interest in the lady on the court cupboard he might then become reconciled to her. Trying to arouse this interest he said one morning, when hope was predominating over experience, that as Christmas was coming, why not move her down into the window and make a feature of her? They could corroborate her with the coffin stool and one or two folios; these would be in keeping – at any rate, their bindings would be. Mr Edom replied that he could do as he pleased.

There was a letter in Mr Edom's hand. It was from Smollet, to say that if the slate-topped chess table was still about he would like it, and that he would look in during the afternoon. Thank God, Collins couldn't get her down singlehanded. Though it was inevitable that Smollet should notice her, at least she would be decently on high.

Smollet noticed her with his first flicking glance; but he said nothing, though his glance had several times reverted, and presently dwelled. Inevitably, Miss Palk tripped in, and began her recital. 'I really must introduce myself. I am one of her admirers, too. I have known her since I was a wee child, when my mother, who was an expert wood carver herself, told me –'

'Now *where* have I seen you before?' murmured Smollet, gazing upward.

'At St Philomena's, at St Philomena's! It's so tragic that she isn't there any longer. We all miss her dreadfully. But she looked far more beautiful there. She's never been quite the same since.'

'Not so long ago, either,' continued Smollet. 'Was it in Bavaria, last year? Or in Luxembourg, on my way back from Aix?'

'Oh, but she's been in St Philomena's ever since my mother –'

'I've got it!' Smollet snapped his fingers, and turned to Mr Edom. 'She's one of the Nine Muses in the Prince-Bishop's theatre at Dudelsacker. Quite a fair copy, too, except for the nose. Whoever put that nose on can't have seen the original article, where it's turned up. That's what foxed me.'

'But . . . but . . .'

Becoming aware of Miss Palk foaming beside him, he gave her a slight pat, and said firmly, 'You ought to go to Dudelsacker.'

Silently, Mr Edom offered him a cigar.

'Thank you. I will. But fancy seeing her here! How did you come by her, Edom? She's not quite in your usual line.'

'It's a long story,' said Mr Edom glancing toward Miss Palk.

After she'd gone, they sat down and he told it. It did him a great deal of good; and as he dilated on Mr Collins' discerning eye and restoring hand, it didn't do Mr Collins any harm. Smollet stood on the stepladder to look more carefully into the restorations. He laughed, but there was technical admiration in his laugh. 'You ought to be in London with me,' he remarked. 'You're wasted down here with the only honest dealer in England.'

'I couldn't do without him,' said Mr Edom.

They agreed to dine together, and Smollet promised to send down his photographs of the Prince-Bishop's Muses, so that Mr Collins could do another nose.

The photographs came. The lady went back to the workshop. Since she never reappeared in the Galleries, it became certain that the Jews had got her. The new nose threw a completely new light on her character, releasing a pagan complacency and elation. No longer an embarrassment to Mr Edom, no longer a Bernini to Mr Collins, no longer a false note, she became, briefly, their private pet. And on Christmas Eve – by which time she had been brightly painted and lavishly gilded – she was taken by car, under a tartan rug, to a Catholic orphanage three counties away. There, in the porch, at 1 A.M. precisely, they left her – a Saint, a Muse and shortly, they hoped, to be as good as a Circus.

A PAIR OF DUELLING PISTOLS

———

'Yes, I see. Take ye in one another's washing.'

Mr Edom had been trying to explain to Mrs Otter why, for professional reasons, he would rather show her duelling pistols to Mrs Vibart, the renowned expert on firearms, than buy them himself. In effect, he had succeeded; she had grasped the central truth. Whether she was aware of what she had grasped was another matter. He had not known Mrs Otter for all these years – of mingled solicitude and exasperated awe – without knowing that she grasped more readily than she attended.

The latest demonstration of Mrs Otter's powers was assembled on his desk: a folding rubber bath, venerably creased and sallow; an equally venerable gibus hat; a massive copy of Foxe's 'Book of Martyrs', five pickle forks, seven kettle holders, a Masonic apron, several flounces of black Maltese lace and a pair of duelling pistols in a rosewood case.

'I simply can't account for their having been in the attic for all these years, for I am constantly in the attic looking for things that might have got there; and you'd think I'd have enough enterprise to poke behind the cistern. But I can be positive they came from my first husband's aunt, who was the last of the Miss MacMahons. She was always buying things at bazaars, when she wasn't selling them. And when they got too much for her she used to send them on to us to be resold in Moses baskets.'

She disentangled a piece of newspaper from the flounces. 'Here you are. The *Northern Whig*. That proves it. She lived in Belfast and used to stand on a balcony saying. "To hell with the Pope!" In fact, that's how she died. Tonsillitis. Goodness, how cheap everything was in the twenties! You could have bought a whole steam laundry in working order for three hundred pounds.'

Mrs Otter fell silent, absorbed in the *Northern Whig*. Mr Collins, the assistant, seized a feather whisk and dusted a crystal chandelier, which jangled.

'So if you approve, Mrs Otter, I will write to Mrs Vibart immediately,' Mr Edom said.

'Mrs Vibart? Mrs Vibart? Oh yes, Mrs Vibart. I knew I'd heard the name; it struck me as sounding so villainous. Yes, do – if you're sure you won't be in any way the worse for it. And of course, love can hurry one into the most extraordinary surnames. I'm Otter. You're sure you don't want any of these other things?'

Mr Edom signified he did not. Mr Collins came forward to help Mrs Otter parcel up the bath, the hat, the apron, the 'Martyrs', the pickle forks, the lace, and the kettle holders. He produced a new sheet of wrapping paper, which crackled under his efficiency, and said repeatedly how glad he would be to take the parcel round that evening. It would be nothing to him. He enjoyed a walk after work. No doubt, thought Mr Edom, George was as anxious as he to be left in peace with the pistols. But he was overdoing his helpfulness. It sounded feverish.

'No, thank you. I can perfectly . . . If you'll just open the . . . Oh! You sweet pet! Mr Edom, there's such a nice buttony little cat on your doorstep. I think it wants to come in.'

Mr Collins, exclaiming 'Shoo!' and 'You're sure you can manage?' and again 'Shoo!,' farewelled Mrs Otter and fended off the cat. In his zeal, he shut himself out and stood on the pavement till he had seen the cat slip through a hole in the yard door. It was a close fit, but he knew she could do it. He had enlarged the hole himself, under the direction of Mrs Knowles the cleaner, who had appealed to him as a man to think what it was like not being able to call your measurements your own. The chorus of infant voices swelled in volume and intensity, then was hushed.

It was all Mrs Knowles' doing. These women, these females, had no sense of the befitting. They are at the mercy of their instincts. There were four kittens, and their voices grew louder daily.

He re-entered the Galleries. Mr Edom was hanging over the pistols. He called to Mr Collins to admire. 'These attics, George. These attics, these box-rooms. People simply don't know what's hidden away under their roofs.'

Mr Collins agreed. And while Mr Edom continued to fondle the pistols, lifting them from the maroon velvet cradles in which they lay so snugly, caressing their ivory butts, expatiating on the workmanship of their case, the exactitude of its hinges, and all in such perfect condition, Mr Collins looked at Mr Edom's trousers. It was profanation even to think of such trousers exposed to kittens who would cover them with hairs. Some dealers – a new school – wore corduroy trousers, knitted pullovers, neckerchiefs, an air of pastoral neglect. Such persons might very well allow cats in their show-rooms – some, in fact, did and made a feature of it. Mrs Althea Budd boasted that she could sell any old saucer by leaving it on the floor with some milk in it, customers being the predatory race they are and always on the lookout for a chance to know better than you do. But Mr Edom's clothes, like his wares, were classical: his waistcoats a breath of the old order, his cravats seemly as collects appointed for Sundays after Trinity. Yet hidden away on this good man's premises was a tortoiseshell cat and four thriving kittens. For the moment, they were quiet, being satiated, but soon they would start their mewing again; and sooner or later Mr Edom must become aware of it. If that very bad cold he caught at old Parker's funeral had not left him slightly deaf, he would have heard them long before.

It was because of the very bad cold that Mr Collins was now the prey of a guilty secret. In Mr Edom's absence (his doctor had kept him at home for a week) Mrs Knowles became conversational.

'Have you seen our Moggie, Mr Collins?'

As she had cleaned the Galleries for over seven years and never broken as much as an item, Mrs Knowles felt herself part of the firm and used the proprietary first-person plural. He looked about him for a Moggie, supposing it was some local term, possibly for a tankard.

'It's ever such a pretty little cat. Taken quite a fancy to us. It's there in the yard every morning when I take out the rubbish. Rubs against me so grateful when I bring its drop of milk, and very partial to kippers. You come and have a look at it.'

It had been early impressed on Mr Collins that Mrs Knowles was above rubies and must not be crossed. He followed her into the yard, where the cat was reposing in a hamper of shavings. She looked plump. No doubt she caught mice.

Unfortunately, the fact that Mrs Knowles was entertaining a cat in Mr Edom's yard made less impression on Mr Collins than that she called it a Moggie and, when questioned, asked what else she should call it. As she mustn't be crossed, he left it at that. A Moggie. Perhaps it was a term for tortoiseshell cats, or for short-haired cats, or even for cats without attachments: Mrs Knowles asserted the cat in the yard had no home of its own, poor thing. Moggie. He consulted the Concise Oxford Dictionary on Mr Edom's desk. There was no 'Moggie' there. He went to the public library and sought the term in books about dialect and books about cats. That evening, he wrote a letter to *The Times*. There was a political crisis, and *The Times* printed his letter, a welcome sprig of ornamental parsley, on the leader page. It drew several answers. One directed him to '*mujer*', the Spanish for 'woman', corrupted to 'Moggie' by the gypsies; another derived it from the Grand Mogul, and said it was applied to Persian cats. Others were quite as ingenious. All the writers agreed in saying that the term 'Moggie' was reserved for she-cats.

He did not realize the force of this till Mrs Knowles asked him to enlarge the hole in the yard door. Even then, he glided onward. Kittens, he knew, were drowned at birth. He would not like to drown a kitten himself, but no doubt Mrs Knowles was conversant with that sort of thing. For all that, he took pains not to be *tête-à-tête* with Mrs Knowles, hiding behind the buttresses of St John's Church or lurking in the tobacconist's till he had seen Mr Edom enter the Galleries. It was from behind Mr Edom's back that she caught his eye as in a mantrap and held up four fingers.

When she went out with the rubbish he made a pretext of autumn leaves choking the gutters and followed her into the yard. There was Mrs Knowles with four doomed innocents squiriming in her apron. They seemed very active for doomed innocents.

'She's been hiding them all this time,' said Mrs Knowles. 'The artful piece. Bless her heart!'

'But –'

'Two tabs, a black, and a ginger.'

The cat stood watching the apron, her embattled soul in her eyes. When the kittens were put down, she cleaned them imperiously. Then she rolled over on her side and gave suck.

'Did you ever see a prettier sight?' asked Mrs Knowles.

That was the worst of it. It was a pretty sight. He and Mrs Knowles, she grossly wallowing in the Life Force, he conscience-stricken at his murderous mind, compared very ill with it.

'What on earth are we to do now?'

Mrs Knowles went on simpering at the kittens.

'You must find homes for them!' he exclaimed. 'Good homes.'

'It's too soon for that, Mr Collins. But I'll look about. Blacks are lucky and gingers are always popular, but I don't know about the other two, the tabbies. If I could have got at them in time, I'd have drowned them. But I haven't the heart to do it now.'

She stooped and caressed the cat. Never before had Mr Collins felt such dislike for a woman as he now felt for Mrs Knowles. As he couldn't murder her, he walked away.

Mr Edom began to worry. George wasn't being his usual self. He was always fidgeting; he moved things about, he polished what was in no need of polishing, he knocked over the wastepaper basket, he even collided with the fine Victorian gong bought at the Tabley Manor sale. He developed a nervous cough. He talked at random. He read aloud from catalogues. He was incessantly industrious and perfectly amiable, yet gave the impression that his mind was elsewhere. It occurred to Mr Edom that George might be going a little deaf; he seemed to be straining his ears all the time as though he heard imperfectly. Perhaps it was love. In that case the loved one must be local, for when Mr Edom suggested a few pick-me-up days at Brighton the suggestion was rejected as if he had spoken of a few days in jail. Mr Edom said no more at the time, but privately decided that whether George liked it or not and whether his malady was in the heart or in the head he would be packed off for a change of air as soon as Mrs Vibart had visited the Galleries. Meanwhile, to take George's mind off his troubles, he talked about Mrs Vibart.

Though the kittens' voices had grown ever louder and more insistent and more difficult to drown; though their mother now left them for longer and longer intervals and came to sun herself on the Galleries doorstep; though a day was bound to come when the kittens followed her through the pop-hole and sat there with her, a bait for public compassion, which might ignore one cat but certainly wouldn't fail to notice five, Mr Collins, intermittently surfacing from his distraction, realized that Mrs Vibart was indeed somebody, and that with a mind at leisure from itself he would have very much looked forward to seeing her.

If she had been a Hester Bateman teapot, Mr Edom could not have esteemed her more highly. She was, he related, self-made – the daughter of a county family who had married a hunting man. The hunting man had a collection of swordsticks. Mrs Vibart, by the process of familiarity, distinguished that many of them were fakes. When he died from an accident in the hunting field, she kept one Andrea Ferrara as a souvenir, sold the rest, and turned her attention to firearms. She frequented auctions, where from time to time, she bought a mixed lot. The Ring was accustomed to ladies buying a mixed lot for the sake of a preserving pan, say, or a garden hose; it was a good six years before the professionals noticed that most of the constituents of the mixed lots knocked down to Mrs Vibart presently appeared at auctions elsewhere. By the time they had discovered what she was up to and begun to hound her, she had outwitted them so successfully that she could afford to outbid them. She was brilliantly lucky, single-minded, the unquestioned authority in her field; it was believed that she had bequeathed her private collection to Girton College, Cambridge.

Mr Collins had never seen Mr Edom in a state so nearly approaching excitement. It could not be snobbery in so cool a man, so it must be veneration. Ambition did not come into it. 'There's nothing in the Galleries she'd look at,' he said with pride. 'It'll be the pistols or nothing.' Mr Collins thought of cups and lips and of how his dear employer might be disgraced in the very moment of his triumph. In dreams he saw Moggie ripping Mrs Vibart's stockings and kittens in molt swarming all over Mr Edom. With greater urgency he besought Mrs Knowles to find homes for them. And Mr Edom wondered if it would not have been better to insist on that seaside holiday. He particularly wanted George to make a good impression and it didn't seem at all likely that he would.

The day of Mrs Vibart's visit came. Mr Edom had on his best waistcoat. He was calm. The case of duelling pistols lay on his desk – the opening would come later. Mrs Vibart was driving from Old Windsor (she scorned London) and would arrive at eleven-thirty. She would be on the dot, said Mr Edom with the confidence of a votary.

At eleven-twenty-five Mrs Dudley, a lady who occasionally wanted to buy something quaint, undulated into the Galleries. Her mien was condescending, her voice assertively kindly. 'I understand you have some kittens to dispose of, Mr Edom. May I have a look at them?'

'Kittens?' said Mr Edom. 'Kittens?' His manner was unruffled, his face serene. 'Kittens.' On this third repetition he changed the accentuation of the word and seemed to be musing on kittens in general.

'I think I can put my hand on some,' panted Mr Collins.

'Thank you, George.'

But the words were lost on Mr Collins, who had rushed out of the Galleries. It was the two tabby kittens he came back with.

'Tabbies,' remarked Mrs Dudley censoriously.

'These are the true old English tabbies,' said Mr Collins, surpassing himself as he hoped never to have to surpass himself again, for it was a dreadful sensation. 'It is rare to find them nowadays, especially with such regular markings and with the butterfly pattern so clear on the back.'

'Oh. Well, I must admit I don't know much about cats. But if you want a home for one of them –'

'Ten and sixpence,' said Mr Edom.

'Ten and sixpence? But I don't want both of them, I just want a plain ordinary cat to keep down mice.'

'Each,' said Mr Edom.

'Two guineas,' said a clear voice from the doorway.

Looking round, Mrs Dudley saw a tall, grey-haired woman who seemed to her very plainly dressed, and instantly took a strong dislike to her. 'Twenty-five shillings for that one!' she exclaimed, and remained with her mouth open, appalled at the words which fury had wrenched from it.

'Five guineas for the pair,' said Mrs Vibart.

'Never, never in all my life . . .'

Unable to specify further, Mrs Dudley left the Galleries, nearly falling over the cat, who had come round to see what was happening.

'Fun while it lasted,' said Mrs Vibart. 'Mr Edom, you must allow me to congratulate you on your assistant. I thought he did admirably. It isn't everybody who knows about the butterfly pattern.'

'I got it out of a book,' mumbled Mr Collins.

'The right way to begin,' said she, 'unless one's a cat and doesn't need book learning. If you can let me have a good deep hamper, with plenty of clean straw, I'll take them back with me. They're fine kittens. I'm delighted to have found them. One should always buy kittens in pairs. They keep each other warm and don't pine.'

Followed by the cat, Mr Collins went off to pack the kittens. Mrs Vibart turned to Mr Edom. 'Now for the pistols.' When he opened the case, she said, 'Ah!'

THE THREE CATS

'It's a sure thing,' remarked Mr Edom 'that if you see something you've never seen before and can't account for, within a couple of weeks you'll run across a match to it.'

Mr Edom's assistant knew that whenever Mr Edom made one of these general remarks something particular would follow on it. Now he saw Mr Edom delve in the pocket of his overcoat and bring out a crumpled blue-and-yellow paper bag. Inside the bag was a small object wrapped in tissue paper. While Mr Edom was unwrapping it, the assistant looked at the bag. It was labelled 'Ye Abbey Gifte Shoppe'.

'It caught my eye in passing,' said Mr Edom. Mr Collins had raised his eyebrows at the bag, so these words took him down a peg, as they were meant to do – though kindly, since Mr Edom thought well of him, and was bringing him on.

The tissue paper was removed, the object placed on Mr Edom's desk. It was a very small object, about two inches high; but the minuteness of the modelling made it seem larger. It was a representation in enamelled bronze of a cat engaged in reading. It was sitting upright on a stool; its tail curved down behind, one of its hind legs was crossed over the other, its front paws supported a folio on its knees. Except for the tail, it partook of the human; but it was also perfectly feline – an ordinary short coated tabby cat, but in an unusual attitude and unusually employed.

'What do you think of it?'

'It looks French to me,' said Mr Collins. 'Nice bit of modelling, too. Very life-like.'

'Just what struck me about it. And look at the finish! That wasn't done yesterday.'

He put it away in a drawer. Mr Collins remarked that a pair of such cats – cats being so much in demand – would be quite a useful item. Pairs, replied Mr Edom, continuing the process of taking down while yet bringing on, were all right for the present; but he wondered where the chimney-ornament side of the trade would be when the Coal Board and modern architects had between them done away with chimney shelves. 'There'll still be window sills,' said Mr Collins who, being young and progressive, felt he must stand up for modern developments.

'Window sills! I pin no hopes on window sills. They bring out the worst. I can remember the days when it was Dying Gladiators. Now it's aquariums.'

A fortnight went by, a month went by, but the metal cat remained unmated. In the end, it was taken from the drawer and added to the Miscellaneous Table, which needed new blood. Later that day, Mrs Otter came in, looking, as Mr Collins had privately commented when he first met her, like a tinker out sleepwalking; and said she wanted a christening present for a baby who wasn't going to be christened. 'But that's no reason why the poor little creature should be robbed of its due – unless, of course, it changes its mind when it's grown up and is dragged through a tank backward. Agnostics' children constantly do.' Here Mrs Otter picked up a shagreen case containing a set of fleams, gazed at it ardently, and murmured, 'Phlebotomy!'

Mr Edom hovered nearer, like a guardian angel ready to intervene. Sales are all very well, but he felt a personal responsibility for Mrs Otter. Prudence Otter, the daughter of an adoring rural dean, the relict of two successively adoring theologians, was one of those women who are sent into the world to turn the heads of ageing men. Her foot was light, her hair was like honeysuckle in its uncontrollable windings, her eyes and her conversation were wild. Ageing men gazed into her eyes and listened spellbound by the unsurmisability of what she would say next. She gave them back their youth, with its wide horizons, where nothing was impossible. The young, including her two sons by her first husband, found no charm in her at all.

As for Mr Edom, he trembled whenever she came into the shop. Not that she broke things; her gestures might sweep a Leeds basket to the brink, her hair on several occasions had become entangled in chandeliers, but she never broke anything. It was his self-confidence she threatened: he never knew when she would not persuade him out of his better judgment and possibly turn out to be right – for more than once she had been illuminatedly right; also he never knew when he

26

mightn't forget himself and address her as his darling. Now he saw with relief that she had abandoned the set of fleams and moved on to the silver table. A spoon is always appropriate . . . She had fastened on the very worst of the lot, a spoon so worn and battered that he would have hesitated to display it if its two initials had not been so nobly engraved. 'It's in very poor condition, Mrs Otter.'

'But the initials, Mr Edom! "C.B." Charlotte Brontë's own tooth marks, for all we know.' She peered with her shortsighted eyes, like an animal looking out of a thicket. 'I can't read the hallmark.'

'Sheffield. 1817.'

'There! I was right. Mr Edom, I must have this spoon. Which reminds me, if you ever see a watercolour of a cormorant looking down on a drowned woman . . . Oh!' Mrs Otter had moved on to the Miscellaneous Table, and was clasping the cat. 'A Grandville! I'm positive it's a Grandville. Did you ever read "Minette et Bébé"? With an angel cat in a long white nightgown struggling for poor Minette's soul on a rooftop? Just like Canon Bowles – you know he broke his leg? So sad for him. Stop! Wait a minute! I've got a feeling – Yes, it's coming back to me. Mr Edom, I've met two of this cat's relations.'

Mr Edom cancelled his dream of giving her the cat.

'But where? I know I was talking about tapioca at the time, but tapioca might be anywhere – unless it was old Mrs Cartwright's St Bernard. Sheepshead and milk pudding. Can you imagine a more horrible menu? Or it might just have been husbands, harking back on their school days – and flushed with rhubarb all through Lent. Tapioca. Tapioca.'

Meanwhile old Major Barnard had come in and sat down with a grunt on a coffin stool. With his stick between his knees and his hand clasping the handle and his chin resting on his hands, he sat listening to Mrs Otter.

'Tapioca. I shall run it down in time. It's just a question of keeping my mind on it. That's a very pretty work-table. Hullo, Henry. Have you been here long? You don't look very comfortable.'

'I've been here for exactly four minutes, Prudence, and I am very comfortable, thank you. I saw you through the window, and came in to ask you to have lunch with me.'

'I'd be delighted. When? Now, instantly?'

'As instantly as you can manage. You're obviously dying of

malnutrition, as usual. Mr Edom, may I see that spoon Mrs Otter was looking at? I want to give it to her. It might remind her to eat. Hmm! Been a bit knocked about.'

'Look at the initials, Henry! Charlotte Brontë's own spoon!'

'Yours now, dear.'

'Oh, Henry, I'll adore it. I'll use it every day of my life. It's exactly the right size for eating essence of chicken out of the pot with.'

'Not tapioca?'

'Tapioca? Why tapioca? Oh, yes! That reminds me. Henry, have I ever talked to you about tapioca?'

'I expect so. One thing leads to another. By the way, Grandville did illustrations and things, didn't he? And caricatures. I've never heard he went in for statuary.'

They left together, Major Barnard carrying Mrs Otter's gloves, her handbag, her books from the public library, and both her shopping baskets, Mrs Otter clasping her spoon and talking about the Colossus of Rhodes. Mr Edom put the cat back in his drawer, handling it with reverence, and went out for his lunch. Mr Collins, who would lunch later, began consulting Mr Edom's books of reference. It was an extraordinary thing about these country fogeys: they knew nothing, hadn't the smallest idea of values, attributed all their family portraits to Joshua Reynolds and took them to be restored by the caretaker at the auction rooms, who did it in his spare time with a cleaner called Roll It Off; and yet, all of a sudden, they'd be at home with some shibboleth like this Grandville, who wasn't even in a book of reference, thought the assistant, seeking for him without his 'd'. Come to that, he wondered how much Mr Edom knew about Grandville.

The spurt of rebellion was quelled that same afternoon, because a dealer, buying extensively, he said, for shipments to Latin America, walked in, and to see Mr Edom putting him down and keeping him there was something Old Masterly.

'He didn't get much out of you.'

Mr Edom straightened his waistcoat. 'The sort of person I used to keep horse brasses for in my younger days,' he observed; and, having entered in the Sales on Commission ledger, 'Turquoise Rabbit Pin, Mrs O. £9. 5. 0.,' made out the cheque, less his ten per cent commission, with a sense that he had not done too badly for her.

When she came in two mornings later, her look of excitement went rather beyond what £8. 6. 6. would warrant, and her voice, when she thanked him, was inattentively enthusiastic. Could she have been expecting more for that shocking trinket?

'And now, Mr Edom . . .' Words had actually failed her. Portentously, she disembarrassed herself of a portentously large parcel.

'Yes, Mrs Otter?'

'Don't look so alarmed, I wouldn't give you a walrus. It's your two cats. I said I'd find them, and I have found them, though tapioca was a completely false scent. You know that place that sells thatched tea cosies – the Abbey Present Shop.'

'Gifte Shoppe.'

'That's it. Gift. Horrid word; one might as well say "donation". Well, I was going past it and thinking of that unchristened baby I told you about, when suddenly I saw its silver lining. If it's to grow up a little heathen, then give it an idol. And as it will be an English heathen, the idol must be furry. And I went in, and found a superb idol, a washable brown walrus with harmless woollen eyes. And while it was being done up I was looking with thankfulness at all the things I needn't buy, and there, among some bead necklaces, were your two missing cats! But they're rather expensive. I didn't know if I should spend so much of your money without asking you. They want three guineas for them.'

Mr Edom's face hardened into professional glassiness. He had bought the first cat for seven shillings and sixpence.

'You were quite right, Mrs Otter. Three guineas would be going too far.'

'Poor pets!'

'But I'll see what can be done. I don't intend to miss them.'

'But if someone else gets there first? We should never know their fate.' Her voice was suddenly maudlin, and tears ran down her cheeks.

'I will send Mr Collins immediately.'

A second inquiry within an hour was impolitic, but he could not bear to see Mrs Otter so upset. Taking the assistant to one side, he told him to go up to twenty-five shillings if necessary.

Mr Collins had long legs, and a steady head for bargaining. By the time Mrs Otter had dried her tears and drunk a little brandy out of the flask she carried in case of street accidents, he was back. Thrice unobtrusively whisking the thumb and fingers of his left hand, he set down the two cats on a small table. Mr Edom produced the first cat from his drawer. It was a solemn moment; even the assistant felt it to be so, and exclaimed, 'Reunited!'

Mr Edom noticed a momentary demur cross Mrs Otter's beaming face, as a wisp of cloud crosses the moon. Shortsighted people have their own kind of acute vision. Perhaps she had seen some flaw in one of the cats, some discrepancy of measurement or handling? He saw nothing wrong himself. They seemed all of the same litter, all studiously inclined. One of the newcomers was bending over a small table, and in its right paw was a quill of really remarkable workmanship; the other was staring at some sort of square-ruled drawing board. All three sat on identical stools with their tails curling down behind. They made a nice little group, were in excellent condition, and quite unusual. Already he foresaw the customer for them: young Mrs Harington, who, as he had reason to know, was prone to cats.

'I'm sure we shall find the others,' said Mrs Otter.

'The Others?'

'The other four: Music, Astronomy, Geometry, and Rhetoric. Here's Grammar, you see, reading the classic authors; that's Arithmetic; and this one is Logic, writing a treatise to account for everything, like Thomas Aquinas. That's why Grandville has given him such a smug ecclesiastical expression.' Perceiving that they were silent, she added, with a slight blush – for she did not like to appear better informed than they – 'The Seven Liberal Arts, you know. In the Middle Ages. To know them was a liberal education.'

'Four more,' said Mr Edom pensively.

'Yes, but we're practically sure of another pair – the two I saw when I was talking about tapioca. I have never seen anything to suggest tapioca in that Present Shop, so it can't have been there.'

'You might have seen them in the window while you were talking about tapioca outside,' said Mr Collins. Mr Edom frowned. He disliked the insinuation that Mrs Otter had only one subject of conversation. It was uncivil; and it was demonstrably untrue. For example, she could talk about these seven liberal arts, which was more than George could.

After she had gone, Mr Edom realized that he had been uncivil himself, for he had forgotten to thank her for finding Logic and

Arithmetic, who, with Grammar, were now in the drawer. Why Grammar and Arithmetic, and, for that matter, Geometry, should be arts was beyond him. Why the artist should have chosen to represent them as cats was a bit beyond him, too, though less so, since artists can be led into the most peculiar expedients; he had seen the Nine Muses as monkeys – a parallel case – in a sale, and had bid for them, though Thompson of Cheltenham got them in the end. Seven Bronze Liberal Cats would not be so commanding an item as Nine Porcelain Monkey Muses, perhaps, but they would be a set – if the other four could be traced, that is. Mrs Otter seemed pretty confident about it, and she might well be right. In a country neighbourhood, sets which have been dispersed still tend to remain within hailing distance; one daughter takes the cups and saucers, another the cake plates, a third, for the sake of sentiment, the teapot, even though it's cracked. And such small objects as these cats, though jolted apart, might not have rolled very far. He inclined to back Mrs Otter. In the past, she had several times been surprisingly right, if at other times surprisingly wrong. Her judgments were those of the heart rather than those of the head, but there is a lot to be said for the heart. The heart has rejected the fake before the expert has had time to say 'Bob's your uncle'; and Luck, that austere goddess, won't do a thing for you if all you've got to go by is head. For all that, and feeling that he would like to have some hand in it himself, he reinforced Mrs Otter's powers by sending a small advertisement to a trade paper, inquiring for 'Bronze Enamelled Figurine Cats, height, two inches'. Mention of Rhetoric, etc., would not be discreet.

However discreetly one frames an advertisement, one cannot prevent its being read by enterprising blockheads, and Mr Edom received offers of cats in all sizes and substances – cats as Christy Minstrels with banjos, china kittens dressed as choirboys, Oxford and Cambridge cats competing in the boat race, several signed drawings by Louis Wain, and a stuffed polecat, 'very lifelike with all faults'. Meanwhile, he saw nothing of Mrs Otter; he supposed she was carrying on the pursuit. But when she next visited the shop, she had nothing to report; she had been having influenza, and felt so miserable that she had come to buy something, just in order to cheer herself up. There were other customers in the shop, strangers to the place, and Mr Edom found himself wishing Mrs Otter would go away, for they looked at her as if they had never seen a lady the worse for influenza before.

Though she continued to come in from time to time, it was most often to bring something or other she wanted him to sell on commission; presently, she brought things she wanted him to buy outright – among these, the spoon with the initials C.B. on it. He could not refuse to buy it; and because the transaction shocked him, paid her more for it than he had charged Major Barnard, saying that the price of silver had gone up. It was not like Mrs Otter to do such a thing. He began to feel a kind of resentment against her; resentment because she did not visit him so often, resentment because he felt impoverished that she did not, or did not seem present even when she did. As for the cats he thrust them into the back of the drawer, saying to himself that she had lost interest in them, and so had he. Major Barnard, taking his daily walks down Abbey Street, came in as of old whenever he saw her through the window. Sometimes he made a pretext of buying, at other times he sat patiently on the coffin stool, waiting till he could take her off for a meal or see her home.

It was early in May, the lilacs were just in bloom, and children coming back from the country walks dropped buttercups on the pavement, when Mr Edom saw Major Barnard halt his venerable Bentley in front of the Galleries and walk in, leaning on his stick and with a carnation in his buttonhole.

'Mrs Otter's meeting me here, at quarter past four,' he said. 'Do you mind if I wait inside? I don't expect she'll be long.' And he sat down on the coffin stool. 'I ought to pay you rent for this,' he said, smiling.

Customers came and went. The beautiful weather had brought sightseers to the town; not many bought, but all were polite and praising because they were happy. The hands of the clock went on to four-forty-five. Major Barnard said, 'Do you mind if I smoke a cigar?'

Mr Edom brought him an ashtray. 'Perhaps Mrs Otter mistook the time,' he suggested.

'Just what I was thinking. She must have thought I said quarter past five. Maybe I did say quarter past five.'

'Are you taking her out in the car? It's a lovely day for it. Everything will be looking its best.'

'She's coming with me to Salisbury. There's some sort of concert in the cathedral. It begins at six, and then we are to have dinner and drive back in the cool. But now we shall miss a good part of the concert. Silly of me to tell her the wrong time. Silly time to have a concert, come to that.'

As the hands of the clock moved toward five-fifteen, Mr Edom tried not to count the minutes till Mrs Otter should appear. At twenty past five a woman who was not Mrs Otter came in. She looked at everything, attentively and in silence. Finally, she began to bargain for an ikon. Mr Edom had no patience with bargainers, but now he nursed her along and dandled her hopes, for she filled a gap – till the moment came when she changed her mind and bought a mug from the Miscellaneous Table and went away. Only then did he allow himself to look at Major Barnard, and at the clock. He signed to Mr Collins to leave by the side door and pretended to busy himself in replacing the ikon. The clocks in the shop, the clocks in the town began striking six; the Abbey bell surmounted them with its leisurely strokes; the street filled with people going home from work. Major Barnard raised his head and stared at Mr Edom as though he had appeared on the margin of a dream.

'I'm afraid Mrs Otter must have mistaken the day, Major Barnard. She would be so concerned.'

'Something's happened to her. There's been an accident.' The old man hoisted himself to his feet and began to walk up and down, clenching and unclenching his rheumatic hands. 'But what can one do? What can one do?' he muttered.

'If you think Mrs Otter may have met with some accident, sir, why not ring up the police station? They would know. And it would set your mind at rest.'

Compelling Major Barnard into his private room, he dialled the number, put the receiver into his shaking hand, and shut the door on him.

It wasn't long before he was back. 'No bad news, I hope,' said Mr Edom, reading calamity on his face.

'She was found unconscious in Fore Street, early this afternoon. She's been taken to hospital – to Pomeroy House.'

'Oh, poor lady!' Pomeroy House was where they took the mental cases, the attempted suicides, the alcoholics.

Major Barnard stiffened himself. 'The truth is –' Staring fixedly at Mr Edom, he had recognized in Mr Edom's face the expression of one

33

engaged in putting two and two together – a mercantile process. 'The truth is, I must be going,' he concluded, and walked out.

Once set in motion, two and two rush into four. By the next day all those acquainted with Mrs Otter knew that they had known for a long time that she was drinking too much; and most of them – for even those she did not charm felt she injured no one and was part of the place – were sorry. Naturally, the quality of the sorrow varied; varied from the desolation felt by Major Barnard, who had lost the delight of his heart, to the pure, fellowly compassion felt by Old Grog, who had lost the dear, sweet creature who never grudged him a couple of shillings toward a drink. Mr Edom's narrower heart was wrung by a more complicated laceration. His grief was an anguish to him because the cause of it was so painful and so shocking. He would have gone to the stake, he averred, rather than think such a thing of that dear lady. His prim uprightness flinched from the picture of a drunken lady lying in a stupor outside the closing doors of the Acorn Inn, and carried away by the police on a stretcher; it was a rape on his respectability.

Six months later, when he heard that Mrs Otter would shortly be discharged from Pomeroy House as cured, his second thought (for the first had been an explosive realization how much he had missed her) was that he didn't know how he would be able to look her in the face.

It was not her face. His memory repudiated it, and she exclaimed, 'Why, Mr Edom, I don't believe you recognize me!' They had returned her fat, healthy, well preserved, and unaccountably lowered in class. Her clothes were spruce, she was made up, her hair had been waved and tinted. The charm was gone. Even her voice was coarsened, and though she talked as much as ever, it was of herself she talked and of the psychiatrist. Mr Edom was too stricken to ease his mind by finding a formula. Mr Collins who had recently come on a lot in judgment and connoisseurship and who was not personally affected by the disappearance of a charm he had never felt, was at no loss for a summary: Mrs Otter looked as if she had been given a thorough treatment with Roll It Off. He kept this opinion unspoken; but later he asserted himself. It was stock-taking time, and they were going through the unlisted articles in Mr Edom's drawer. 'Three bronze enamelled cats,' he called out. 'How do I enter these?'

'Incomplete set,' replied Mr Edom.

Mr Collins placed them in a row. 'You know, I'm not altogether so sure about that,' he said. 'I think you should take another look at them.'

Mr Edom approached, gloomily, and did so.

'It's my belief,' went on the assistant, 'that they are a set just as they are. Look. Reading, Writing, and Arithmetic.'

For a moment, Mr Edom was convulsed. He seemed about to take hold of Mr Collins and strangle him. Then, recovering himself, he looked at the three figures – soberly, professionally – and said, 'I daresay you're right.'

SOPWITH HALL

Mr Edom handed the telephone receiver to his assistant, Mr Collins, saying, 'It's for you, George. From somewhere in Perthshire. A personal call.'

He then withdrew and busied himself at the other end of the shop. Even so, he could not avoid hearing Mr Collins exclaim in a loud tone, almost a yelp, of anguish, 'But, Baby, it's impossible!' From this he deduced that the call must be on such a private matter that tactful disregard would be best. George was not the first to have a Baby in his life. Mr Collins put back the receiver, a changed man. His face was pale, his hair was rumpled. His clothes no longer appeared to fit him. Fortunately, it was still early in the day, so no customers were likely to come in just then and see Mr Edom's valued assistant in such an unprofessional state of mind.

'The most appalling thing has happened,' said Mr Collins. 'My great-aunt has died.'

Mr Edom made a befitting noise of sympathy.

'And I'm her executor!' continued Mr Collins. 'She never warned me, but I'm down in the will. And that's not all. The other executor is in a home for seniles. And poor Baby – she's my second cousin once removed – is no better than a hen; she'll be swindled out of everything if I'm not there to see to it. God save a man from Scotch relations! I haven't seen any of them for years, all I knew was socks at Christmas – and now I've got *this* on my hands.'

'Today,' said Mr Edom composingly, 'is Tuesday. When is the funeral?'

'Tomorrow! Some nonsense about catching a minister. How on earth–'

'You must go off and pack, catch the midday train to London, and take the night express. Have a sleeper to calm your mind. And stay as long as you need to, George. Death's death and the Law is the Law, and there's an end of it. We can't escape these things. Take warm underclothes.'

There is a certain stimulus in a return to an earlier way of life. In the course of six years, Mr Edom's Mr Collins had graduated from a young man who had a lot to learn to being the trusted companion addressed as George, who could lift lead-lined wine coolers without effort, keep his head at auctions, supply details without seeming officious, recollect who it was who had asked for a set of spillikins, and gauge the requirements of local ladies who came in quest of something that would do for a confirmation; but left to shift for himself, Mr Edom found he could manage very nicely. He hoped that George in similar circumstances was doing as well. Method is nine-tenths of the battle, and he had got George into good ways. Picture postcards of glens and braes under very blue skies told him briefly that it rained incessantly and that George had no idea when he would be through with it all. Then came a letter recounting what George had been going through.

'The house is crammed with tartan penwipers and gifts from Oban and Baby has to tell me a story about each of them. I counted twenty-seven paperweights, and nineteen pebble brooches. Quaichs. Sporrans. Thistles. Stags (Eve and Bay) in beads on hassocks. A landscape of heather hills, done entirely in heather. But some items are worth attending to, and I suggest I buy them at the probate valuation and bring them south. Baby would be glad of the money and it would be a sin to leave them here. God knows how I'll pack them, there isn't a tea chest within miles. It would work out at about £250. Do I act? Please wire.'

Mr. Edom replied, 'PLEASE ACT INCLUDE HEATHER LANDSCAPE IF CONDITION FAIR.' He itched to be at Coire Cottage himself. It was the kind of adventure he sometimes imagined when falling asleep.

He had not imagined, he had not expected, two such punch bowls, nor such a cobweb-spun Belleek basket, nor such a rabbit tureen, such a boulle boudoir clock, a shagreen étui in such perfection of completeness, a brace of such potpourri jars, such a Pontypool tray. The heather landscape done in heather, too, surpassed his experience of conspicuous waste of time and industry: the perspective was obtained by using heather bells of different tints, and a white heather waterfall gleamed among bell-heather rocks. Mr Collins had also unbent to some

37

small absurdities which he judged as likely to appeal to Mrs Otter and be given to her by Major Barnard. Concealing his pride, he expatiated on the exploit of finding tea chests. The third tea chest contained a complete scenic dessert service which might well be Minton: twelve plates, two comports, two oval platters, and three standing dishes – twenty-one vignettes (the comports had two apiece) of a gentleman's seat, its stables, its summerhouses, its shrubberies, its rustic bridges, its park, its village church. The seat was mid-Georgian, though an invading romanticism had influenced the summerhouses and the church. The season was summer. The scenes were painted in shades of green and sepia; their bases and surrounds were nut brown. That, at least, was the term used by Mr Edom in listing the service, though when Mrs Otter saw it she declared that the colour was filemot. She also declared that the mansion was named Sopwith Hall.

It was unfortunate that Mrs Otter should have come in on the heels of Mr Harington. Mr Harington seldom visited the Galleries; he bought even seldomer, and never without deliberating the deed. But merely to be hovered over by Mr Harington – merely to be stalked from a distance – was an accolade. His horses, his dwelling, his car, his wife, his suits, and, eminently, his shoes expressed the same stern pursuit of a rarefied ideal. As for Mrs Otter, he found her detestable. She was eclectic and put her clothes on anyhow. Mrs Otter's random charm was chiefly felt by ageing men, but at no age would Mr Harington have become aware of it. As a dotard, he would still have rejected her. Plainly, he was rejecting her now; but as his manners were as scrupulous as his taste, he would keep up a semblance of hovering till he could be gone without having appeared to go.

Not wanting to embarrass the gentleman, Mr Edom continued listening to Mrs Otter, till, glancing round to make sure that Mr Harington had gone, he saw that Mr Harington was still there, and apparently listening to Mrs Otter, too. For when she repeated the words 'Sopwith Hall' he stiffened, as if from his hovering he would swoop on her like a falcon. He remained till she went away, and went away himself soon after.

'I'll tell you something,' said Mr Collins to Mr Edom. 'My Lord Harington is after that dessert service.'

'I doubt it, George. I very much doubt it. It's not up to his mark.'

'That's as may be. But while Mrs Otter and you were talking, he was watching it as though it would get away if he took his eye off it. And I heard him say to himself, "I must have it."'

Mr Edom remarked they needn't rush to conclusions; Mr Harington would have to make up his mind first, and it might be weeks.

Within two days, Mr Harington was back. Under cover of the Pontypool tray he stalked the dessert service for some ten minutes, then advanced on it.

'I don't think I've seen this before, have I?'

'No, Mr Harington, I daresay not. It's only been in for a few days.'

'Charming. I like the colouring. Where did it come from?'

'From Perthshire.'

'Perthshire . . . Perthshire.' He repeated the word as if in time he would get used to it. Mr Edom showed him the heather landscape and said it came from Perthshire, too. Mr Harington looked at it with sombre gravity and said, 'Indeed.' There were some engravings of architectural and landscape subjects on a table near the door, placed there for non-buyers to get away by. Mr Harington paused, examined them, selected a Harlech Castle, paid, and went away.

Mr Edom said, 'Wrong guess, George. It's not the dessert service he's after. It's the house.'

For a moment, it almost appeared that Mr Edom was licking his lips. Then two ladies who had been studying the window came in, and Mr Edom became as usual.

He had been waiting for some years for an opportunity to feel malicious about Mr Harington. It was not the hoverings nor the withdrawals from a purchase he took exception to, for it is as hard for the rich to know what they want as it is for them to enter the Kingdom of Heaven; and for Mr Harington it was peculiarly hard, since his taste was so good and so cultivated that his likings were cowed by it and never really got a look-in. But this was no excuse for pouring his good taste like cold water on Mrs Harington, that lovely young creature, whenever she set her heart on something he didn't approve of. Mrs Harington also had taste – much of it so bad that it promised to become excellent, given time and rope enough. But the rope was never given. Any other man, thought Mr Edom, would have walked a hundred miles barefooted and rejoicing to buy her another little heart-shaped box, a Parian cat on a cushion.

And why shouldn't she have them, if she wanted them? But Mr Harington silently rebuked such lapses by giving her a pair of black basalt urns or a jade water buffalo – if he deigned, that is, to notice her tentative 'Isn't this rather ...' at all. Now Mr Harington had seen something he wanted. Wanting would do him good, thought Mr Edom. Let him want, let him languish. Let him go to Perthshire!

Though Mr Harington's determination to own the property on the dessert service burned like a fever, it did not make him precipitate. Instead of driving through the night to Perthshire, he wrote to the secretary of the Georgian Society to ascertain the whereabouts of Sopwith Hall. The secretary replied there was no evidence that a Sopwith Hall existed or ever had existed. This was a blow, but mitigated by the fact that he could dismiss from his mind all thoughts of being under an obligation to Mrs Otter. By any other name, the house would be a great deal sweeter. Meanwhile, its anonymity made it harder to inquire after: it would have to be sought by eye. He rang up old Anselm Tipping, and set out for Devizes.

At Devizes, in Wiltshire, was the Tipping Collection – a private museum containing Mr Tipping's lifework of making a photographic record of eighteenth-century domestic architecture in Great Britain and Ireland: castles, manors, town and country houses, rectories, almshouses, stables, dower houses, follies, judges' lodgings, lockups, etc. The photographs were stuck in massive albums, and indexed under Counties, Known or Reputed Architects, Styles, Purposes, Main Aspects, Number of Saloons, Materials, and Particular Features – i.e., ironwork, plasterwork, panelling, scagliola, statuary, Romford grates, coats of arms, rocaille, moss huts, bone houses, etc. With all these categories and aids to elimination, plus Mr Tipping's obliging inattention, it promised to be pretty easy to assemble the requirements – mid-Georgian, oblong, stone-built, three story, cornice, plain fenestration of sash windows, modest central portico with Doric pediment, the whole distinguished by symmetry and restraint – for the house of the dessert service. By the end of the day, he had accumulated quite a number of houses (none in Perthshire, however; Edom was growing careless and relied too much on his man) complying with these requirements. Each in turn seemed to be the house he sought, then wasn't. Each successively weakened his recollection of it. It faded like the Cheshire cat; only the regularity of the fenestration remained, like the teeth in the cat's grin. He told Mr Tipping he would be back in the morning, and went to the Bear Hotel, where he dined moodily and dreamed he had inadvertently bought the Alhambra.

Next day he resumed the search. It yielded another dozen houses or so which almost answered to the dessert service, but not one of them evoked the instant, uncontrovertible acknowledgement of recognition. The type swallowed the individual. He went through the albums again, growing drowsier and drowsier, as if he had been counting a flock of pedigree Southdowns. It was raining, too, and he had an ache in his shoulders from turning over so many pasteboard pages. Yet while his energies foundered in discouragement and fatuity, his purpose burned in fantasies of power. Not only would he, against all discouragement, find his house, but against all obstacles he would possess it, ejecting orphans, lunatics, contemplative orders, convalescent trades unionists, delinquent boys, milk-marketing boards, and all such riffraff who under a Welfare State squat in stately homes which private owners can't afford to keep up. Once he was in it, moreover, there should be no National Trust trippers, no throwing open of gardens for charitable purposes. He would be king of his castle, with the Georgian Society itself kept out.

Driving home that evening, he came to a decision: he would buy the dessert service. It was not an easy decision to accept. The dessert service was not the sort of thing he bought. The standing dishes were stumpy, the oval platters not a perfect oval, the margins were too wide, the gilding of poor quality. Yet he must have it. If at Devizes he had had a platter to consult or the plate with the rustic bridge in the foreground, identification would have been irrefutable and achieved in half the time. Have it he must – and put up with the ignominy of appearing to admire it. He had no sooner decided to make this sacrifice when an alternative presented itself. The dessert service could be bought by Lizzie, the helpmate God had given him. He had long ago left off trying to improve her taste, and Edom knew it so well that he positively pandered to it. So tomorrow Lizzie should be taken to the Abbey Galleries to notice the dessert service, exclaim over, it, purchase it, while he stood indulgently by.

By the time he reached home, she had gone to bed and was asleep. He woke her, explained why the dessert service was necessary to his happiness, and rehearsed her till she was word-perfect. She expostulated a little, asking idiotically what sort of soil the house would be on and if the climate would agree with the children.

He rehearsed her again after breakfast. She had got it into her head that the service had pink surrounds, and this idea had to be got rid of. As a result, they did not reach the Galleries as early as he had intended. That old bore Barnard was there, and a couple of dealers. The dealers stared at Lizzie. Lizzie lost her head.

'Mr Edom, I hear you've got a tea set with –'

'Dessert service.'

'– a dessert service, I mean, with views on it, and my husband thinks it is just what I should like. Is this it? Oh yes, I like it very much. Look, Richard! The knobs on the lids of the tureens are little gold apples. And what pretty landscapes! I never knew Perthshire was so peaceful somehow. Richard, I think I must have this dessert service.'

'Mrs Harington, I am very sorry to disappoint you. But the service is sold.'

'Oh dear.'

One of the dealers nudged the other. Cold as ice, Mr Harington reflected that it wouldn't be hard to settle with him – though the delay was annoying. But having to vent his exasperation with Mr Edom for selling the dessert service he observed, 'Of course, it's not Perthshire. I can't imagine why anybody should suppose it was.'

Mr Edom bridled; he was vexed at having sold to a dealer what would have pleased Mrs Harington. 'I think there was a slight misunderstanding. You asked me where the service came from. It *came* from Perthshire, where it was in the ownership of the late Miss Stiven, Mr Collins's great-aunt. But I should say the vignettes undoubtedly represent an English estate.'

'Mr Collins's great-aunt?'

Mr Harington had no particular animus against Mr Collins and wished no more than to be disagreeable to everybody. Mr Collins took it otherwise, and flushed.

'My great-aunt,' he said. 'My great-aunt was in domestic service. She began as a housemaid and raised herself to being a housekeeper. She was housekeeper to a succession of English families, and they thought so well of her that when she left them, to better herself, they often gave her family possessions as a parting gift. The dessert service was one of these. The boulle clock there was another. It was customary in those days.'

With one exception, everyone present felt that Mr Collins had properly rolled on Mr Harington. The exception was Mr Harington. A great hope had shone on him: the house of the dessert service was within his grasp. 'Did your great-aunt tell you the name of the family who gave her the dessert service? Or the name of the house?'

'I never heard her mention either.'

'Do you think you could possibly find out? I am really extremely anxious to know. It would mean a great deal to me.'

Mr Collins thawed to the suppliant. 'Actually, I wanted to know myself. It would have made the service more interesting. But when I asked my great-aunt's legatee she could tell me nothing.'

'She had no idea even what part of England it was in?'

Major Barnard had lumbered over to look at the dessert service which was arousing all this feeling. 'It's in Leicestershire,' he said. 'Purefoy House. I shot my first partridges there, I'm not likely to forget it. Another thing I'm not likely to forget was the shooting lunches. If Mr Collins's aunt had a hand in them, she was a benefactor. Leicestershire is a cold county. There was always cherry brandy, and it was homemade. You ought to have some cherry brandy yourself, Mrs Harington. You're shivering.'

'In Leicestershire,' she said slowly. 'I don't know anyone in Leicestershire. Purefoy House is a pretty name.'

'All gone now – unless there's a Purefoy Street somewhere about. It was too near Leicester for its own good. It's a residential suburb now, all natty little bungalows and – Don't be frightened, I've got you, Mrs Harington. Just sit down and keep your head between your knees. You'll be all right in a moment.'

Mr Edom hurried up with a bottle of smelling salts. It was a slight comfort to Mr Harington that nobody noticed *him*. One cannot be pitchforked from the very threshold of Elysium without manifesting some sign of mental disarray.

When they were again alone together, Mr Edom said to Mr Collins,

'Your ears are better than mine, George. Did you happen to catch what Mrs Harrington said, just before she went off into that faint?'

'"Oh, thank God!" That's what she said. "Oh, thank God!"'

ONE THING
LEADING TO ANOTHER

The onion, the apple, the raisins, the remains of the cold mutton neatly cubed were simmering over a low heat, and Helen Logie had opened the store cupboard and was about to get down the tin of curry powder when the telephone rang yet again. With a sharply drawn sigh she moved the pan to one side and ran up the basement stairs. The caller was Miss Dewlish, who wanted to consult Father Green about something that might seem rather silly, but something else really quite important might hang on it, so unless he had started lunch . . .

'He's out. Both their Reverences are out.'

But as she spoke, Helen sat down – Miss Dewlish would not be dismissed as easily as that – and as one can rest one's feet and yet be usefully employed, she cast her reviewing eye over the hall, where she noticed that the frayed end of the mat had once more escaped from its binding and that Father Green's snuffbox lay open by the telephone, empty and appealing. She put it in her apron pocket, to be replenished from the tin in the store cupboard. The presbytery was a damp house, and the kitchen was the best climate for snuff. Meanwhile, Miss Dewlish was explaining why the purchase of a different brand of floor polish (costing an extra sixpence, but on the other hand the tin was oval, so it probably held more) from Mr Radbone who kept the small grocery shop at the bottom end of King Alfred Street (at least, from her house it was the bottom end, though from the presbytery it might seem the top end; it depended on the way you looked at it) might bring Mr Radbone back to his duties as a Catholic, for while buying some tapioca (she always felt it a duty to go to small shopkeepers if it was humanly possible) she had discovered that he was a lapsed, so it had immediately occurred to her that if he could be got into Our Lady of Ransom, just to see how splendid his polish looked (she for one would gladly give an extra rub; no doubt the others of the Church Guild would do the same) – well, at any rate, it would be a step, wouldn't it? And we all had the conversion of England at heart, hadn't we?

When there was no reply to these inquiries, she remarked, 'I'm afraid I'm keeping you?' To which Helen vouchsafed in her tight Scotch voice, 'Well, yes, you are, rather, just now. If you don't mind,' and put back the receiver as soon as she could interpose a goodbye among Miss Dewlish's understandings of how busy she was and how wonderfully she managed to do all she did.

Sublimating her feelings into a 'God help his Reverence', she hurried down to the kitchen, put in the rice to boil, stirred up the mutton, and got out the curry powder. The telephone rang again. This time it was the coal merchant, inquiring if it would be all the same if he brought boiler-nuts.

'At six shillings a ton more? It will not.'

He was easier to quell than Miss Dewlish, but for all that, when she returned to the kitchen the rice was just about to boil over. At the same moment she heard the street door open and Father Curtin come in.

'Miss Logie.'

'What is it?' she called back, shaking in the curry powder. Let him bring himself downstairs on his long legs, she thought. He was, God forgive her, but the curate. She heard him doing so.

'Miss Logie, I've a message for you from Mrs Ward. She wants to know – I say, that smells good!'

He approached the stove, and the steam from the boiling rice clouded his spectacles.

'It's about the Catholic Women's Bazaar. She says she's already taken orders for five dozen of your scones, and would you be able to make as many again for sale on the stall, as well as the shortcake and the treacle tarts? And we've been promised another bottle of whisky for the tombola. We'll get those kneelers yet, Miss Logie.'

She drained the rice. Each grain was separate. She stirred the curry. It was thickening to perfection. She would not be eating it – her digestion was not what it was – but it gratified her to see it doing her credit. She loaded the chocolate shape, the custard, the big loaf of bread, and the jug of water on the tray, and started upstairs with it. He did not attempt to take it from her, and she would have been affronted if he had. They had both grown up in good God-fearing homes, and knew

46

their places, his in the sanctuary, hers in the kitchen.

Father Green entered the house, saying 'Well, Helen, that smells very appetizing, whatever it is.'

'Mutton curry, your Reverence.'

'Splendid! Any telephone calls?'

'More than enough. But nothing that won't wait till you've had your food.'

When the meal was served, she went back to the kitchen with a clear conscience, saying to herself that the worst half of the day was over.

She had finished her own meal and was about to make the tea when she noticed the tin of snuff on the cooking table. That curate had been after her raisins again, taking out the snuff tin to get at them and forgetting to replace it. Half laughing, half angry, she jumped up to ascertain how far down the raisin jar he'd been. There, on the shelf, was the curry powder!

Never doubting the worst, but as a sort of judicial formality, she went across to the sink, passed her finger over the side of the saucepan, and licked. Yes she had taken the wrong tin; the curry had been made with snuff.

'Mother of God!' she said, and sat down, utterly daunted. How had she come to do such a thing? But it was plain enough. In her flurry she had snatched up the tin that came first to hand; and then, wondering how she would find time for all that extra baking, she had failed to notice any difference in the curry, vaguely thinking to herself that if it looked darker than usual it must be that the onions had caught while that Dewlish body was prating. God forgive her! – it might have been ratsbane and two men of God dying in agonies. As it was, there would be two men of God sitting behind great helpings of curry they couldn't eat – not to mention the waste of a tablespoonful of Father Green's only luxury.

The kettle boiled. 'I'm getting past my work, that's the truth of it,' she said, and rose up as if her limbs were lead, and made the tea and carried it upstairs.

A few grains of rice remained in the dish. Two well-scraped plates had been put by, and the two priests were tranquilly eating their pudding.

All she had meant to say in apology and contrition was annulled. She put down the tea things, collected the used plates, and tried to get away unintercepted. Something in her demeanour struck Father Green. He had inherited her with the presbytery, he knew her worth, he also knew that she must be kept in with. Breaking off an anecdote about a prize begonia, he said, hastily, 'An excellent curry, Helen.'

'Never ate a better one,' added Father Curtin.

'And, Helen. What were those telephone messages?'

'They're down on the telephone pad, your Reverence, all but the last two. The coal merchant, he was trying to foist boiler-nuts on us, but I soon settled his hash. And – and –'

The word 'hash' nearly undid her. If they could eat snuff in a curry, what wouldn't they swallow in a hash?

'Well? What was the other?'

'Miss Dewlish, your Reverence. I just couldn't get all of her down. But the gist of it was that she wants you to buy the church floor polish from Mr Radbone, because he's a lapsed Catholic.'

'Oh, is he? H'mph. But what's the floor polish to do with it?'

'He'd come in, she said, maybe, to admire the floor. Then he'd stay in.'

'It might be worth trying,' said Father Curtin. 'Throw a sprat, you know ...'

Father Green coughed. 'I'd rather you didn't talk like that, if you please. It's unbecoming. Helen, do you know anything about this Mr Radbone?'

'Only the outside of his shop, and that's no recommendation. The polish is sixpence a tin more.'

'How large is the tin?' asked Father Curtin. 'If it could be stretched out over a fortnight, sixpence more wouldn't be a great obstacle.'

'It might not, your Reverence. But taking away a regular order from Mr Vokes, who never misses Sunday or Saint's Day, and brings that great tail of a family after him, to give it to Mr Radbone, who's never been near the church – and who's to say his polish will fetch him? – I'd call that an obstacle.'

Quenched anew in his zeal for souls, Father Curtin said nothing. Father Green said, 'That's a point, too.'

'Miss Dewlish wouldn't stop to think of that. But new brooms are always on the fidget.'

'Helen, that's no way to speak. There are a great many converts who put us cradle Catholics to shame. Use a pinch more charity, Helen.'

Now why, thought Father Curtin, should Miss Logie, rebuked with this homely and appropriate metaphor, look as if the Devil had entered into her? – unless she was jealous of Miss Dewlish? A simple spinster of canonical age, a Child of Mary, a valued housekeeper, and busy from morning till night, you'd think she'd be over such feelings; but unfortunately, those ones were often the worst.

Helen hated Miss Dewlish as habitually as she scrubbed the doorstep, but in a spirit equally removed from emotions of jealousy. The air of private elation observed by Father Curtin was, in fact, precisely due to private elation, to a surging acknowledgement that she was feeling like a new woman – as though the snuff curry had been a kind of brief holiday to her, a release, a levitation, such as she might snatch from smelling the sea or hearing a skirl of passing bagpipes. Feeling like a new woman, she went through the rest of the day's routine as if she were a blithe stranger to it, a sightseer in her own kitchen. And up in her bedroom at last, standing barefooted for the ease of it, and combing out her hair, as flamingly red and almost as thick as when she was a girl, she found herself staring with a new recognition at the two photographs on her dressing table: Jimmy Stott, whom she had loved so hard and sore and could not marry because he would not give over being a Presbyterian, and Father Ewing, whose housekeeper she had been, here, in this very house, for five proud, blissful years, till he had a call and went off to a mission in Africa, where she could not follow him. Every night she looked at them, every night she remembered them in her prayers, but it was a long time since they had had any reality to her. Now they were real again. Their reality was reflected back from hers, from the unique reality of the woman who had made a snuff curry.

Though the alarm clock, going off as usual at six A.M., reclothed her in the sameness of another day, a new element was at work in her mind. She began to speculate. Snuff was not all. Invention, not mere accident, could play a part in cookery, and that not just with the accepted anomalies – the pinch of salt that seizes the flavour of a chocolate icing, the trickle of anchovy essence that gives life to stewed veal – but by more arresting innovations and bolder departures: caraway seeds in a fish pie, for instance; a lentil soup enriched with rhubarb; horseradish in a tapioca pudding. It would be a way of getting oneself attended to, she thought. The snuff curry, while releasing her into the pleasures of fancy, had also imposed on her a new, raw awareness that to be relied on is not the same thing as being attended to, and that to be relied on by those who do not notice the difference between snuff and Indian spices is no great compliment.

However, she went on being as reliable as before. It was her lot, and there was no escape from it, whether or no she liked it. The gay bubbles of speculative fancy continued to rise and break on the surface of her mind, and harmed no one, since they went no further. And though an almost culinary impulse to vary the sameness of her sins once made her mention in confession that from time to time she got silly fancies, Father Green's assurance that the best way to overcome fancies was to pay no heed to them quelled any faint stir there might have been in her conscience. In fact, when at last one of the bubbles rose beyond the surface of her mind and made its way up to the ground floor, she had been paying so little heed to it that only when she was back in the kitchen again and getting on with the ironing did it strike her that the table spread for their Reverences' tea had not looked quite as usual. Had she perhaps forgotten the sugar tongs? The last of the heavy ironing was done and she was trifling with pocket handkerchiefs when a mental picture showed her that nothing was lacking from the tea table, but that a tureen of mint sauce was there, too.

Though once again she said, 'Mother of God!' and sat down, it was not because she was daunted but because she was so shaken with laughter that she could not stand; and instead of bewailing that she was getting past her work, she exclaimed, 'It'll no be accidental-like next time, that's for sure!' adding, after a moment of rapt consideration, 'Rissoles, is it? That heeltap of the coffee extract will do fine.' Henceforward, the whet of excitement that parishioners got from staking a weekly shilling in the St Thomas à Becket Orphanage Football Pool Helen Logie enjoyed – and without paying a penny for it, either – by laying bets with herself how far she could go before Father Green and Father Curtin noticed anything uncanonical. She kept strictly within her own regulations. She bought nothing out of the usual, and except when she sauced a boiled suet pudding with cough linctus, she used no extraneous ingredients. All was wholesome and homemade, the same thrifty traditional home cooking she had been practising for years. A religious scruple stayed her hand on days of fasting or abstinence, and an innate artistry forbade her to be too emphatic with her personal touches, or too frequent in her offerings. The snuff curry remained her model: something hitherto unthought of but not blatantly uneatable. To serve uneatable food would be waste, and Helen hated waste.

She won every bet. If, instead of betting against herself, she had been betting against St Thomas à Becket at two to one, she would have made at least fifty shillings to add to her savings, where every little helps. After a while, these victories began to pall. She longed, just for once, to lose a bet and gain the substantial crown of an exclamation of horror, a protest, an inquiry – a grimace, even. Having served up a wager, she would hang about, hopefully on the watch, or come back halfway through a meal on the pretext of thinking she had been called, to search their faces for some token of acknowledgement. Sometimes she would seem to catch a glint of disaffection behind Father Curtin's spectacles. Sometimes he would pause and glance inquiringly across at Father Green. But Father Green ate steadily on, and Father Curtin returned to the faith. If it had not been for Father Curtin's intimations of uneasiness, and the fact that he went out to tea more often than of old, and the biscuit crumbs she occasionally found in his bedroom, she would almost have believed that miracles of intervenience were wrought halfway up the kitchen stairs.

She left them unassailed during the holy and taxing season of Christmas, and began again in the new year. But she was no longer laying light bets with herself. Still honourably observing her own regulations, she now staked her soul on the event, and lay awake half the night racking her brains for some new abnormality, some arresting concoction that would extort from the two men she served an acknowledgement, if not of her skill, then at least of her labours, an outcry of wrath and amazement that would prove their occasional attention to what she cooked and they consumed. As one of Father Curtin's New Year resolutions had been to subdue the flesh and not think so much about what he liked or did not like eating, she had not even the support of a biscuit crumb. She cooked. They ate. That was all there was to it.

'I'll just waste no more pains on them!' In those words she accepted and disguised defeat. It was necessary to disguise defeat, since she did not like to admit herself inferior to Miss Dewlish in moral stamina; for when Father Green had remarked, 'Well, Miss Dewlish, after thinking it over for this long time, I've come round to your opinion, so we'll try that Cinderella polish,' and then dashed the cup of victory from her lips, and in front of all the Guildswomen, too, by adding, 'But for the present we'll get it from Vokes.' Miss Dewlish had not relinquished her purpose, and had since been engaged in trying to bring back Mr Radbone by calling on him daily for small quantities of groceries and reasoning with him over the counter. 'He's weakening. She'll have him yet' was the report of Willy Duppy, who, being employed as errand boy by the fishmonger opposite Mr Radbone, was able to keep a close observation on this fight for a soul. Father Green's flock included a number of Irish immigrants, and Willy Duppy, the youngest son of a widowed mother, was a favoured lamb. On the mornings when Willy served at Mass he got his breakfast in the presbytery kitchen; and if his reports from the Radbone sector of the Catholic Front were a trifle over-sanguine it was not to be wondered at. His heart was in it, and other military correspondents have been the same.

It was the middle of February, and Father Curtin was gratefully discovering that it was easier than he would have supposed to subdue the flesh and eat what was set before him without considering whether or no he liked it, and a packet of candles had appeared in Mr Radbone's window – which showed, said Willy, what his mind was dwelling on, since why should they be there otherwise? – and people with time for it were having influenza and others were just keeping about with bad colds, and Father Green under doctor's orders had been forced out of the ranks of the latter and been put to bed, when a last belated bubble of fancy rose in Helen's mind. Twelve dozen Seville oranges had simmered in the copper and she was about to begin on the business of scooping out the pulp and chopping the rinds, when it occurred to her that a dash of mustard might make an interesting addition – not to the marmalade she made for sale (her marmalade was in great demand and brought in almost as much to the parish funds as her baking did) but to an experimental pot for use upstairs. It was a poor weak bubble, and by the time it had weakly exploded she had already lost interest in it. There was a long afternoon's work before her, and the best she could hope was that by the time she had done with scooping and chopping and stirring she would be too tired to worry about that ache across her shoulders.

She was not at Mass next morning. She's down with influenza, thought Father Curtin. Though he was slightly appalled at the thought of being neither led nor fed, he was young enough to like the idea of showing his single-handed worth. However, the living-room fire was burning, the breakfast table was laid, and from below came the sounds and smells of breakfast preparing. He warmed his hands at the fire and waited. Steps approached. The door was pushed a little way open, and a tray appeared in the opening. He waited for Miss Logie to follow the tray. The tray remained where it was, and Miss Logie's voice – crisper, he thought, than usual – announced, 'Here you are, your Reverence. Your breakfast.'

As there presently seemed nothing else to do, he advanced, and took hold of the tray. As he took it, he nearly dropped it. It was proffered to him by what seemed at first sight a perfectly unknown woman with a great deal of rather tousled red hair streaming over her shoulders.

'I can't get it up,' she said. 'I've the rheumatism in my shoulders, and I can no more reach to the back of my head than to this ceiling.'

'I daresay I could tie it back for you, Miss Logie, if I had a piece of string.'

He set down the tray and began searching in his pockets. At the same time, he began searching in his mind, for there was something else, to do with Miss Logie's hair and yet not to do with it, that should be dealt with immediately if he were to prove his single-handed worth. 'I've got a rubber band.' At the sound of a cough overhead, he realized what it was that had to be dealt with. 'I'll tell you what I can do. I'll take up Father Green's breakfast.'

It was harder than he supposed to carry a tray upstairs; as for shutting the door after him with his foot, he could not manage it at all. It must be one of those womanly knacks that a man has no need for. At the clatter of the sliding crockery, Father Green opened his eyes.

'Miss Logie has got a touch of rheumatism, so I thought I'd spare her the tray.'

'Well, well. That's very kind of you. I'm glad it doesn't prevent her from cooking.'

Father Curtin felt that he had shown both presence of mind and good judgment. The doctor had spoken of a strain on the heart. It could have been a very dangerous shock to Father Green to see his housekeeper looking like the repentant Magdalen – partially, at any rate. From the chin down, she was as neat and buttoned-up as usual, though, oddly enough, this didn't make her appearance a whit less disquieting; it made it more so.

When he came in to lunch, her hair was up, though it did not look very secure. He commented on this – at least, he expressed his relief that her rheumatism was better.

'It's no better at all, your Reverence. It's just the best that Willy could do, when he brought the kippers.'

'Oh! Isn't there anyone else who could –'

'And he's coming again tonight, to take it down. And early tomorrow, so that I can get to Mass.'

He could not feel that this arrangement was very suitable, but he did not feel that to question it would be very suitable either. That evening – an impulse of chaperonage impelled him to sit up later than usual – he heard Willy being let in at the back door. Willy seemed to be staying a long time, as long as if he were putting Helen's hair up instead of taking it down – which the force of gravity made ridiculous. At last he could bear it no longer. He went unobtrusively to the head of the kitchen stairs. He heard a steady mutter of two voices, apparently conversing with phenomenal glibness. Going a step or two down the stairs, he realized that Helen and Willy were saying the rosary. Well, that was very nice. But what was that other recurrent, swishing sound? It could not be ... But it was. It was Willy brushing Helen's hair. A moment later, Father Curtin heard himself being called from above stairs. The call was sharp, and urgent. Father Green must be having a heart attack. He hurried to the bedroom.

'Who's that downstairs at this hour of night?'

'It's Willy Duppy.'

'Well, what's he doing? He's been there for hours.'

'He's taking down Miss Logie's hair.'

'What?'

It was a comfort to disburden himself, for there are certain problems that only an experienced priest can deal with, and an experienced housekeeper is one of them. They were still talking when Helen, her two plaits finished off with two blue bows – Willy had a grateful heart, and took this opportunity to show how much he appreciated the breakfasts – went past on her way up to bed. The door was shut. But without straining her ears or disgracing herself by stopping to hear more, she heard enough to know that she was being talked about – she herself, not just her ability to provide bacon and eggs.

'I wouldn't care to cross her,' the younger priest said.

And the elder replied, 'We'll have no crossing, I hope. But you're right, all the same. She hasn't got that red hair for nothing.'

'She's what I'd call sensitive.'

'Well, that would be one word for it. Anyway, the best thing you can do is to keep out of it, for she's got more tricks up her sleeve than you'd be equal to.'

So that was the secret! All a woman need do to get herself attended to was to have a fit of rheumatism that would make it impossible for her to put her hair up. Well, now she knew it. And if she didn't rivet their attention this time, she'd have only herself to blame.

Next morning, Father Curtin inquired after Helen's rheumatism – but cautiously – and said nothing of carrying up Father Green's breakfast. With a grieved face and a dancing step, she went up with the tray, and as she needed both hands to carry it, she could do nothing when another hairpin lost its footing and fell out.

'Good morning, Helen. What's all this about your hair?'

'Good morning, your Reverence. I hope you had a better night.'

'Passable, passable. I don't mind telling you, your hair kept me awake for part of it.'

'I'm sure I'm sorry to hear that. Your Reverence has enough to worry you, without thinking about me. What's a little rheumatism? It doesn't prevent me from cooking, or washing or ironing, or the housework, except that I can't dust above my head. But that's no matter. Don't give it another thought, your Reverence. As for my hair, what's her hair to a woman of my age? Nothing, nothing at all.' She shook her head disclaimingly, and several more hairpins fell out.

'And what's all this about Willy?'

'Yes, indeed. It's Willy I have to thank that I could get to Mass this morning. He came round early on purpose, to put it up for me. He's a very obliging lad, your Reverence. There's nothing he wouldn't do to help us.'

'Willy's well enough. But he's got other things to do than put your hair up.'

'A true word. That's what makes it so obliging of him.'

'And take it down again, when he ought to be in bed and asleep. Besides, it's not properly up at all, as far as I can see.'

'Poor Willy! He does the best he can.'

'If you can't manage it yourself, you ought to get some other woman, who'd know how to do it.'

'Well, yes, I daresay. But I wouldn't care to flout Willy, when he's been so obliging. As I've heard your Reverence say, Willy's a boy in a thousand.'

'Some other woman –'

'Excuse me, your Reverence. That's the street bell.' She turned to the door, and her movement shook down a long tress.

'Helen. stop! You can't answer the door, looking like . . .'

But it was too late. Looking like a comet with a burning tail, Helen was gone.

When the doctor came, later in the day, Father Green gave him a searching look and inquired if he knew of a quick cure for rheumatism. The doctor, a rather prosy man, replied that there were a great many different kinds of rheumatism, and that the more one studied the disease, the more mysterious it became. For instance, some people got rheumatism if they drank cider; others if they drank cider were cured of it. After a while, he perceived that his patient had lost interest in the subject and introduced a new topic.

'Remarkable hair your housekeeper has got. I've never seen it down before. She told me she'd been washing it.'

It was a fine explanation, but scarcely one for daily use. When on the morrow Helen's rheumatism quitted her as abruptly as it had seized on her, she was not sorry. She could always recall it if she wished. Meanwhile, it was a comfort to have her hair, and Willy, too, firmly back in their right places. Willy was a good quiet boy, but their Reverences had spoiled him, and he must not be encouraged to suppose himself indispensable.

It seemed, however, as though she were in a way to be as much attended to with her hair in its usual knob as when it flowed unconfined. Father Curtin and Father Green, who was now up and about again, rejoiced in her recovery and showed a great deal of solicitude in warning her not to sit in drafts, get wet feet, or do anything beyond her strength. It was but solicitude, though sharpened by anxiety, that impelled Father Green – after Willy, in the course of delivering a smoked haddock, had stayed for half an hour at the back door, imparting how Mr Radbone had sent away three of his regular suppliers without ordering as much as a packet of starch – and what could that mean but a mind distracted towards more spiritual things? – to inquire what on earth Willy had been chattering about for so long.

'Willy?' said Helen, in affable tones. 'Willy? Oh, aye, I remember. He came while Miss Dewlish was upstairs talking to your Reverence. But I didn't pay any attention, my mind wasn't on him at all. I was wondering when Miss Dewlish would go, so that I could get on with cleaning the parlour windows. But there, she stayed on, so I must just do it tomorrow. Tomorrow'll do as well.'

She could afford to be affable. Tomorrow would see her rheumatism back, and his Reverence dancing and praying for Willy Duppy to come again, and no questions asked, either.

Father Green did not see himself as dancing and praying. It seemed to him that he was exercising a proper amount of authority, while keeping his temper remarkably well for a man who had only just got over influenza.

'Helen, I am sorry to see you are having trouble with your hair again. And I don't think Willy Duppy is a fit person to put it up for you. It needs a woman to deal with it. So you had better ask one of our good neighbours – one of the ladies of the Women's Guild, for instance.'

'Your Reverence, I wouldn't have one of them touch me.'

'Your rheumatism may be painful. I daresay it is. But I can't believe you're as sensitive as all that. In any case, we can't go through life avoiding pain.'

'I'm thinking of the talk. They'd say it was dyed.'

'Helen, this is ridiculous. You must either consent to have your hair put up or –'

'Or what, your Reverence?'

'Or you must stay in your bedroom.'

'Oh well – if your Reverence insists . . .' Helen spoke with more submission than he had dared to expect. Her glance, avoiding his, strayed about the room and lighted on the wastepaper basket, which needed emptying. She picked it up; then, with a shake of the head and a sigh, she put it down again and moved slowly toward the door.

'If you need the tin opener, it's on the dresser, your Reverence.'

Three days, she judged, would be about right. Less than three days would not give them adequate time for repentance. More than three days would mean such havoc in the kitchen that she, too, might be driven to repent.

Three days' leisure took some getting rid of, but she passed the time by overcoming a great heap of darning, and writing letters to her relations. At due intervals she crept downstairs, sad and unshriven, to get herself something to eat. She timed her descents to the kitchen so that she would either find Father Curtin getting a meal or Father Green and Father Curtin together washing up. Abashed and silent, she would then hang about in the doorway, a shameful spectacle that would not intrude itself upon them by any offers of help or advice; and after a minute or two retire, until the kitchen was vacated, when she could have a grim look round on the aftermath, cook something with a strong declamatory smell, like toasted cheese, and leave whatever she had used in a state of ostentatious cleanliness, polished and shining like a good deed in a naughty world.

Three days, as it turned out, was a little too long, for on the evening of the third day they disconcerted her by being invited to supper by Mrs Ward, who was celebrated for keeping a good table. When Helen served breakfast the next morning with her flowing locks back where they should be, she sensed that the situation had curdled, and that next time she would have to go about it more circumspectly. When Mrs Ward's car drove up just before lunchtime and Mrs Ward stepped out of it carrying a covered basket, she knew what had happened. She was no longer the only cook in their Reverences' lives.

So it was unfortunate that, less than a week later, Helen should wake up with another attack of rheumatism in her shoulders, as genuine and inhibiting as the first. Gritting her teeth, and calling on St Jude, the patron of seemingly lost causes, she somehow managed to bundle her hair into a chignon and fling a scarf over her head. St Jude had also provided Willy. Though this was not one of Willy's mornings, the usual Thursday server had failed, Willy had been called to replace him, and was now at the back door, waiting to be let in for breakfast, and bursting to communicate the latest news about Mr Radbone.

'Trying to sell the business? Hoots, why should he want to do that? I don't believe it.'

'It's true as I stand here. And ready to take whatever he can get for it, he's that wild to get away.'

'Where does he want to go, then?'

'Anywhere out of here. The fact of it is –' Willy lowered his voice and glanced behind him. 'The fact of it is – and I wouldn't like to be telling anyone but you, Miss Logie – the fact of it is . . .'

'Oh, hurry, boy, don't make so many bobs at it. And twist harder than that, or it will never stay on my head.'

'The fact of it is, it's her. She's been going at him too hard, every day and twice a day, and telling him in front of the commercial traveller that she's put another novena on him, till it's got so that he breaks out into a sweat every time she goes in for a tin of cocoa or a pennyworth of birdseed. No, she's been too savage for him; she'll never get him now, he's lost.'

'Well, now! That will fair break Miss Dewlish's heart,' said Helen briskly, and went off with the breakfast tray.

People rapturously savouring the misfortunes of others cannot help betraying it by an expression of morbid primness. When Father Curtin looked up to say 'Good morning', he found himself recalling the occasion when it seemed to him that the Devil had entered into Miss Logie. But this morning it appeared as though the Devil had been comfortably lodged in her for some time.

Father Green also said 'Good morning', but did not look up. He did not want to look at Helen, he did not want to hear her voice, he did not want to be aware of her in any shape or form except in the form of works. Ever since the day when she had shot madly from her sphere – her befitting womanly sphere of being his housekeeper – and turned into a

59

baleful, red-maned comet, she had compelled far too much of his unwilling attention, forcing him to struggle not only with her vagaries but with, on his own part, an obsessive, uncomfortable, and totally unmanly exasperation. He looked at his plate of porridge, so calm and daily, and then he unfolded his newspaper and propped it against the teapot and looked at that.

Thus, when Reggie Mendoza, the son of a local landowner, and in the tadpole stage of conversion, arrived that afternoon for an hour's instruction, and was shown in by Helen with her hair in a state of nature, Father Green was unprepared for the shock, and said, 'Sit down, Reggie' with such controlled force that Reggie felt with a delicious thrill that he was really being addressed by the Voice of the Church, and almost knelt down instead. Reggie's reason for becoming a convert was that he doubted the validity of Anglican Orders, and as Father Green did not even give them the benefit of the doubt, one might have supposed that everything would be straightforward. People who feel such doubts, however, do not like to have them too emphatically endorsed; at an unwary assent, the doubter will fly to the defence of what he is proposing to abjure, as when if too heavy a weight is cast on one end of a seesaw the person at the other end will fly upward and possibly fall off. Though Reggie did not fall off, the conversational seesawing required patience and delicate adjustment, and Father Green, with the thought of Helen hammering in his brain, found these much harder than usual to supply. At long last, he got Reggie to the doorstep and saw him off with a blessing. Then, after a pinch of snuff and a couple of reviving sneezes, he summoned Helen to his study.

'Shut the door, Helen,' he began, in much the same compressed tones as when he said, 'Sit down, Reggie'. She was, in fact, already shutting it, but in this conversation he wished to assert his authority from the start. There she stood, her unrepentant tresses flowing and her small grey eyes fixed on him – a revolting, an embarrassing, spectacle.

He had decided on a preliminary pause – such as he made use of, on solemn occasions, in the pulpit. The pause was broken by Helen saying, 'Well, your Reverence?'

He disregarded this, and continued to pause. Helen continued to stare. Then her glance veered to his snuffbox, and her lips curled slightly, as though she were sneering at his only self-indulgence.

'Ahem! What I have to say can scarcely come as a surprise to you. Your conscience will have told you already that I have cause for uneasiness – painful uneasiness.'

'My hair, I suppose.' Her Scottish intonation, dragging out the word 'hair', gave this a cynical ring. 'Or would it be my rheumatism?'

'I have spoken about this already. I had hoped not to have to speak again. But I see I must. Helen, this cannot go on. I cannot have you going about with your hair streaming down your back. It is unseemly. I don't like it.'

'I don't like it myself, your Reverence. But what way can I get it up if my rheumatism won't let me and I mayn't have Willy?'

'It is not your rheumatism that stands in your way, Helen. It is your obstinacy. The parish is full of women who would put your hair up for you.'

'It can be fuller yet, your Reverence, before I'd let one of them near me.'

'Think twice, Helen. Do you seriously mean those words?'

'Indeed and I do.'

'Very well. In that case, there's only one way out. Your hair must be cut short.'

'Cut off my hair? Never! I don't know what your Reverence is thinking of. St Peter said women should keep their hair long.'

'St Peter said nothing of the sort. And if it's St Paul you want, St Paul said that a God-fearing woman doesn't adorn herself with plaited hair, but with modesty, sobriety, and good works.'

'Let them plait their hair that can get their hands round to it! See for yourself if I can plait my hair!' She wrenched up her arms with such fury and vehemence that the pain made her cry out.

The door opened. Father Curtin looked in. 'Is there anything wrong? Has something happened to Miss Logie?'

'Just this – that I've come to the end of my patience. And both your Reverences can hear what I've got to say. Here and now, I'm giving you a month's notice.'

She stamped out of the room, her face white as a bone and her hair streaming like a banner.

Father Curtin turned to Father Green for reassurance. He got none. Father Green's face was purple, the veins stood out on his forehead, and he was breathing like an embattled ram. Presently he glanced at his watch. 'About time to say our vespers.'

On the morrow, Father Green rang up Mrs Ward and said in a voice that was perhaps a trifle calmer and louder than ordinary that he would be grateful if she would help him to find a new housekeeper. To her condolences he replied that it was indeed quite a blow, and that he had no doubt Helen's baking would be missed throughout the parish, but that the work was getting beyond her strength and that she had well earned a reposeful old age.

The news that Helen was going made a considerable stir, but the news, coming soon after, that Mr Radbone had gone, nobody knew where to, made a greater, since there was also Miss Dewlish's frustration to be canvassed, and the question of what she would take up next.

Presumably, Helen was relieved to be out of the limelight; at any rate, about the time of Mr Radbone's departure she was observed to grow less morose, and as Lent wore on, her disposition sweetened to such an extent that instead of triumphing over Mrs Ward's failure to catch a housekeeper, she mentioned a Cousin Isa, who would come on trial if their Reverences thought fit, learn what was required, and, if she gave satisfaction, take over after Helen went. As there was now less than a fortnight left of Helen's month, this was agreed to.

Isa arrived, gave satisfaction, and was engaged. Wearing a new suit and an unexpectedly dashing going-away hat, Helen made a round of farewell calls, in the course of which she said a great deal that was proper and civil, and nothing that was informative. Her demeanour was so grave and reserved that a number of people believed she had been dismissed for some sudden lapse it would not be kind to inquire into, and some among them even thought that Father Green had been too hasty with an old servant.

Her farewells appeared to be final, so it was a pleasing surprise when, soon after Easter, Mr Radbone's redecorated shop opened its doors for the sale of light refreshments, cooked meats, cakes, jams, scones, and bannocks, and there was Helen presiding over it, assisted by Willy Duppy. The business throve, the money she had borrowed to complete the purchase was soon paid back, and Willy was felt to be as good as made, since Helen allowed it to be known that when he had learned the trade, and put by a decent nest egg in the Post Office Savings, and married a nice steady girl, he would become her partner and ultimately inherit the business. True, Willy's vocation to the priesthood, which at one time had seemed so promising, was mislaid in all this; but as Willy himself had never felt altogether sure of it, things were probably for the best.

SOME EFFECTS OF A HAT

Jorge de mi alma,

We have just been doing a little rescue work by moonlight; for it suddenly turned so smitingly cold that I thought of my tender vegetables, and what the brisk smack of frost could do to them. So the cocoa beans were housed in Indian bed-spreads, and I brought in a trugful of courgettes, and both the oak leaf geraniums, and the baby myrtle and the even more baby tangerine, and things I can't get in till daylight helps are overdecked with sheets of *The Times*. And what the garden will look like tomorrow with its paperings and Indian bedspreadings to the morning postman I know not and care not. Anyhow, as he brings the letters into the hall, he already has the American Gentleman's hat to occupy his mind.

The American Gentleman, with two American ladies, turned up over a week ago, having heard of Valentine's antique shop and found their way to it. They didn't buy anything, but they were all very nice and amiable and well-beseen. And after they'd driven away, Valentine found that the gentleman had left his well-beseen hat behind him. We had to go out that afternoon, but we supposed he would come back for it, so we left it conspicuously disposed in front of the house, in shelter and on an eminence where the cats would not sleep on it . . . but when we got back, there it was. So then we supposed, since one of the ladies had taken Valentine's shop card with the telephone number, that he would ring up about it. Not a ring. And next day, not a letter, not a postcard.

So it sits in the hall, where for a few days it was a feature, and now is imperceptibly melting into the general aspect of the things we keep in the hall – including the machete I prune trees with and the chapeau de paille d'Italie I walk round the garden in when we have visitors; and I suppose it will end by being another of the things I dust from time to time.

Such a beautiful hat – I don't know how any man could forsake such [a] hat, all the more so since he had scarcely taken its virginity. It is a homburg, made of a solid, slightly furry felt (I think the term is brushed), a subtle shade of green olive on its way to becoming black olive, with a fancy Petersham band round it and a feather incident – and a lining of turquoise blue. Dunn's, Piccadilly. I long to wear it myself. It is only a trifle too large for me, and immensely becoming. But I can't persuade Valentine to agree, she says it would make me conspicuous. What else does she suppose I want a hat to do? What other purpose has a hat? But there it is, I am too kind to wear a hat that would even incidentally associate her with conspicuity; and the gentleman won't reclaim it, I despair of him now. Unless he has had a motor accident and only when consciousness returns to him will he cry out, My hat, where is my hat? And by that time they will have mislaid Valentine's card, and he will be carried onto a Jet airliner on a stretcher and never see his hat again.

If he hasn't reclaimed it before Christmas, would you like it? It is a very handsome hat.

Letter from Sylvia Townsend Warner to George Plank. (see p. vi)

Above the porch of the Wesleyan chapel at St Petrock was a marble tablet: 'REBUILT, 1910'. The graveyard was much older. It sloped uphill, and Lennie Soper, a child given to strange ideas, wouldn't go past it at dusk, alleging that it was like people at the cinema. Perhaps the ranked headstones, rising one behind another, did have a certain resemblance to a sombre audience, attentively motionless. It was many years since anyone had been buried there. But it was kept neat. The grass was scythed at regular intervals, and for the rest, Miss Mary Daker weeded the paths, sheared the mounds, and scraped the moss off the headstones. She did this the more willingly since it absolved her from taking part in livelier activities – Bright Hours and Ladies' Committees. Her father, twenty years dead, had been Minister, and she had lived on in the place of her birth, at first with her mother, afterward alone. The Dakers were Derbyshire stock, and after forty years Mary was still looked on as a foreigner, and imperfectly chapel. John Wesley had visited St Petrock on his way to Cornwall and made many converts there; no one in St Petrock had ever heard tell of his going to Derbyshire. That she was imperfectly chapel no one knew better than

Mary herself. That she was a foreigner would have surprised her. Having spent her best days in St Petrock, she supposed she would age and die there, living in No. 3 Chapel Row, and earning a livelihood by the hand-woven tweeds and woollen scarves she supplied to a firm in Torquay.

The stranger heard the clack of her loom as he let himself into the graveyard, and wondered what the noise was. The noise ceased. She had paused to put in a fresh bobbin and seen him from her window. A mist was drifting off the moor, and it enlarged and darkened his form; moving slowly along the brow of the graveyard, he seemed portentously tall, tall beyond human stature. He was going systematically from one stone to another. Plainly, he was looking for a particular name, a particular grave. It would be only right to help him – and on such a dismal afternoon, too. Carrying her weeding basket as a pretext, she walked up the centre path toward him. As she approached, he dwindled. By the time she neared him, he was no more than a rather tall man, who lifted his hat and said, 'Good afternoon.' He spoke with an American accent.

'Good afternoon. Are you looking for someone?'

'Why, yes. That's just what I am doing. I'm looking for my great-great-grandfather. And it's quite an undertaking, for I don't even know if he lived in St Petrock. But it was some place in this locality, some place between Totnes and Moreton Hampstead.'

'What was his name?'

'Prosser. Ezekiel Prosser.'

'Also Susan Amelia, wife of the above. Yes, they're along here.'

'Well,' he said admiringly. 'You know more about them than I do. I'd been told she was a Susan, but I never knew she was Amelia. Say, are we related? Are you a Prosser, too?'

She shook her head, and stood back to give him an uninterrupted view of the tall stone with its deep-cut, dogmatic lettering.

He copied the inscription into a notebook. Then he produced a pocket camera and took several photographs. That done, he looked attentively round him.

'And did Ezekiel and Susan Amelia worship in that chapel?'

'No – not exactly. In an earlier one, pulled down fifty years ago. But it stood in the same place.'

66

He put back his camera.

'I've got a photograph of the old chapel, if you'd like to see it.'

'I certainly would.'

'It won't take you a minute. That's my house there, with the blue door.'

She was proud of the blue paint; she had laid it on herself. But hearing him stumble over her Wellington boots and dislodge a pile of books as he tried to find somewhere to put down his hat, she wished she had carried out her intention to make the narrow entry rather less like a burrow by whitewashing it. The photograph of the old chapel hung in the parlour, above her father's desk. She unhooked it, and carried it to the light of the window. There was little to be said about it, but what there was he said, and thanked her, and repeated how fortunate he had been to meet her in the graveyard. 'By the way, didn't you have a basket?'

'So I did. I must have put it down somewhere. Never mind. It's quite used to being forgotten.'

He looked for a moment as if some revelation, some light from Heaven, had flashed on him. But it could not have been her small joke that he found so enlivening, for his answering laugh was quite perfunctory. Perhaps he had realized that he could now go away – for he did so, rather hurriedly, though thanking her to the last.

She replaced the photograph, and lit a cigarette, thinking about her father, and the bitter romanticism with which he cherished this relic of a building he had never seen and delighted in every malfunctioning of the amenities of its successor. Then she remembered the weeding basket and went out to fetch it. The mist had thickened into a small rain. It was no weather to whitewash in. But for all that, this very evening she would clear and sweep that deplorable burrow, and tomorrow she would lay on the first coat. Entering, she switched on the light and looked round at the scene of action. On the table lay the American gentleman's hat.

Its colour was a rich, muddy green, and its felt had been surfaced into close, lustreless mossiness. Round the crown was a band of fanciful braid, and into the braid was tucked a wad of partridge breast feathers. It was obviously a very grand and superior hat. She took it up, cautiously, with the feeling that anything so grand must also be fragile, and was astonished at its combination of lightness with solidity, and at the unassaultable curve of its brim. A hat for all time, a hat like a monument.

Turning it over, she gave a cry of pleasure. The crown was lined with pale-blue satin, smooth and blue as a duck's egg. The inner band was of fine leather, and stamped on it in gold was the name of the maker and an address in Piccadilly. Moreover, there was no trace of wear. The hat appeared to be perfectly, impersonally new.

And yet, in the elation of finding Ezekiel and Susan Amelia, he had left such a hat behind! But by now, or at any rate before long, he would realize his loss, turn his car, no doubt as grand as the hat, and come pelting back for it. This was no time to prepare for whitewashing. Instead, she would lay out a tea tray with two cups, give a lick and a promise to her parlour, and sit down to await the American gentleman and the pleasure of bestowing. Strictly speaking, the hat was his, and not for her to bestow. The pleasure of reuniting. But she thought of it as a pleasure of bestowing, because bestowing, except in the restricted shape of giving to the collection, or to the jumble sale, was a pleasure that rarely came her way.

But the American gentleman did not come back.

Perhaps he would ring up the police. Or the post office – though by now it would be shut. Or Mr Woodward, the Minister. He could scarcely write or telegraph to her, since he did not know her name. Though she presumed his to be Prosser, there was no immediate help in that. During the evening, she thought of a great many expedients which might or might not occur to him when the loss of his hat burst – as sooner or later it was bound to – upon him. By far the simplest and most practical would be to come back for it, and she had little doubt that this was what he would do, for he had struck her as a practical-minded man. Practical-minded, and also determined; not a man to relinquish his purpose. If he had set himself to visit every village between Totnes and Moreton Hampstead in search of a great-great-grandfather, and had already, as he mentioned, visited seven before trying St Petrock – if he could do all that for a name on a headstone, he would not abandon a substantial hat. And such a hat, lined with such blue satin and bought at heaven knows what a price in Piccadilly. He would certainly come tomorrow.

He did not. But it was a Sunday. A true-blue Prosser, he might repudiate Sunday travelling. So he would certainly come tomorrow. She got up early, in case he came at cockcrow.

68

He had not even come by noonday. And this was a first Monday in the month, when she was due to deliver her month's work to Homecrafts, Ltd, and bring away the yarn for the next order. She waited till the last moment, wondering what to do and doing nothing. Finally, she carried a chair out onto the doorstep and placed the hat on it, under a light veiling of tissue paper. It was a fine windless afternoon. No harm could come to it.

When she arrived home, no harm had come to it. The fear which had seized her the moment after the bus started, that a cat would come and lie on it, was unfounded. No one had come. She hurried the hat withindoors before the dews of night could get at it, and as an expression of her sense of guardianship she locked the door. Mrs Raiment, arriving half an hour later, had to knock for some time before Mary distinguished her knockings from the noise of the loom. Mrs Raiment had called round, she explained, because, not having heard a sound all day from Mary's side of their common wall, she was afraid something might have happened to her. She brought some rock cakes, too, as she had been busy baking all that afternoon.

Still the American gentleman did not come. Still his hat remained on the table in the passage. Mary had brought back an unusual amount of work; it allowed no time for the whitewashing project, for speculation, for remorse. Remorse set in two Sundays later. Returning from the morning service, Mary realized that for some time she had been walking past the hat without even being aware of its presence. She stopped dead. This was shocking. This was fatal. It meant that already the hat was joining the dull mass of things that were where they were because they had got there somehow and somehow had never been dealt with. Squatters. Like the inexplicable key on the bathroom window sill, the dog-eared packet of wallflower seed behind the parlour clock. But the hat was a different matter. She had not even the excuse of having bought it at a bazaar. Full of remorse, she carried it up to her bedroom, to give it a good brush. Poor thing, it needed it! Having still some energy in hand, she removed her own hat, considered it, and with a fine sense of turning over a new leaf threw it into the wastepaper basket. So much for that! But meanwhile here was the American gentleman's hat, snatched from oblivion but still unloved. She put it on. A transformed Mary looked back at her from the mirror. The hat swallowed up her high forehead; it shadowed her eyes and contained her untidy wisps of hair. She looked jaunty, challenging, and slightly rakish. Instead of resembling a sheep, she resembled a goat. She took it off. Back, mild and forgiving, came the sheep. She put it on again. There was the goat; and it looked at her as much as to say, 'Aha!' It did not come from Piccadilly for nothing, that hat. She longed to wear it, and to experience the new character it would give her, a character that could sit at ease in a public house instead of growing flyblown in a teashop, that could reject flabby fish and sleepy pears, and command attention at Woolworth's, and never call out those abhorred words 'What I like about Miss Daker, she's always just the same.' Perhaps, one day, if its owner never reclaimed it, and if instead of selling her tweeds she had a length made up by a proper tailor, she could wear the hat in Torquay; or, better, in London, revisiting its birthplace. But not in St Petrock, where people would look at her queerly. Meanwhile, she must buy it a hatbox. Meanwhile, she carried it downstairs and put it back on the table in the passage.

She had not noticed that people were already looking at her queerly. If she noticed anything, it was just that they were even more than seasonably inclined to bring her vegetable marrows.

'And is it still there?' they asked one another.

Mrs Raiment nodded and looked charitable. 'Yes, poor soul! It's a thing I've heard tell of, more'n once – that old single maidens keep a man's hat inside the door, to scare off thieves and murderers. Well, let's hope it's some comfort to her.'

Not everyone accepted this hypothesis.

'And is Mary Daker's hat still keeping off burglars?'

Mrs Soper pursed her lips and looked knowing. 'Well, if that's what she says it's for, it's not for me to deny it. But from what I've read in those scientific bits in the Sunday paper, it isn't only to scare off burglars that old maids like to keep a man's hat about.'

'Never! You don't say so!' exclaimed Mrs Honeyball, not very certain what in fact Mrs Soper implied, but sure it was something one wouldn't want to believe about a friend; and, having called to present a pot of apple jelly, came away saying, 'You know what Mrs Soper said about that hat, and I could hardly credit it? Well, I won't go so far as to say whether 'tis so or 'tisn't. But this I can swear to. The hat's still there.

And what's more, it's been moved a good inch to the right since I saw it last Tuesday.'

'That doesn't surprise me,' said the fishmonger's wife. 'I reckon Mary Daker does more with that hat than keep it as an ornament – that is, if you ask me.'

'Yes, but a man's hat wouldn't walk into a house on its own,' said her sister-in-law. 'How did she come by it, that's what I want to know. She never bought it; she's too near to spend all that money. And it must have cost a packet, for it comes from a shop in Piccadilly.'

'In Piccadilly? You don't say so. How do you know it does?'

'I looked inside it.'

'You've got a nerve! Suppose she'd caught you?'

'And the dust on that table, I could have written my name in it. Any man who took up with her and her old curiosity shop . . . Well, he wouldn't be very choice.'

'True, true. Still, there's no accounting for tastes. And some sort of man there must be, for how'd the hat get there otherwise?'

'If you ask me, she must have stole it. I'm sure no one's ever seen her about with a man.'

'I have! I have!' piped Lily Soper.

'Lily!' said Mrs Soper sternly. 'You oughtn't to be listening, let alone knowing about such things. Where were they?'

'In among the graves.'

'Among the graves! Outrageous! What were they doing, child?'

'He was taking photographs of her.'

When they had worn out the hat, they still had plenty to fall back on: her penuriousness – which ballooned out into immense secret riches; her reserve – she was so stuck up, she'd barely speak to you; her nonattendance at Bright Hours and social occasions – she didn't dare look people in the face, and no wonder; her activities in the graveyard – and we all knew the reason for them. In a small community, a topic for scandal can grow into a subjugating obsession that gathers impetus from itself, like a fire or a pestilence. All through October, St Petrock was swept by the scandal of Mary Daker, and could think of nothing else. She alone escaped.

She had had so much weaving to do that on the first Monday of November there was more than she could easily carry to the bus stop, and she asked young Peter Raiment to lend her a hand. Rather to her surprise, he hesitated; and though he complied, he walked at some distance behind her and whistled loudly all the way. It was November 5th. As she was getting into the bus she noticed the bonfire heaped and ready in Mr Puddock's field nearby. It occurred to her that this must be the first year she had not been asked to contribute fuel to it; she had seen the boys going round with their barrow, but for some reason they had not come to her. It was a huge bonfire, and finishing touches were still being added, for Lennie and Alan Soper were rolling tyres towards it, and out from the fishmonger's yard door came his errand boy carrying an old washstand.

'When are you going to light it?' she asked Peter.

Compelled into speech, he said, 'You'll be in plenty of time.' A look of greed, triumph, and apprehension suddenly lit his face, and was as suddenly gone.

'Even then,' she said, talking it over with Bill, a couple of months later, 'even then, I didn't suspect anything. I suppose I was very stupid.'

'You weren't very bright, love.'

In fact, she had sat in the return bus feeling childishly elated, pleased to be bringing back such a large cheque, and looking forward to the rockets. At the turn of the road, she saw that the bonfire was newly lit. Sluggish, uncertain flames staggered about in clouds of smoke. The fire hadn't yet taken hold, was feeding here and there on appetizers of brushwood and oily rags. The crowd was so dense that the bus could scarcely make its way to the stopping place. Because of her bale of yarn, she stood back to let the other passengers alight. A voice in the crowd said, 'Isn't she come?' A hand steadied her as she descended. Dazzled by the flames, now leaping out in all directions, she could not recognize whose friendly hand it was. Then she heard Mrs Soper's loud 'Good evening, Miss Daker,' and Mrs Raiment's fat voice. 'Here you be, my de-urr! Don't 'ee go home-along yet. You bide here with me, and zee the vun.' Mrs Raiment had put on her most exaggerated Devon accent; it was as though she were addressing a stranger from whom she hoped for a tip. But a salvo of rockets went up, and with her consciousness hanging on their scatter of fiery pollen Mary disregarded the oddness of Mrs Raiment's greeting. Other voices were greeting her, too, all telling her she must stay, must stay and see the fun. She was so thronged about that even if she had intended to go home she would not have been able to. Elbowed, encompassed, she was propelled forward till she stood in the front row of the crowd, with the heat and glare of the flames on her face. By now, the bonfire was fully alight. It burned with a grinding roar, and the shouts and wolf whistles and yelling voices of children seemed merely a fringe of sound waving in its wind. Suddenly, a movement went through the crowd, as though a tide stirred in it. Everyone began looking to the left. Lennie Soper's screech went up like a rocket: 'Here comes the guy!' Out of the fishmonger's yard and down Fore Street came a procession of boys clashing saucepan lids together, beating on tin trays, rattling petrol cans with pebbles in them. They had blackened their faces, and trails of black crêpe paper hung from them like mourning scarves. The crowd had fallen silent, so completely silent that a cow in a distant field could be heard lowing. After the band came the men carrying the guy. They, too, had blackened their faces, and wore overcoats hind part before. The guy, strapped to a chair, was borne on a platform supported on their shoulders. As it came into the light of the bonfire, there was another outburst of wolf whistles. Mrs Raiment's clasp tightened on Mary's right arm, Mrs Honeyball's on her left. 'Why, I do believe ... Oh, the impertinence!' exclaimed Mrs Raiment. The guy was Mary, and it was crowned with the American gentleman's hat. The hat was fixed on the back of the wobbling head, the brim like a halo above the high sheep's forehead and wisps of tow hair. They set down the platform. The guy in its chair was lifted on a couple of pitchforks, displayed this way and that, then dumped on the summit of the bonfire. Little tongues of fire licked up it, its limbs began to writhe, the locks of tow blazed and vanished, squibs packed in the straw stuffing exploded in a volley of belches, and as the flames sprang up, the chair tilted sideways and the hat fell off.

'It was the hat that saved me,' continued Mary. 'I was so furious about the hat that I could think of nothing else. As if I should ever wear a hat at the back of my head like the village idiot!'

Cold and impassive in her fury, she stood like a stone till the crowd gave way from around her – and then she walked home. The lock had been forced, but her door had a bolt; she bolted herself in, and with a mind as clear as ice she began her night's work. Before dawn, everything was done: the house swept and bared, her loom dismantled, her suitcase packed, the necessary letters written, the few things she wished to keep locked into her father's desk, the rest burned in the kitchen fire or crammed into the dustbin. She thought from one immediate act to another, certain that she was going away and of nothing beyond, thankful that in her loveless life there was no animal dependent on her. Once or twice, she caught herself wishing, and with great reality, that she had got the hat; for now she could have worn it, in its startling becomingness. Earlier in the night, she had laid out a meal for herself. When everything was done, she ate it, washed up, set her alarm clock, and lay down in her clothes. The bank didn't open till ten; she could have four hours' sleep.

She slept like a log, and when she woke, a further stretch of her future had been decided for her. To begin with, she would go to Torquay, return the yarn to Homecrafts, and buy herself some decent new clothes. From Torquay she would go to London, from London to Derbyshire. As the American gentleman had sought his stony Prossers she would seek flesh-and-blood Dakers. She was better circumstanced than he – with only a hearsay locality to guide him. She had the name of a town: Chapel-en-le-Frith. One way or another, she seemed to be doomed to chapels; but this couldn't be helped.

At ten o'clock, she was at the bank, cashing her cheque, drawing out her balance, and arranging for the withdrawal of some shares in a Housing Society. The bank manager was red in the face, and flinched from looking at her. At ten-twenty, she was with Mr Prudlock, the solicitor. The law is a hardening profession; he neither reddened nor flinched. But he was sufficiently unmanned to find himself consenting to do several things outside his capacity, such as getting a padlock fixed to her door and seeing that the electricity meter was read, the cistern drained, and the water supply turned off. At ten-forty-five, she was drinking coffee and eating a ham sandwich at the Devonia Café. At eleven, she caught the Torquay bus. It is the habitualness of life, tying one down as the Lilliputians tied Gulliver, that impedes action. Like a knife cutting butter, Mary bought new clothes, slept in strange beds. Four days later, she was looking at Derbyshire from a coach.

The coach took her as far as Buxton, where she dined and spent the night in a temperance hotel. The hotel was very warm, with enormous coal fires. Outside, it was very cold, with a dry air and a nipping wind – a variety of cold she had never experienced before. Several times, listening to people in the street, she could have sworn she heard her father speaking. But one can't interrupt a conversing stranger and say, 'Are you a Daker?' In that respect, the American gentleman, with tombstones abiding his question, had the easier part. Next morning, it was so dominatingly cold that she went out the moment the shops were open, bought a woollen vest, and changed into it before leaving the hotel. Immediately, she was filled with confidence. The bus to Chapel-en-le-Frith twirled her along a road of dramatically sharp bends through a landscape of dramatically steep contours, and set her down in a town which was larger than she had expected, and quite singularly prosaic. But, supported by the vest, she told herself it looked sensible. After a lifetime of the Devonshire climate this dry, unequivocal atmosphere made her feel a different being. In fact, though she was unaware of this, its effect on her was that of a double gin. Feeling clearheaded and capable, she explored Chapel-en-le-Frith with a brisk step and almost total inattention, from time to time smiling idiotically because over a row of slate roofs or at the end of a street a steep bare hillside had caught her eye. Having made an early breakfast, she was now growing hungrier and hungrier. Nothing if not practical, since she was hungry she would eat; and as her new life had begun, she would walk into the first public house instead of wandering in search of a bun shop. The first public house was called The Plume of Feathers. It had a solid stone front, sash windows, and no garnishments whatever. Stepping over its whitened doorstep, she happened to glance up. There, above her head, neatly painted in italic on an oval label, were the words, 'William Wilfred Daker, Licensed to Sell Wines, Spirits, Beer and Tobacco'. She read them between one step and the next, and was into the house before she had time to think it a coincidence.

William Wilfred Daker – she had no doubt about him – was sitting behind the bar, reading a newspaper. Hearing her step, he got up.

'Half pint of bitter, please,' she said, as to the manner born.

'Draught or bottle?'

'Draught.'

He filled a tankard, and handed it across the bar.

'And I should like something to eat – something solid.'

'What about a fresh cut of pork pie, Miss?'

It was strange. Just as she knew he was William Wilfred, he knew she was Miss.

Returning from a sort of pantry with a napkined, furnished tray, he said, 'Come into the snug, Miss. You'll be warmer in there.'

In the snug was another of those great coal fires, an upright piano, and an array of potted geraniums. He saw her look at them, looked toward them himself, gave a sigh. 'They want watering again,' he murmured. On the window sill was a glittering brass hot-water can. He took it up, found it was empty, shook his head, and went away with it. Presently, he came back and watered each geranium with exact care. His look was full of melancholy and self-blame.

'I've never seen such splendid geraniums,' said Mary.

'Yes, they're fine specimens. This is Guardsman. This is Queen of the Pinks. But they take looking after. They're nesh.'

Nesh. Her father's word, meaning 'delicate'. *The girl looks nesh.*

He had turned back to her, with a resumption of his former expression. 'Is the pork pie to your liking?'

She could only nod, for her mouth was full. As soon as she could speak, she spoke.

'"Nesh". That's a word my father used. He was born here – in this town. His name was Daker. Like yours.'

He came up and grasped her hand. 'I'm very glad to meet you, Miss Daker. There's a fair lot of us – all the better for another one.' There was real pleasure in his face.

Customers had come into the bar, and were calling, 'Bill!'

'I'll be back in a minute,' he said.

She sat disentangling the sound of his voice from theirs. It was lower-pitched than her father's and gentler. Though he spoke to the same tune, his accent was not so marked. When he came in again, he drew up a chair to the table and looked at her with frank curiosity. 'You're like a Daker, too, now that I come to study you. But not in your speech.'

'I was born in Devonshire, and I've lived there all my life. My father was in the Wesleyan ministry.'

'And now you've come back,' he said, brushing the rest aside. 'Excuse me. I'm wanted.' He was gone again.

That's all he thinks of, she reflected; that I've come back. I don't suppose he'd even wonder why. She liked him very much – only it was a pity he had such an interrupting profession. On his third appearance he brought two glasses of cherry brandy. On his fourth, an album of photographs of the Peak. The bar kept him busy. Presently, he darted in to put more coals on the fire. 'My trouble is, I'm single-handed. Here's all this time gone, and I don't know your Christian name.'

'Mary. And I mustn't keep you from your work. I've been thinking. I'll go for a walk round the town and come back this afternoon, after you've closed – if I may.'

She unclasped her bag. He caught back her wrist. 'None of that, Cousin Mary Daker. But you're right, we'll be more comfortable between hours. I'll let you out by the house door; you needn't go through the bar. It will be to this door you come back. Mind and be punctual.'

She was punctual. But the first freedom was gone; they were not so easy with each other. Thinking to help out conversation, she asked if there were other Dakers in the town. It was as if his glance had said, 'I was waiting for this.' Flushing and frowning, he said, 'There's quite a few. But there's more in Glossop.'

'I might go on there then. Is there a hotel in Glossop?' For apparently she had outstayed her welcome.

His look of constraint deepened to anguish. He stared at the geraniums, and then at his feet, and then at the geraniums again. 'I'm ashamed that I can't ask you to stay here. It's what I'd like to do, and ought to do. And there's a room, with a view of the church and all. But it wouldn't be fit for you. It wouldn't be what you're accustomed to. I'm single-handed, like I said. My wife died, a matter of six weeks ago – '

'I'm so sorry.'

' – and everything's been at sixes and sevens ever since. I manage to keep the downstairs clean, and fend for Lucy and Simmy – they're my two daughters, eight and ten – but the rest of the place has got beyond me. All I can say for myself is that I know it.'

'But don't you know anyone who'd help you manage? Can't you get some sensible woman to cook and clean for you?'

'There isn't a woman in the place – not one that I'd have here – who'd come near the house.'

'But – ' She stopped herself.

He saw her confusion, and laughed. 'My wife. She'd fallen out with every woman in Chapel-en-le-Frith, God rest her! I should say that at one time or another, they've all sworn their Bible oaths never to cross this doorstone again. And we're a stiff-necked lot, up here. When we've said a thing, we stand by it. You see – she was a terrible cleaner.' He turned back the keyboard lid of the piano. 'Just look at those brass hinges! She was like that all through. Thorough! And if people didn't come up to her ideas, she'd tell them so. She'd got a polishing tongue.'

So that's why he didn't take up my question about the other Dakers, Mary thought.

'So that accounts for the flower-pots!' she exclaimed.

'Damp-flannelled every morning. Mind you, though, I won't have a word said against her. She was a very kind woman in the house, whatever she was outside it.'

'And not double-faced,' said Mary, thinking back to St Petrock.

He got up, saying he must get tea for the children. Mary remained sitting, and so he had to ask her to stay for it. She accepted without a blush, remarking that she would like to meet two more Dakers. They came in, two ramping, stamping little girls, sparkling with the cold, and were introduced to their Cousin Mary from Devonshire. Tea was substantial but brisk. Just before opening time, Mary rose. 'I've remembered my suitcase. I left it at the bus depot. I must go and fetch it.'

He accompanied her to the door. 'Where are you spending the night?' he asked.

'Here. At The Plume of Feathers.'

'You can't, Mary, you can't! It's not fit for you. The bed isn't even aired.'

'I'll make it. And air it. I'm over forty, I ought to know how to air a bed by now. I'm your Cousin Mary, and I've come up from Devonshire to keep house for you till you can find someone local. And as good, of course. And a Daker.'

To assert his manly authority, he called back into the house, 'Lucy! Simmy! Get your coats on and go down to the depot with your cousin, to help carry her traps.'

Six months later – and as in that moment she had ordained – he married her.

By then, in Rhode Island, Mrs Eldred Prosser had given up

reproaching her husband for his carelessness in mislaying the splendid British hat she had bought him. But she still could not understand why he had done nothing to retrieve it, however often and however patiently he pointed out that he had visited nearly a dozen places between Totnes and Moreton Hampstead in the search for his great-great-grandfather, and might have left it at any one of them. As, indeed, he might have done; though it happened to be at St Petrock that the expedient had been vouchsafed to him how to get rid of that deplorable, that frightful hat.

THE MAHOGANY TABLE

The moment had come for Mrs Carrington to look at her wrist watch. 'Heavens! I must fly. We've got people coming in for drinks this evening, the morning's gone and I haven't as much as salted an almond. Why can't I be efficient like you? But of course, you're marvellous, quite marvellous. No, no! Don't get up. I can see myself out.'

The car went up the lane, its horn blaring. She had stayed her usual quarter of an hour and deposited her usual small cottage cheese. Letitia Foley carried it to the larder, and sat down again. Her glance traversed Mrs Carrington's wake: a dislodged cushion, a trail of white chalk mud, a tissue handkerchief, a paper clip. Paper clips rained from the poor woman as hairpins would have done in an epoch when hair was a crowning glory. Though there was no immediate call for a paper clip, paper clips come in handy at some time or other; meanwhile they accumulated in the Cloisonné box. All things in their season. When the mud had dried, she would deal with Pansy Carrington's wake. She sat and let the stiffening of attention ebb out of her limbs and imagined the reply she could have made to the parting assurances that she was marvellous.

'I am not marvellous at all. I am merely tidy, methodical, and an early riser. I get up at seven, I wash and dress and strip my bed to air it. I go down to the kitchen, which is clean because I left it in order overnight, and eat a sensible breakfast because a sensible breakfast is the best beginning for an active morning. I listen to the weather forecast and the news; if the post has brought me any letters I read them and decide how to answer them. I plan my meals for the day, and how best to use any left-overs. I make it a rule to keep no left-overs lying about. What with one thing and another it is now time to walk to the village to buy what I may need. I buy a packet of five cigarettes every morning; a regular walk means that I have to polish my shoes and keep myself in trim. By half-past eleven I have finished the housework and have the rest of the day before me to do as I please in. I never find time heavy on my hands; there is always something to do, polishing, or mending, ironing, spraying the window-plants, turning out a cupboard; there is always something interesting to do, and always time to do it in. *Ohne Hast, ohne Rast*, as the saying is. Sometimes I talk German to myself, to keep in practise.'

But such exemplary replies were never spoken. There was no call for them. Satisfied that she was marvellous, her visitors left it at that, talked about themselves, and went away.

There had been a time when a neutered cat called Dinah had twined through Miss Foley's systematic days. Dinah grew old and died, and was not replaced; for by then Letitia Foley too was growing old; and wondering what would happen to a cat who might outlive her would have been painful. A few years later she was forced to come to a similar prudent decision about her garden. It was a small well-flowered garden, in front of the house; if it had been at the back, she could have kept it as a private pleasure, an eccentricity of self-will; but from the day when a dandelion yielded so abruptly that she fell on her back and had to struggle to get up again, she recognized that weed as she might and be envied for her lilies and clove carnations, the garden was growing too much for her. No one had marked her fall; but she might not be so lucky another time. Brushed and polished and wearing gloves, she visited the local builder, and told him she wanted the garden levelled and put under concrete. 'You want a patio,' he said, all-knowingly. She said she wanted an estimate.

Dinah had died a quiet natural death; the garden was noisily slaughtered. But self-respect does not allow one to regret an act one has paid a great deal of money for, and by not thinking about the garden she contrived not to grieve for it. She missed not listening to the weather forecast. It had been a companionable voice; but now it was no more to the purpose than the news.

She brushed away the traces of Mrs Carrington's visit. For lunch she had planned a poached egg, but now substituted the small cottage cheese, and a healthy apple, and then satisfaction; for this was her afternoon for polishing the sitting-room furniture.

If the house was too large for a single woman, the furniture was undoubtedly too large for the house. She had known it all her life, and for much of her life had polished it. The pair of tallboys had come into the family with her Swedish great-grandmother. They were pale and classically plain, and so tall that to reach their cornice she had to stand on a chair. When she was a child they were known to be ugly; now she understood they were estimable. Deducing the great-grandmother from the tallboys, she grew up convinced that the great-grandmother had been a dislikeable character, harsh and ungiving, with none of the rich fruit-like glow of the mahogany table under which she and Cecily used to play houses. When she and Cecily set up house together after the parents were dead, Cecily had insisted on the mahogany table. Neither of them wanted the tallboys; but as belated twins at the end of a long family they had to take what was allotted and be grateful for it.

Moving to a small villa in a county without associations, they lived a happy slatternly life till the day in 1918 when Cecily brought in her limping expeditionary American. He was a Californian, large and polite, politely concealing his astonishment at the speed with which Cecily had caught him. Cecily was not in the least astonished. As though she were speaking a part in a play she told Letitia that everything was settled, that she had never been so happy in her life, that as soon as Dexter's new leg had settled in they would marry and leave for California. Dexter hoped that Letitia would visit them.

The invitation ripped open Letitia's sense of injury. 'Will you be taking the mahogany table?' she asked. The words were no sooner out of her mouth than she blushed for them. Cecily appeared to consider. 'Dear old thing . . . no, I don't think so. Dexter swarms with furniture he calls missionary.' Her triumphant satisfaction wadded her against reproach; one might as well be sarcastic to a cat with a bird between its jaws. It was so painful to be alone with her, in surroundings where they had always been together, that Letitia, concentrating her resentment into hating Dexter, was thankful for his company.

One evening after she had farewelled him with an almost genuine 'Must you go already?' Cecily looked up from the night-dress she was embroidering for her trousseau. 'Must he go already? Do you suppose he enjoys sitting here while you mope at him? Can you think of nobody but yourself?' They hurled themselves into a violent quarrel, each knowing where to wound. Cecily won. Having allowed Letitia to rant to a standstill, she remarked cheerfully, 'Thank God we shan't have to make this one up,' and went on with her embroidery. To the last, she was conscienceless and Dexter was kindly. At last they were gone and Letitia was alone in a house littered with remains of packing. By the time she had set it to rights, method and economy had fastened on her. On alternate Tuesdays she wrote to Cecily. Cecily's letters came intermittently: she had had a child; she had bobbed her hair; there was wonderful news but it must wait till the next letter. The next letter came from Dexter's mother. Cecily had been killed in a road accident; Dexter had taken an overdose.

Wisps of the past had become entangled in the routine of her days, and recurred as regularly, to be acknowledged and ignored. A chipped dinner plate was Dunkirk; a hearth rug, the first raw misery of being alone. Cecily with her hair in pigtails was an adjunct to polishing the mahogany table. Today, as on every other Wednesday, the act of taking off the heavy tablecloth and folding it, uncovered Cecily waggling the moveable table leg and saying the roof of their house was about to fall. It was a large oblong table, the two moveable legs supported its hinged flaps. All four legs were made of an inferior wood, and she always polished these first, looking forward the while to the smooth sweeping pressure and rewarding glow of polishing the top. The glow had again rewarded her, she had seen her face reflected – though wanly; for the day was clouding over. It was working up for rain and presently she would hear the first raindrops patter on the concrete square where the garden had been. It was on such afternoons that she and Cecily were told to stay indoors and played at houses. She had put back the tablecloth and was replacing the cap on the canister of polish when there was a loud rap at the door – so loud, so startling, that her hand shook as she put down the canister.

Village people always knocked instead of ringing the bell, but this crack of doom summons was intolerable. She flung open the front door, too incensed to know what she would say, but knowing it would put the fear of God into whoever had knocked. There was no one in sight, there were no runaway footsteps. Large separate raindrops spotted the concrete. She stood on the threshold long enough to recover her breath and grow chilled. Shrugging her shoulders, she slammed the door, and went back into the house which had lost that much daylight by slamming it. What little was left seemed to exist in the cold pallor of the tallboys, as though the polish she had put on them had turned to ice.

The canister stood on the very edge of the table, so hastily had she set it down. The cap was gone; it must have dropped from her hand. Groaning, she went down on all fours, and groped about for it. The carpet was threadbare; if the cap had fallen on its rim it might have rolled some way. It might have rolled under the table. She poked her head under the tablecloth, and peered. There, lodged against the further leg, was the cap. She crawled in and seized it.

It was not that she was unfamiliar with the underneath of the table; she was there every day with the dustpan and brush. But that was in the morning, and daylight came in with her, for the tablecloth was rolled back. This was in the late afternoon, the tablecloth enclosed a compacter darkness than the dusk of the room, and she had no purpose to be there – only the trivial accident of the strayed canister lid. And she was feeling quite remarkably tired. If she had been one of those women who lie down after lunch ... She subsided, warily; there was still head-room enough. She sat down, amid the smell of polish, under the noise of rain, in the obscurity, holding the little cap, she drooped her head toward her knees and curled herself up and fell asleep. She knew where she was and the little cap was still in her hand when Cecily came by, and remarked, 'Identical twins always quarrel. Think of Jacob and Esau.' Cecily walked on, but the words stayed in the air, and Letitia accepting them in her depth of sleep thought, 'When I wake up everything will be all right,' and saw rancour and remorse detach themselves and rise out of her like two dark bubbles that would burst on the surface of waking and be gone.

By that time Mrs Carrington had poured out the first round of sherry and handed cheese biscuits (the salted almonds had been a failure), stuffed olives, rings of onion, little sausages on sticks, and was retailing the neighbourly deed but for which there would have been a greater variety of things to eat.

'I have no idea how old she is, but she must be well on in her eighties, and getting quite appallingly stiff. And there she is, stuck at the end of that lane like a hermit-crab – or do I mean limpet? – anyway, there she is, without a relation in the world to come and look after her. I lie awake for hours wondering how to make her see sense, and go into a Home. But what can one do, what can one do? Of course, I do my best, but she ought to be in a Home. There's that delightful place at Booton – Sorrento, or something. Mercy Bradshaw says it's ideal.'

About the time when Mrs Carrington's guests were driving homeward, Letitia awoke under the impression she was in Sweden, for nowhere else could it be so cold; yet at the same time she was under the mahogany table, smelling polish and the thick smell of the tablecloth. She stirred. An agonising pain darted up her thigh, nailing her to place and identity. She was that old fool, Letitia Foley, with an attack of cramp; but such knotted cramp that she was afraid to move, could only grit her teeth and wait. One after another her stiffened muscles creaked into anguish. In fragments of reason, she knew she must escape from beneath the table, stand, pull herself together, turn on the light, drink something hot, fill a hot-water bottle, creep into bed with an aspirin. To get up, she must get onto her knees, for that she must have something to haul on. Still sitting, she writhed about directionless till she felt a table leg. Clutching it, she tried to hoist herself. It reeled away from her, the flap of the table fell, and knocked her senseless.

In the lounge of Sorrento, some days later, Marina Wickstead filched the local evening paper from the woman beside her, and read the report of an inquest, headed 'Peculiar Death of an Elderly Recluse'.

'Some people have all the luck!' she exclaimed – so passionately that Matron offered her another cup of tea.

THE SEA IS ALWAYS THE SAME

'It's wonderfully kind of you. And in this beautiful car, too. Green is quite my favourite colour, and travelling so smoothly, and with that dear little clock. So utterly different to a bus. *Atkins. Wreaths and Crosses.* What enormous chrysanthemums! – though they always make me feel a little sad. Another summer gone. *Removals to All Districts.* Oh! How quickly you got by that van! But of course you could in this splendid car. You dear young things, just because I happened to mention that I hadn't been to Wimpole since I was a child. And I might never have happened to mention it, might I, unless the conversation had happened to turn that way? But actually to be going there after all these years – a lifetime, really, a lifetime. Blaizeworth!' Miss Belforest read out the name on the sign-post so fervently that Tom slowed down.

'Is that a turning I should have taken?'

'No, no, I don't think so. I don't think I've ever heard of Blaizeworth till just then. Or do you think we ought to take that road?'

Tom increased speed and Miss Belforest went on talking in her voice like a cracked flute.

'No, I don't think that can have been the right turning, Mr Blake. I think it would have taken us inland and not to the sea at all. To think that I am going to see the sea – and the sea at Wimpole! Such a special sea! Oh, how happy I used to be there, paddling, you know, and building sandcastles, and eating hard-boiled eggs. Oh, it is so kind of you! Almost strangers, for I never feel that in a hotel one – *The Arden Café. Teas.* But it does trouble me to think you are using your petrol. Such a price! And Mrs Blake, too, sitting at the back. I really can't think why you are doing it.'

Glancing at Tom's sad flat face in the driving-mirror, Lavinia Blake couldn't think why, either. Happiness softens people – so she had heard said. It was nearer the truth, she thought, that happiness intimidates people, especially a happiness almost lost; and in the incredible bliss of Tom convalescent, Tom well enough to demand a fortnight's holiday at a hotel, with no invalid cookery, no trays, no cares, Miss Belforest was being taken to revisit her special sea as a form of insurance. Meanwhile Miss Belforest was still performing her breathless cadenza, reading aloud every printed word that caught her eye, and apparently seeing nothing else of the autumnal countryside.

'The son of *Dean* Coldbath,' she now exclaimed. 'But he should never have become a schoolmaster, far too absent-minded. He had two drawing-rooms, and a friend of my mother's was shown into the back drawing-room by mistake, and after a long time Dr Coldbath came in, and sat down, and rang the bell – *The Pixies' Tavern, Open till Midnight.* Till midnight! Fancy that! – and when the maid answered it he said, "Louisa, bring me my slippers." *That* boy never went to Boxhall.'

Tom laughed, and even sounded amused. But these insurance policies that I take out, thought Lavinia, it's Tom who pays for them. And the petrol we're spending on this old claptrap might have taken us to the sea by ourselves. Though not to Wimpole. Already she knew that there was nothing to be hoped from Wimpole.

'Can we get lunch there?' she asked.

'Lunch? Dear Mrs Blake, how thoughtful you are! You think of everything. If Mrs Tapper knew we were coming, how delighted she would be to give us lunch. She always had everything so clean, and the fish so fresh, and shell-boxes in the bedrooms, real seaside lodgings. But of course she must have been dead for years, poor thing! Oh, look, look; I do believe it's the golf course. *To Upper Wimpole Golf Course Only.* Yes, it is. Daddy used to go there, to get some peace and quiet, he used to say. He rode on his bicycle. I remember it all so clearly! Everything! Our dear old Paddy – he was a retriever, and could swim like a fish, and so faithful, and one day he insisted on bringing home a dead skate, and he wouldn't put it down for anyone until he put it down among Mrs Tapper's begonias and tried to bury it. And the day Nanny's hat blew away, and going to the harvest festival. Such a lovely little church, a real gem, and such quaint epitaphs. *Price and Modderworth, Funeral Furnishers.* Do you know, I believe I remember them, only it wasn't here at all, but next to the little house that had a canary and was painted blue. *Dangerous Hill, Engage Low Gear.* Oh, Mr Blake, did you see that? It's the hill down, we always used to walk up it to spare the horses. Foxgloves all along the side of the road, and those little blue flowers I used to call Fairies' Pincushions. They were just like pincushions. Round this next corner there's the first peep, such a wonderfully beautiful peep! Oh, I can hardly believe that I'm going to see it all again. Such a dear spot!'

The sea swung into sight, rising smoothly and rapidly as though lifted by machinery.

'Wimpole!' announced Miss Belforest. *'Oster's Garage. Caravan Corner. Hot and Cold in All Bedrooms. Bide-a-Wee Café. Whist Drive, November 7th* – why, that was yesterday. *The Lobster-pot. To Sanatorium Only.'* Material for readings aloud bristled on either side of the descent into Wimpole.

'Of course it's changed,' commented Miss Belforest with bright resignation. 'There's the church, though. Dear thing!'

Confronted by an ogreish specimen of Victorian gothic, Lavinia tried to catch Tom's eye in the driving-mirror. The eye was not to be caught. Tom was always like that until he had found somewhere to park – secluded in a purposeful inattention, like a cat going to kitten.

'Here we are,' he said. His voice even conveyed a sense of arrival, and he opened the door for Miss Belforest with a flourish of letting joy be unconfined. Out she skipped, and exclaimed – she would – 'There's the sea!'

Slamming to the rear door, Lavinia received a full charge of melancholy and ozone. The raw smell hurt her nose. The flap of a wave furling itself on the shingle smote on her hearing. It seemed so final, so exhausted, that there could never be another wave. But almost immediately there was.

'And there,' cried Miss Belforest, indicating a groyne, 'is where Daddy used to sit. I can see his legs at this very moment.'

Two dogs and a distant man were occupying the beach at this moment. *Flap*, went another wave. Turning inland, Lavinia scrutinized a row of stucco boarding-houses.

Tom was leaning against the railings of the esplanade, as though waiting for the late Mr Belforest's legs to swim into his ken like some new planet. 'With the wind in the north,' he said, 'that would be a very comfortable place to sit.'

Flap-flap-flap, went another wave, breaking less successfully. The boarding-houses were called Elmont, St Ronan's, Cartello, Westward Ho! and Buckingham Court. All of them except Cartello catered for outside visitors. All of them without exception could be and would be read aloud by Miss Belforest. Meanwhile she was still gazing at the indecipherable ocean. And when the silence was broken, it was Tom who spoke.

'But where were your lodgings? We must find them. I want to see where Paddy buried the skate.'

Miss Belforest gazed about like a hound or a prophetess, and said, 'Along there. Up a little side street, near the chapel.'

Staggered by gusts of wind, they persevered along the esplanade. The first turning was wide, and had a cinema at the corner. Miss Belforest shook her head. The words, *glamorous* and *today*, were blown in fragments from her lips, and she walked on. The second turning led to a public garden, with public conveniences on either side of the entrance. Miss Belforest again shook her head.

'I see a chapel,' said Tom.

Miss Belforest darted up the third turning, her bag swinging, her fur stole flying, her conversation spattering.

'Not that we ever *went* to the chapel. But we used to hear them singing on Sunday evenings, with potted shrimps and the singing coming through the windows. Bertie, my brother Bertie, he died. couldn't hear them because of his deafness; but he was such a happy child, he used to sit reading aloud out of a book of Mrs Tapper's – oh, Mrs Blake, did the wind blow my fur into your eye? I'm so sorry!' Lavinia desisted from clawing the air at the mention of yet another literate Belforest, and said, brightly, 'My hat.'

'Yes, it was called *Home Medicine*, and really I don't think we were supposed to look at it, for it was all about carbuncles and smallpox and thrush and consumption. But now I come to think of it, I believe the consumption was in another book, called *The Dark River*, that we couldn't come to the end of, because the last pages were missing, you see.'

'*The Dark River*,' said Tom. 'That's a splendid title.'

'Azrael, the Angel of Death. He was in it. Rather low church, now I come to look back on it. It's further than I thought, but I think it can't be far off now. Such a dear little house, a row of them, really, with wooden palings and box windows and such a jessamine. *Repent ye, for the day of the Lord is at hand.* Can it be down here?'

'Isn't this hell?' said Lavinia, while Miss Belforest peered down one shabby street and then down another.

Raising her voice above the wind, she said that now they would go and find a hot lunch. Miss Belforest came away with docility, alarmed by the interest her bobbing researches had aroused. 'Good people, no doubt,' she said. 'But rather rough. Not like real Wimpole people.'

Anecdotes of real Wimpole people, who were all such characters, wearing seaboots and dropping courtesies, wafted them over a poor lunch. The anecdotes flowed more freely because Tom had ordered a bottle of white wine, which after a little civility Miss Belforest put away pretty much as a matter of course. Now that this is over, we can drive back, Lavinia thought. On the heels of that reflection Tom said, 'Now we will run Mrs Tapper to earth. But it's too cold to hunt on foot, so I'll go and fetch the car.'

Lavinia dived for her bag and gloves, and followed him out. To be alone with him, even for five minutes, would be heaven after hell; and heaven would last longer than that, for at least they could stay long enough in the car to smoke one cigarette before returning for Miss Belforest.

'Darling,' she said, and took his arm. He did no more than let her take it. He's got another chill, she thought, he's going to be ill all over again. 'I'm so sorry,' she said.

'I *am* so sorry,' she repeated. 'Tom! what's the matter. Are you ill?'

'I'm trying to keep my temper.'

'My God, yes! But you're keeping it so beautifully. You've behaved like an angel. I've never seen anyone so good at not screaming out loud.'

After a pause he said, 'I'm trying to keep my temper with you, Lavinia.'

'With me?' she said, genuinely astonished; and then, less astonished, she went on defensively, 'If I had known. . . . If I had thought for a moment . . . Oh, when shall I learn not to rush into kind actions? But it was a good plan to make her tiddly.'

'I made her tiddly in the hope that I might make her less aware of your bad manners. Your intolerably bad manners,' he said, shaking her arm out of his. 'I don't know what to do with you, Lavinia. I despair of you! I want to beat you, have you no pity in your heart?'

'Not enough to want to beat you, if that's your idea of pity.'

'Very well, you've got no pity. Well and good! And you're as lazy and as selfish as a Blue Persian Queen on a cushion. Well and good again! I knew all that when I married you, as it happens. But at least you might put up some show of wifely interest, you might exert yourself to seem civil, instead of grimacing at me behind the old woman's back. As I was crazy enough to think of giving her a day's pleasuring . . .'

'You? *You* thought of it? Do you mean to say that you suppose that this hideous outing was *your* idea?'

'Whose else was it?'

'This is outrageous! It was my idea. I'd thought of it long before you did, I said to you that really one ought to . . .'

'Thought! Said! Ought to! And how much further would it have gone if it had been left to your initiative? You would still be licking your lips over how pathetic the old thing was, and how like something in Tchekov, if I hadn't asked her. Who asked? I say, Lavinia, who asked her?'

'Oh, have it your own way. And I wish you joy of it!' She got into the back of the car, pale with rage and mortification. Tom started the engine with the controlled delicacy of a virtuoso beginning a slow movement, and then remarked, 'Now we will find the right chapel.'

When they got to the restaurant Miss Belforest had left the table. After they had sat waiting for ten minutes Lavinia broke the silence to say that doubtless the old fool had locked herself in. Tom said nothing. Presently the waitress appeared, and suggested they might like more coffee.

'We're waiting for the lady,' said Tom.

'I expect she'll be back soon,' the waitress said, glancing towards the street door. 'She said she was only going out for a little stroll.'

After another ten minutes Lavinia suggested that Miss Belforest might be waiting in the car.

The car was empty. Lavinia, by force of habit, got into the front seat. Tom, by force of habit, offered his cigarette case. They were still unable to speak to each other. Gusts of wind shook the car. On the wall of the restaurant was a hanging sign, that creaked as the wind swung it to and fro. The street ran steeply down on to the esplanade, and beyond the esplanade was the groyne where the late Mr Belforest's legs had been immanent to the late Mr Belforest's daughter; only now there was not so much of it, for the tide was coming in, and the waves cast themselves more sternly, more purposefully, on the darkening shingle.

'You don't . . . you don't think . . .' Lavinia said, and could say no more. Apparently Tom did not think.

After stubbing out his third cigarette he sighed profoundly, and said, 'I'm sorry I lost my temper, Lavinia. Now I suppose we'd better drive to the police-station.'

Lavinia said, 'Oh God!' and began to cry.

'I can't drive if you cry,' he said wearily; and a moment later he said, 'There she is.'

The onshore wind detached her like a fragment of dried seaweed from the esplanade railing where she had hung, and fluttered her up the street towards them. Even before Tom got out, her lips were moving.

'GBY 695. Here I am. I'm afraid I have kept you waiting, but I knew you wouldn't mind being left alone together, after putting up with me for so long. Yes, I've found everything. The chapel, and Mrs Tapper, and the jessamine, and the shop where we bought our buckets. Everything! All just as it used to be, not changed at all, or scarcely at all. A bit of real old-time Wimpole. No, no, Mrs Blake. I insist. You promised that I should sit in the back for the return journey.'

Tom's hand closed on Lavinia's wrist as she made to change places. 'Yes, I found it all in the end, only I had to walk about a little, you know, picking up the trail. Everything was there, only in the opposite direction. So silly of me, dragging you all that way for nothing before our nice lunch. But I was sure I should find it, if I gave my whole mind to it, and found the right chapel. Congregational. The other was Baptist. Not the same thing. Besides, I didn't want you to waste any more petrol, you've spent far too much as it is, giving me this delightful day. And on my way back I stopped for a real good look at the sea. Just as I remembered it, though actually we only came here in summer. Yes, I looked at the sea, and almost saw myself again, running about so happily in brown holland, Nanny smocked so wonderfully, and Paddy hauling along the dead skate. So delightful, so refreshing! Just the same sea – but the sea never changes. A rug? Oh, how kind of you, Mrs Blake. You think of everything. Really, I'm not in the least cold, but if you insist on spoiling me ... Oh! Headlights look so pretty. They light everything up so. *Bide-a-wee*. We saw that on the way down.'

But after a little Miss Belforest ceased to read aloud. She had carried it off, she thought, pretty well. Those poor dear young things, spending all their petrol, would never know that the chapel and the jessamine, the window with the canary in it, the steps up which Paddy had so impetuously rushed in the vigour of his youth and the pride of that very smelly skate, all, all were gone, quite gone. Only the sea – and Daddy's legs, though afterwards she had thought it must have been another groyne, a groyne much further to the left: and now the golf course, where Daddy had gone on his bicycle to get a little peace and quiet. *Only*. Darkness swallowed the inscription: *To Upper Wimpole Golf Course Only*. Her lips framed the final word, but she was too tired to speak it.

A BREAKING WAVE

In the bare landscape of the downs the house stood out plain as a bullseye. Below it the hillside hollowed itself into the curves of an amphitheatre. Zigzagging across the slope was the path made by the Butler children walking down to catch the school bus in the morning, walking back in the afternoon. Their feet had burnished the grass, and here and there had scuffed the thin turf off the chalk, so that the path looked like a strand of silk with a few pearls threaded on it.

It was because of the Butler children that Mrs Camden was now walking up this path. As a rule she was glad enough to agree with her husband that parishioners who did not come to church would not want to be visited by the parson or the parson's wife. But the Butlers appealed to her as a special case. It was so enterprising of them to settle in that derelict house and send their children to the village school. 'Even if they don't come to church,' she had argued, 'they send their children to a church school.' Henry had replied by asking where else they could send them. Evading this, she had repeated that the Butlers were a special case. The truth was that the Butlers sounded unusual, and after seven years in a west of England country parish Mrs Camden felt that the unusual would do her good. 'I shall make it clear that I'm not going there as the Parson's wife,' she added, 'but just as one woman to another.'

As an undenominational visit of womanly good-will her visit had been left rather late. The Butlers had been on their hill top for six months already. They must by now be sufficiently at home to feel that their home was their castle.

At this moment, she thought, they may be watching me approach and wishing I didn't. If the Butlers disliked being visited the oncome of a stranger must seem like a very slow arrow; for any approaching figure must be seen long beforehand, and with the certainty that it was directed towards them since it could not be directed to anything else. She had got

94

thus far in her thoughts when a dog in the house began barking. If it had not been for her conviction that she was being watched she would have turned back; but it would look so very odd to come halfway and then retreat; so she went on, trying not to look at the house which was the only thing to look at.

The hollowed hillside was full of March sunlight. The air was windless, but cold. The appearance of warmth and revival was no more than a gauze laid over the uncomplying landscape. The greyish turf, the heaving downland contours, the sense of a close-lipped solitude extending on every side, evoked an impression of mid-ocean in which the house on the skyline seemed to be poised on the summit of a wave. The dog continued to bark, and Mrs Camden continued to approach, passing a patch of newly-dug ground, a heap of builders' sand and a galvanized tank which lay on its side with a waterlogged teddybear in it. The Butlers' door was painted a gay green. When she knocked her knuckles clove to it, and she saw that she had left a mark on the wet paint. The dog snuffed at her under the door, and a high-pitched voice, impersonal as an oboe, said, 'Come in. He won't hurt you.'

The dog was a red setter, young and highly bred. Its brilliant coat emphasized the poverty-struck antiquity of the small stone-floored room within. Four doors and a flight of stairs led out of it, and except for a kitchen chair without a back it was entirely empty. She stood and waited, and the dog walked round her smelling her skirt. On the walls stains of ancient damp glowered through a coat of whitewash. A broken lath and tufts of cobwebby reeds protruded from a hole in the ceiling. Presently the dog's attention was distracted by a beetle, and it began to follow it round the room, diligently breathing on it. Mrs Camden coughed, but to no purpose. She was counting ten before coughing again when a woman came slowly down the stairs. She was great with child and a tattered overall hung on her with classic dignity.

Good heavens, thought Mrs Camden, is she going to smell me too? For the woman had now come close up to her, frowning slightly, and remaining perfectly silent. 'I am sure you must wonder who I am,' Mrs Camden said. The woman continued to regard her without a trace of speculation. 'I am – I mean, my name is Camden. Mrs Camden. I ought to apologise for being on this side of your door, but someone asked me to come in.'

'My father-in-law,' said the woman. 'He's in here.' The room they entered must have been the farmhouse kitchen, and now it was furnished in affected concordance with its former use. There was an oak settle, some stained deal chairs with patchwork cushions, a dresser displaying brass candlesticks and bakelite mugs. A modern shotgun lay on the old gun-rests above the hearth. An old man sat by the window in a wheeled chair with a rug over his knees, and the sunlight streamed into the room, obliterating the small fire under the cavernous chimney.

'This is my father-in-law, Colonel Butler. Father, this is Mrs Camden.' Having completed her introduction Mrs Butler lapsed into silence. Bowing from the waist, the old man excused himself for not getting up. Too profusely Mrs Camden said, No, no, of course not.

'My legs are still there,' he said, glancing down at the rug, 'but they might as well be in New Guinea.'

Mrs Camden said, 'Oh dear,' and bit back a parish-visiting impulse to remark that the wheeled chair must be a great convenience. While she was hesitating what to say instead Colonel Butler added, 'Or Tibet.'

'Tibet? Have you been to Tibet?'

'I don't think so.' His calm face became troubled. 'Emma! I haven't been in Tibet, have I? Emma, have I been in Tibet? Have I, have I? Emma, why don't you answer me?'

'No, father. You have never been in Tibet.'

Moving towards the window Mrs Camden began to expatiate on the view, and this enabled her to turn round to Mrs Butler with a suitable topic. 'I have always longed to live in this house myself. It seemed such a pity it should stand empty for so long.'

'We had looked everywhere for a house,' said Mrs Butler.

'Yes? And then you found this? How thrilled you must have been.'

'It was all we could find.'

Her manner of speech and frowning attentive gaze might have seemed childish and rudimentary if they had not so patently been vestigial, the gawky remnants of an earlier candour and dutifulness. 'There's a roof,' she continued, 'But it leaks. There are no drains, the floors are rotten, and the well has rats in it.'

'Rats?' exclaimed Mrs Camden, struck by the novelty of this last complaint.

'Dead rats.'

'But the situation,' said Mrs Camden, falling into her parish-visiting tone; 'I'm sure the situation must appeal to you. Such a view! And such seclusion!'

Mrs Butler flushed. Mrs Camden became aware that her reference to seclusion might be construed as applying to the old gentleman in the wheeled chair. The old gentleman now intervened, saying in a tone at once stately and airy, 'The house is well enough, but it's too high up. I don't like that because of these atom bombs.'

Unable to stop herself Mrs Camden enquired, 'Why because of atom bombs?'

'One's so much nearer to them. Doesn't do, doesn't do!'

Mrs Butler had now picked up a basket overflowing with ragged socks, and was thrusting her finger through one hole after another, as though measuring herself for a ring. Frustrated in her intention of finding a fellow-soul, Mrs Camden tried to get what satisfaction she could from pitying a fellow-creature. Her life was already well-supplied with pitiable fellow-creatures, but Mrs Butler's claims could not be set aside, one must be sorry for any woman so unattractive, so plainly poor, with three children, and another coming, one might say, immediately, who had to live in a house perched like a piece of driftwood on an ocean billow with a crazy father-in-law and a well with dead rats in it.

Just now the crazy father-in-law struck Mrs Camden as particularly regrettable. If he had not been there she could have got into a conversation about anaesthetics and breast-feeding, which might have made her visit seem more purposeful and rewarding. But there he sat, combing his beard with very thin and unnaturally tapered fingers, so that in order to find something to say she had to look at the chimneypiece and ask, 'Does you husband shoot?'

'Sometimes. Mostly, he sets snares.'

They poached! Unfortunate creatures, they poached! In general she approved of poaching (both the Camdens belonged to the Labour Party) as being the nearest one could get in village life to Merry England and Robin Hood. But the poaching of the Butlers was another matter. For one thing, they were gentlefolk. For another, Mrs Butler had no resemblance to Maid Marian.

'I see you are getting ready for a garden. I think you are so fortunate in being able to start your garden from the beginning. When we came here we inherited a garden so encumbered with Portugal laurels . . .'

The door burst open, and a man came in, saying, 'Emma, Emma! Where's the iodine?'

Spilling all the socks Mrs Butler leaped to her feet. Her dull face was illumined with a look of such agonized despair that it was as though the devil had spitted her.

'Isn't it in the blue box? Oh dear, one of the children must have taken it! Where on earth? . . .' She searched about the room with a heavy fluttering movement, like a singed moth.

'Never mind. I'll give it a wash, and chance it.'

'Oh, but the soil! Oh Phil, you know they told us it was full of tetanus.'

Mrs Camden produced a phial of iodine from her bag, and then a clean handkerchief, and finally accompanied Mr Butler to a very dubious basin in the back-kitchen, where she applied her first aid to the jagged cut in his wrist. She thought she had never seen a hand so deformed with cuts, scars, bruises, and chilblains, nor so white and well-shaped an arm. Looking at his broken fingernails she recalled Colonel Butler's taper fingers. But there was nothing but satisfaction in Philip Butler's asseveration that he was a jack of all trades and master of none. Before she had finished tying the bandage he was opening cupboards and pulling out drawers to display his handiwork.

'Has Emma shown you round? No? But you must have a look at the place. Through here is what used to be the dairy. Just now we use it for a sort of rubbish-collection, but as soon as I can patch up the roof, and fix a better door, and stop the rat-holes it's to be a dairy again. We're going to make cheese from goats' milk. I mean to have a lot of goats, and do the thing properly. I've got a set of bells for their necks already. Now through here – I say, I hope you didn't twist your ankle – we really must clear these tins away, Emma? – through here there's a fine old pigsty. I only found it last week, when I was lopping the brambles. Well, I'm going to make a wire top for it, and keep snails. Snails make very good eating. And the place is alive with them, it's just a matter of collecting them and popping them into the snail-pen to grow fat. I'd like a fish-pond too, but water is the difficulty. But later on I mean to try my hand at making a dew-pond. Even if we couldn't keep fish in it, it would give us some soft water. The well water is so hard that Emma has a desperate job with the washing. It takes most of the family soap ration to get me a clean shirt.'

'You could get rain-water off the roof,' said Mrs Camden.

'Not till the roof's mended, and I can fix up some gutters. At present most of the rain comes indoors. By the way, Emma, that reminds me, do try to keep the children out of the end room. I haven't got round to fixing those boards yet, and I don't altogether trust the joists.'

'How the children must love this place.'

'Oh they do, they do! I suppose they're growing into young savages, but at the same time they're learning to make themselves useful. They pick up sticks – that's Emma's worst headache up here, worse than the washing, worse than the mud! It really is a problem how to find enough wood to keep fires going. And my poor old Dad feels the cold. But all that will be easier in summer.'

They turned the corner of the house, and the view extended before them.

'What a view! What a distance!' exclaimed Mrs Camden.

'There's a rabbit,' said Mrs Butler. 'Shall I get the gun?'

'I don't know. It's a difficult shot. Shooting down hill is always tricky. Besides, poor bunny! – he's enjoying himself. How do you think these fruit bushes are looking? I put them in last week. They don't look too good to me, but I daresay they'll come to something. Raspberries, gooseberries, black currants, three dozen of each. We ought to get enough home-made jam out of that, even for the children. Besides, there are always brambles. Here's our hen. The foxes got all the others, so now I am going to make a dovecot. Of course what one really ought to keep up here is a couple of falcons. Hawk, horse, and hound: that's what I aim to have in time.'

Mrs Butler who had gone indoors now came out with the gun. She took a careful aim and fired. The rabbit rolled over, picked itself up, and ran.

'You aimed a bit too low, dear.'

She fired the second barrel.

'Nowhere near him! Never mind! Better luck next time.'

Breathing unsteadily she broke the gun, took out the cartridges, and put in two more. Mrs Camden said again, 'What a view!'

'Yes, isn't it? Not a house in sight. That's what I like. Robinson Crusoe, that's my idea of the good life.'

Turning to Mrs Crusoe, Mrs Camden remarked, 'I always think it's so fascinating to remember that this was once the most densely populated part of England. You know, there are ancient British villages and earthworks all over these downs.'

Philip Butler's face lit up. 'I say, Emma! That's an idea! That's what we'll do. We'll pick a site, and do some excavating. Yes, that's what we'll do next!' He was so delighted, and Mrs Butler remained so unforthcoming, that Mrs Camden had not the heart to tell him that amateur diggings were discouraged by the local archaeological society. Besides, she did not suppose he would get very far with it. Everything that she had seen about the house indicated that Philip Butler was a man of many beginnings and no completions. This conclusion was strengthened when a noise of tapping on the window behind them was followed by the crash of the window falling out from its frame. Colonel Butler, blinking in the pure sunlight, remarked through the aperture, 'There! Did you hear that one? It blew the window right off its hinges. I was just going to tell you that the fire's gone out again. That's all.'

'I suppose I shouldn't have trusted to the string,' Philip Butler said. 'Though it has lasted a long time. I've been meaning to get round to it for weeks, but there's always been something else.' He picked up the shattered window and considered it. 'Wonderful workmanship! I should think it's eighteenth century at least. Well, it wouldn't have lasted much longer anyhow. All right, father,' he added. 'I'll fix up some sort of shutter. There's that bit of corrugated roofing on the shed that got loose in the gale. I could use that. Emma would be thankful not to hear it banging any longer – wouldn't you, Emma?'

She was picking up broken glass, and did not answer. Colonel Butler peered out at them, looking like some abstruse hothouse variety of orchid exposed to the open air and fast becoming the worse for it. Mrs Camden said she really must be going.

When she discovered that her host was determined to walk down as far as the lane with her she felt a twinge of social conscience. As though instantly aware of this, he said that he would get some sticks from the hedge. Emma would need more sticks. Now he wanted Mrs Camden to tell him about mushrooms. During the autumn he had gathered all sorts of mushrooms and most of them had turned out to be edible, but some had not. Mushrooms led to wild flowers and a design of naturalizing opium poppies on the downs, opium poppies led to home-grown tobacco, home-grown tobacco to water-divining, and in the middle of water-divining the curve of the hillside reminded him to tell her about his plan for fitting out his children with roller skates and kite apiece, which would teach them the rudiments of managing the glider-plane he meant to buy as soon as he had finished paying for the house. By the time they reached the lane Mrs Camden felt that Mr Butler quite made up for her disappointment in Mrs Butler. The readiness with which he blew up the tyre of her bicycle, which had deflated since she left the bicycle under the hedge, made her think differently of his practical abilities: the crooked shelves, the window tied with string, the smudges of paint, the litter of half-baked projects, now seemed the expression of a courageous man battling with adversity. It was a pity that Mrs Butler was not better fitted to live with such a man in the wilderness. But at least, she loved him. That moment of looking for the iodine had revealed a degree of love which Mrs Camden, searching her mind for the right word, finally classified as *raw*. Yes, raw was the word. Raw, like a wound suddenly pulled open. A disagreeable analogy, and a disagreeable kind of love to bear one's husband, but that, undoubtedly, was how Mrs Butler loved Mr Butler.

Mrs Camden had just settled this when the report of a gun ripped through the silence. Mrs Butler must have seen another rabbit. Mounted on her bicycle Mrs Camden was able to look over the hedge into the valley. She saw Mr Butler roll over, exactly as the rabbit had done. But unlike the rabbit, which had picked itself up and run, Mr Butler got slowly to his feet and seemed uncertain what to do next. A second shot rang out. Mr Butler dropped rapidly, and began to move obliquely on all fours. Really, thought Mrs Camden, it was too much! Of course with three children and two men to feed, one would take almost any risk to secure a rabbit: but Mrs Butler was going too far. There she was, poised on the crest of the wave, and seemingly looking down into the valley at Mr Butler travelling on all fours. A thread of light shot from the gun barrel, and now, good heavens! Mrs Butler had reloaded the gun and raised it to her shoulder. Mrs Camden, doing what she could, rang her bicycle bell. Like an unproportioned echo a third shot answered it. But she could not see what was happening, for the bicycle had carried her round the bend in the lane, and there, on the road ahead, was the school bus, pausing to set down three children who must be the Butler children.

Mrs Camden dismounted. The children stopped and looked at her enquiringly. 'Are you the little Butlers?' she asked. One of them nodded. 'I – I thought you must be. I've just been visiting your father and mother.' They regarded her exactly as Mrs Butler had done, as though they were smelling her. She listened, smiling at them, delaying them without alarming them. There were no more shots. 'I think you've got a lovely house,' she said. 'I wish I lived in it. I saw your dog, too. He's a beauty.'

There were no more shots. She re-mounted her bicycle, and saying, 'Goodbye, children! Goodbye!' rode on.

A VIEW OF EXMOOR

From Bath, where Mr Finch was taking the waters, the Finches travelled by car into Devonshire to attend the wedding of Mrs Finch's niece, Arminella Blount. They made a very creditable family contribution – Mrs Finch in green moiré, Cordelia and Clara in their bridesmaids' dresses copied from the Gainsborough portrait of an earlier Arminella Blount in the Character of Flora, Mr Finch in, as his wife said, his black-and-grey. Arden Finch in an Eton suit would have looked like any other twelve-year-old boy in an Eton suit if measles had not left him preternaturally thin, pale, and owl-eyed.

All these fine feathers, plus two top hats, an Indian shawl to wrap around Arden in case it turned cold, and a picnic basket in case anyone felt hungry, made the car seem unusually full during the drive to Devonshire. On the return journey it was even fuller, because the Finches were bringing back Arminella's piping bullfinch and the music box that was needed to continue its education, as well as the bridesmaids' bouquets. It was borne in on Mr Finch that other travellers along the main road were noticing his car and its contents more than they needed to, and this impression was confirmed when the passengers in two successive charabancs cheered and waved. Mr Finch, the soul of consideration, turned into a side road to spare his wife and daughters the embarrassment of these public acclamations.

'"Pember and South Pigworthy",' Mrs Finch read aloud from a signpost. 'The doctor who took out my tonsils was called Pember. It's so nice to find a name one knows.'

Mr Finch replied that he was taking an alternative way home. After a while, he stopped and looked for his road map, but couldn't find it. He drove on.

'Father,' said Cordelia a little later, 'we've been through this village before. Don't you think we had better ask?'

'Is *that* all it is?' said Mrs Finch. 'What a relief. I thought I was having one of those mysterious delusions when one half of my brain mislays the other half.'

Mr Finch continued to drive on. Arden, who had discovered that the bars of the bird cage gave out notes of varying pitch when he plucked them, was carrying out a systematic test with a view to being able to play 'Rule Britannia'. Cordelia and Clara and their mother discussed the wedding.

Suddenly, Mrs Finch exclaimed, 'Oh, Henry! Stop, stop! There's such a beautiful view of Exmoor!'

Ten-foot hedges rose on either side of the lane they were in, the lane went steeply uphill, and Mr Finch had hoped that he had put any views of Exmoor safely behind him. But with unusual mildness he stopped and backed the car till it was level with a gate. Beyond the gate was a falling meadow, a pillowy middle distance of woodland, and beyond that, pure and cold and unimpassioned, the silhouette of the moor.

'Why not,' Mr Finch said, taking the good the gods provided, 'why not stop and picnic?' It occurred to him that once the car was emptied, the road map might come to light.

The Finches sat down in the meadow and ate cucumber sandwiches. Arden wore the Indian shawl; the bullfinch in its cage was brought out of the car to have a little fresh air. Gazing at the view, Mrs Finch said that looking at Exmoor always reminded her of her Aunt Harriet's inexplicable boots.

'What boots, Mother?' Cordelia asked.

'She saw them on Exmoor,' Mrs Finch said. 'She and Uncle Lionel both saw them; they were children at the time. They were picking whortleberries – such a disappointing fruit! All these folk-art fruits are much overrated. And nobody's ever been able to account for them.'

'But why should they have to be accounted for?' Clara asked. 'Were they sticking out of a bog?'

'They were in a cab.'

'Your Aunt Harriet –' Mr Finch began. For some reason, it angered him to hear of boots being in a cab while he was still in doubt as to whether the map was in the car.

'Of course,' Mrs Finch went on, 'in those days cabs were everywhere. But not on Exmoor, where there were no roads. It was a perfectly ordinary cab, one of the kind that open in hot weather. The driver was on the box, and the horse was waving its tail to keep the flies off. They looked as if they had been there quite a long time.'

'Days and days?' Arden asked.

'I'm afraid not, dear. Decomposition had not set in. But as if they had been there long enough to get resigned to it. An hour or so.'

'But how could Aunt Harriet tell how long –'

'In those days, children were very different – nice and inhibited,' Mrs Finch said. 'So Aunt Harriet and Uncle Lionel observed the cab from a distance and walked on. Presently, they saw two figures – a man and a woman. The man was very pale and sulky, and the woman was rating him and crying her eyes out, but the most remarkable thing of all, even more remarkable than the cab, was that the woman wasn't wearing a hat. In those days, no self-respecting woman could stir out without a hat. And on the ground was a pair of boots. While Harriet and Lionel were trying to get a little nearer without seeming inquisitive, the woman snatched up the boots and ran back to the cab. She ran right past the children; she was crying so bitterly she didn't even notice them. She jumped into the cab, threw the boots onto the opposite seat, the driver whipped up his horse, and the cab went bumping and jolting away over the moor. As for the man, he walked off looking like murder. So what do you make of that?'

'Well, I suppose they'd been wading, and then they quarrelled and she drove away with his boots as a revenge,' said Clara.

'He was wearing boots,' said Mrs Finch.

'Perhaps they were eloping,' Clara said, 'and the boots were part of their luggage that he'd forgotten to pack, like Father, and she changed her mind in time.'

'Speed is essential to an elopement, and so is secrecy. To drive over Exmoor in an open cab would be inconsistent with either,' said Mr Finch.

'Perhaps the cab lost its way in a moor mist,' contributed Arden. 'Listen! I can do almost all the first line of "Rule Britannia" now.'

'But, Clara, why need it be an elopement?' Cordelia asked. 'Perhaps she was just a devoted wife who found a note from her husband saying he had lost his memory or committed a crime or something and was going out of her life, and she seized up a spare pair of boots, leaped hatless into a cab, and tracked him across Exmoor, to make sure he had a dry pair to change into. And when Harriet and Lionel saw them, he had just turned on her with a brutal oath.'

'If she had been such a devoted wife, she wouldn't have taken the boots away again,' Clara said.

'Yes, she would. It was the breaking point,' Cordelia said. 'Actually, though, I don't believe she was married to him at all. I think it was an assignation and she'd taken her husband's boots with her as a blind.'

'Then why did she take them out of the cab?' inquired Clara. 'And why didn't she wear a hat, like Mother said? No, Cordelia! I think your theory is artistically all right. It looks the boots straight in the face. But I've got a better one. I think they spent a guilty night together and, being a forgetful man, he put his boots out to be cleaned and in the morning she was hopelessly compromised, so she snatched up the boots and drove after him to give him a piece of her mind.'

'Yes, but he was wearing boots already,' Cordelia said.

'He would have had several pairs. At that date, a libertine would have had hundreds of boots, wouldn't he, Mother?'

'He might not have taken them with him wherever he went, dear,' said Mrs Finch.

Mr Finch said, 'You have both rushed off on an assumption. Because the lady drove away in the cab, you both assume that she arrived in it. Women always jump to conclusions. Why shouldn't the cab have brought the man? If she was hatless, she might have been an escaped lunatic and the man a keeper from the asylum, who came in search of her.'

'Why did he bring a pair of boots?' Cordelia asked.

'Ladies' boots,' said Mr Finch firmly.

'He can't have been much of a lunatic-keeper if he let her get away with his cab,' Clara said.

'I did not say he was a lunatic-keeper, Clara,' said Mr Finch. 'I was merely trying to point out to you and your sister that in cases like this one must examine the evidence from all sides.'

'Perhaps the cabdriver was a lunatic,' said Arden. 'Perhaps that's why he drove them onto Exmoor. Perhaps they were *his* boots, and the man and the woman were arguing as to which of them was to pay his fare. Perhaps – '

Interrupted by his father and both his sisters, all speaking at once, Arden returned to his rendering of 'Rule Britannia'. Mrs Finch removed some crumbs and a few caterpillars from her green moiré lap and looked at the view of Exmoor. Suddenly, a glissando passage on the bird cage was broken by a light twang, a flutter of wings, a cry from Arden. The cage door had flipped open and the bullfinch had flown out. Everybody said 'Oh!' and grabbed at it. The bullfinch flew to the gate, balanced there, flirted its tail, and flew on into the lane.

It flew in a surprised, incompetent way, making short flights, hurling itself from side to side of the lane. But though Cordelia and Clara leaped after it, trying to catch it in their broad-brimmed hats, and though Arden only just missed it by overbalancing on a bough, thereby falling out of the tree and making his nose bleed, and though Mr Finch walked after it, holding up the bird cage and crying 'Sweet, Sweet, Sweet' in a falsetto voice that trembled with feeling, the bullfinch remained at liberty and, with a little practice, flew better and better.

'Stop, all of you!' said Mrs Finch, who had been attending to Arden, wiping her bloodstained hands on the grass. 'You'll frighten it. Henry, do leave off saying "Sweet" – you'll only strain yourself. What we need is the music box. If it hears the music box, it will be reminded of its home and remember it's a tame bullfinch. Arden, dear, please keep your shawl on and look for some groundsel, if you aren't too weak from loss of blood.'

The music box weighed about fifty pounds. It was contained in an ebony case that looked like a baby's coffin, and at every movement it emitted reproachful chords. On one side, it had a handle; on the other side, the handle had fallen off, and by the time the Finches had got the box out of the car, they were flushed and breathless. His groans mingling with the reproachful chords Mr Finch staggered up the lane in pursuit of the bullfinch, with the music box in his arms. Mrs Finch walked beside him, tenderly entreating him to be careful, for if anything happened to it, it would break Arminella's heart. Blithesome and cumberless, like the bird of the wilderness, the bullfinch flitted on ahead.

'I am not carrying this thing a step further,' said Mr Finch, setting down the music box at the side of the lane. 'Since you insist, Elinor, I will sit here and play it. The rest of you can walk on and turn the bird somehow and drive it back till the music reminds it of home.'

Clara said, 'I expect we shall go for miles.'

Seeing his family vanish around a bend in the lane, Mr Finch found himself nursing a hope that Clara's expectation might be granted. He was devoted to music boxes. He sat down beside it and read the list of its repertory, which was written in a copperplate hand inside the lid: 'Là ci darem la Mano'; 'The Harp that once through Tara's Halls'; the Prayer from *Moïse*; the 'Copenhagen Waltz'. A very pleasant choice for an interval of repose, well-earned repose, in this leafy seclusion. He ran his finger over the prickled cylinder, he blew away a little dust, he wound the box up. Unfortunately, there were a great many midges, the inherent pest of leafy seclusions. He paused to light a cigar. Then he set off the music box. It chirruped through three and a half tunes and stopped, as music boxes do. Behind him, a voice said somewhat diffidently, 'I say. Can I be any help?'

Glancing from the corner of his eye, Mr Finch saw a young man whose bare ruined legs and rucksack suggested that he was on a walking tour.

'No, thank you,' Mr Finch said. Dismissingly, he rewound the music box and set it going again.

Round the bend of the lane came two replicas, in rather bad condition, of Gainsborough's well-known portrait of Arminella Blount in the Character of Flora, a cadaverous small boy draped in a blood-stained Indian shawl, and a middle-aged lady dressed in the height of fashion who carried a bird cage. Once again, Mr Finch was forced to admit the fact that the instant his family escaped from his supervision they somehow managed to make themselves conspicuous. Tripping nervously to the strains of the 'Copenhagen Waltz', the young man on a walking tour skirted round them and hurried on.

'We've got it!' cried Mrs Finch, brandishing the bird cage.

'Why the deuce couldn't you *explain* to that young man?' asked Mr Finch. 'Elinor, why couldn't you explain?'

'But why should I?' Mrs Finch asked. 'He looked so hot and careworn, and I expect he only gets a fortnight's holiday all the year through. Why should I spoil it for him? Why shouldn't he have something to look back on in his old age?'

CHLOROFORM FOR ALL

When Mr Finch retired and bought a house in the country he and his family knew nothing about the country except that it was where one went for country holidays. Mr Finch was a Londoner. Mrs Finch whose mother was a violinist had spent her girlhood in European capitals. Fortunately Mr Finch was widely read in the English novelists, and now his reading enabled him to guide his family to a correct conduct of country living. That was why he said, 'I think we should go to church next Sunday.' His three children said, 'Why?' Mrs Finch said that it would be delightful – but it turned out afterwards her mind was elsewhere. The warmth of her assent moved Mr Finch to add that one must go to church twice a year or so, in order to be civil to the parson.

They went to church, and were herded into one of a large assortment of empty pews, where they behaved very creditably, except for Mrs Finch. Mrs Finch gave too much both to the hymns and to the collection, and she should not have said to her daughter at the close of the Ten Commandments, 'I have been trying to remember the name of the strange cat who came in through the skylight in Ebury Street. Was it Violet?' But her speaking voice was low, and though of course she should not have used a speaking voice in the hearing of God and his congregation Mrs Mulliner, wife of the Reverend Felix Mulliner, was ready to overlook a good deal in her satisfaction at beholding a Christian Family. The Bishop attached great importance to Christian Families; Mrs Mulliner attached great importance to the Bishop, rightly so, since the living was in his gift and Felix was not the kind of man who makes his way in the world. A Christian Family is a family where the number of the children exceeds the number of the parents (families where the number of the parents exceeds the number of the children are Pagan Families, families where there are two of either are just families).

What was so particularly gratifying about the Christian Family of the

Finches was that it had come to church. It was tragic indeed that just when the Bishops, and Mrs Mulliner's Bishop in particular, had been laying so much stress on the importance of rearing Christian Families, such a number of young people were marrying and rearing families which were quite soon numerically Christian but really not Christian at all, being brought into the world for no better purpose than to be sent to Dartington Hall and to grow up as communists and free-thinkers.

Mrs Mulliner hastened to call on the Christian Finches, and after a few preliminaries she invited Mrs Finch to join the local branch of the Mothers' Union. It would mean, she said, so much to the Mothers. Once a fortnight they had such pleasant little meetings, and from time to time quite delightful outings. Mrs Finch glanced round for help. Why couldn't Henry come in and explain her essential unsuitability for either meeting or outing? – he was ready enough at other times to discourse on punctuality. Why couldn't Cordelia, who was also punctual, do something beyond staring at Mrs Mulliner's chest, which glittered with what must be Church of England amulets?

'I'm afraid I'm not really suitable. I've got three children, you know. And Arden is horribly delicate. The instant I take my eye off him he develops something, or falls off a roof, or drinks so much cider that he has to be put to bed. He's got no head at all, poor child. Neither has Henry. I can drink Henry under the table with ease.'

'He will get stronger in country air,' said Mrs Mulliner firmly.

'Then there's the garden – and the piano-tuner.'

While Mrs Mulliner was finding the answer to the piano-tuner Mrs Finch reflected further, and added triumphantly, 'And my husband.'

As though Mr Finch were a thing of nought, Mrs Mulliner said that she would expect Mrs Finch on Thursday week, adding again that it would mean so much to the mothers to see a new face among them.

'Wouldn't Cordelia do as well?'

'I'm afraid it wouldn't be quite the same thing, would it?' said Mrs Mulliner, thereby assuring Cordelia's implacable resentment. 'Now, Thursday week, Mrs Finch. And we shall count on you for a few words.'

After Mrs Mulliner had gone Cordelia said that her father would be furious. Cordelia was furious; Cordelia and Mr Finch often had very similar reactions. Mrs Finch broke it as lightly as she could to Mr Finch that she had undertaken to join the Mothers' Union. 'Not that I really mean join. I told her I couldn't do that without asking you first, in case you didn't approve.'

'I don't approve.'

'I hoped you wouldn't. It makes it much easier. I will just go this once, I had to promise that. And I will explain to them that I shan't be able to come again because you don't approve. Do you think it would be enough if I quote that bit about plaiting one's hair with subjection? It's in the marriage service. Don't you remember? You must have heard it when we were being married, you were certainly there, and *you* hadn't got a wasp under your veil. I wonder what you were thinking about all the time. Well, Henry, do you think it will be enough for me to plait my hair, or shall I have to explain why you don't approve of Mothers' Unions. What are they, do you know? Something to do with mothers uniting, I suppose. Shall I say you don't approve of people being forced into unions and having to pay levies?'

'You can say what you like provided you don't bring me into it.'

'Oh! Oh, very well, I'll think of some other reason, some quite unmarried reason. I'll say – '

'But the obvious expedient is to wait till the day before and then send a note explaining that you have a cold in your head.'

'You've not seen that Mulliner female, Father. She'll only begin again about next time.'

'With a little management, Cordelia, there need not be a next time.'

Mr Finch was about to be elected to the Parish Council, Cordelia and Clara were always going out to play tennis, Arden was inseparable from Mr Cumfrey the village carpenter: Mrs Finch alone had failed to strike root in country life. So far, indeed, the piano-tuner was her only conquest – for one could not count as a conquest old Major Tyrawley who talked of nothing but the Empire League and was in consequence famishing for anyone to talk to. Being her mother's daughter Mrs Finch's soul dwelt naturally in marble halls with vassals and lords at her side. However much she shrank from the thought of Mrs Mulliner she could not contemplate without simpering, the vista of all those mothers to whom she would mean so much, and lying in her bath she found herself fluently inventing the things she might say to them if she had wanted to meet them. But in the course of the next few days she forgot the whole subject and would not have have given it another thought if

Mrs Mulliner, flashing past the post office on her bicycle, had not cried out, 'See you this afternoon, Mrs Finch. My mothers are so looking forward to your little talk.'

'My little talk?'

'Surely you're not shy? Just a little talk. *I* will introduce you.'

Saying to herself that it was too late to do anything about it, Mrs Finch went home to lunch and said nothing. Later on she changed furtively into a black dress and a broad-brimmed hat of an essentially unpastoral nature, made up her face more attentively than usual and, carrying a pair of gloves and a few sheets of notepaper, left the house by a side door, pausing in the kitchen garden to bolt some figs with a strong sensation that she was stealing them.

That afternoon Mr Finch found himself alone with the teapot. After he had waited a little he shouted, and after he had shouted a little he rang the bell. Janet reminded him that Miss Cordelia and Miss Clara had gone out to play tennis and supposed that Master Arden was down with Mr Cumfrey. She had no idea where Mrs Finch was. Mrs Finch had not mentioned anything. After three cups of strong cold tea Mr Finch became a prey to uneasiness. He roamed through the house and through the garden. House and garden alike were full of clues, and all the clues irresistibly suggested to his trained legal mind a probability that something or other must have stirred Elinor up. What else could you make of a suede glove dangling on a fig tree, a soup ladle on the bathroom windowsill, Elinor's right-foot shoe lying on the bed in company with a prayer book, and a half-sheet of notepaper on which she had written: *Rhus. Tex. Old-fashioned bell-ropes. Anchovies? Onions for hornets. Reproach laundry. Mme de Brinvilliers, Mrs Beeton. ?? Clytem-naestra. Remember my bodkin. Chloroform for All.* This last entry had an emphatic little hand pointing to it.

When she walked into the room she was looking so elated, not to say rollicking, that he recalled those pencilled notes and wondered how far she had got in her programme.

'Where have you been, Elinor?'

'Cucumber sandwiches,' she replied. 'Thank God you've left me a few. I have been saying a few words, and I am ravenous. Where's Arden?'

'Elinor, where – '

'About kangaroos. And I've seen the sweep and he's coming on Monday. He's such an interesting man.'

'And why are you dressed up like that?'

'Arden said they all wore black. Mr Cumfrey had shown them to him last time, and he asked Arden if he had ever seen such a lot of old tea-leaves. So I thought I'd better be a tea-leaf myself, like doing in the Vatican as the Pope does, only I didn't hire a mantilla. The Mothers' Union, Henry. Don't you remember?'

'You've been to that thing after all? Have another sandwich.'

'I had to. You forgot to remind me to write and tell them I'd broken my leg. You've got a head like a sieve, Henry, no one remembers anything in this house except me. You won't believe it, but I was a great success. I was, really. I was astonished at myself, I didn't think I had so much eloquence in me, or that I knew so much about them. I've always been devoted to zinnias because they remind me of Elvas Plums, but now I shall love them for themselves alone. Of course, if you could imagine a pale Elvas Plum it wouldn't be altogether unlike Major Tyrawley.'

'Was Major Tyrawley also at this meeting?'

'How could he be, Henry? He isn't even a childless widow. No, I met him on my way there, and as I had started far too early because of stage-fright, and the way you always intimidate me with punctuality, when he said, would I like to see his zinnias, I said I'd love to. And while we were having a drink (he mixes very strong drinks, it's a mercy I've got such a good head, not like you, my poor darling!) I told him how I was on my way to the Mothers' Union and hadn't the least idea what to talk about. I'd never thought of the Empire like that before, I'd always assumed it was full of people like anywhere else, except of course where it was uninhabitable like the Desert of Gobi. But Major Tyrawley began at once to explain how neglected it was (I must say he made it sound perfectly delightful), and how important it is to encourage mothers to have large families, fathers too, of course, but mothers need more encouraging, because of populating vast open spaces with young men leading free wallaby lives, and so on. And as a result I arrived rather late and Mrs Mulliner was cold to me, and not in black at all but in a very unbecoming flowered hula-hula. A horrid woman, Henry. I am beginning to wonder whether we shan't live to regret going to her church. But the mothers were charming, and so responsive I felt so sorry for you, having had to waste yourself on those inanimate juries.'

'Thank you, my dear. It was often very mortifying. Did you talk for long?'

'When I got up to begin, Henry, I felt so odd, so dizzy. It must have been stage-fright. And then suddenly I got going. I remembered all the right words, I knew such quantities of facts, everything became so clear and lifelike. I positively saw them.'

'Saw who, Elinor? The mothers?'

'The kangaroos. The kangaroos in Australia, Henry. Bounding about all over Australia with their babies in their pouches. Believe it or not, Henry, I talked for over half an hour about kangaroos, and wasn't once at a loss. I even remembered they were called the Marsupialia. The mothers were entranced, they saw at once how much more practical it is to have pouches, so convenient and labour-saving. So now I am going to take them all to the zoo, and I think I shall ask Major Tyrawley to come with us, because if I hadn't met him I shouldn't have been half such a success.'

'I suppose not,' said Mr Finch, more earnestly than gallantly. 'I hope you are not tired out by all this. Would you like to lie down before dinner? Shall I turn on a bath for you?'

'I'll just put my feet up.'

Thoughtfully twirling the broad-brimmed hat in his hand Mr Finch ran over the clues. The glove, the prayer-book, Mme de Brinvilliers, Mrs Beeton, Clytemnaestra, the chloroform... one by one they sank into place. The bodkin was probably related to the earlier domestic entries, the laundry and the hornets. Though on the surface Elinor might appear inconsequential she had a remarkably purposeful sub-conscious, and in all probability Mrs Mulliner would have been quite as much estranged by Mme de Brinvilliers as by any kangaroos. But the soup ladle remained unaccounted-for.

'Elinor. Why ... '

She was asleep.

MR MACKENZIE'S LAST HOUR

Mr Finch was not a man for visitors. As a dinner host, he was excellent, and under favouring circumstances he could be tolerably hospitable to those staying the night, provided they left after breakfast. After that, his house in Kent became his castle, and the guest, for the remainder of his stay, was consigned to the oubliette – in other words, to Mrs Finch. But when hospitality gave out, compassion replaced it. The longer people stayed, the more Mr Finch condoled their wretched lot and grieved over their sufferings. He was now grieving for a Mr Mackenzie, a professional acquaintance, whose first visit Mr Finch was sombrely convinced would also be his last.

All this, said Cordelia Finch in colloquy with her younger sister, Clara, was Father's wishful thinking. He would rather suppose visitors were miserable than face the thought that they might want to come again.

'But he's just as sorry for them if he's brought them in himself, like this one,' said Clara. 'If anything, he's worse.'

'Of course he's worse. He's struggling with a guilt complex into the bargain,' replied Cordelia. 'Haven't you noticed the way he says, "Ah, Mackenzie, so here you are," whenever the poor man crosses his path? That's the equivalent of murderers feeling compelled to haunt the scene of the crime.'

'I haven't noticed him haunting Mr Mackenzie between meals,' said Clara, and added, 'Where is he now?'

'Lurking in the vinery, I think.'

'No. Mackenzie.'

'Packing. What else could he do, after the pointed way Father talked about not keeping that sister-in-law waiting?'

Mr Mackenzie, in addition to having complied to its full extent with Mr Finch's invitation to make it a long weekend while he was about it, had fallen into the further condemnation of proposing to remain till after lunch, when his sister-in-law could pick him up in her car while on her way to London. Learning of this, Mr Finch extended his compassion to the sister-in-law, saying that it would add twenty miles to her journey and that he dreaded to think what the road over Donkey Common would do to her tyres. When Mr Mackenzie explained that Agnes liked breaking new ground, Mr Finch fell back on the peculiar suffering of those who enter London through its south-eastern suburbs.

A little later, the last lunch having been hurried through, coffee was being dragged out in the library and Mr Finch was regretting that all this rain would make it next to impossible for Mr Mackenzie's sister-in-law not to skid in the Old Kent Road, the more so because, being delayed by having to come so far out of her way, she would be there in the rush hour. Mrs Finch remarked, more cheerfully, that if they had an accident, and liked jellied eels, she had noticed there were very fine ones in the shop next to the pawnbroker who hung out coats. Mr Mackenzie shuddered. For one thing, he was Scotch, and the Scotch do not readily eat eels; for another, the weeping, sweeping gale made the thought of anything jellied abhorrent. Noticing the shudder, Mrs Finch continued, 'I've been told there's a law about fumigating them before they are sold. But what's fumigation? It wasn't any help to that unfortunate young woman in the Apocrypha who was always losing her husbands before she could marry them. Especially if they are fur-lined. And yet when their owners deposit them, it must be like tearing off an old friend. Besides the indignity of having to pay for the pawn ticket, which I consider an outrage, don't you?'

Suppled by three days of Mrs Finch's attentions, Mr Mackenzie replied, as calmly as if his feet had never left the ground, that if you pay for a thing, you are less likely to mislay it.

'Theft is a good preservative,' said Mr Finch. 'Stolen umbrellas cling.'

'The things that visitors leave behind are the most clinging of all,' remarked Cordelia.

'Yes, that's very true,' Mrs Finch said. 'All manner of things. Bones. Did you happen to notice the bone in your wardrobe, Mr Mackenzie? It's been with us for years, but how we came to have it and who has been remembering it with tears ever since, we shall never know, because we only came on it after a mother superior of an Anglican sisterhood, the last person in the world to cherish riding boots – '

'Dear me! I hope I haven't overlooked anything,' Mr Mackenzie said. 'Perhaps I had better have a last look round.'

'No, no, don't trouble to do that. It would be a waste of time,' said Mr Finch. 'I expect your sister-in-law will be here at any moment now.'

'No, no,' said Mrs Finch. 'Have some more coffee, instead. And don't think anything of the clock. Henry likes to keep them a little in advance.'

'He advanced them all this morning,' added Clara.

'That's why I think hourglasses would be so much more satisfactory,' Mrs Finch said. 'You can't tamper with them.'

'You might forget to reverse them, Elinor,' said her husband.

'But, Henry, it would still be an hour, whenever I began it. An hour is all I ever want to know about. Think of all the things you could do in an hour, besides boiling twenty successive eggs. You could hem a bath towel, or you could plant half a dozen oak trees, or you could learn Wordsworth's "Ode to Duty" by heart, or you could conduct the first act of *Tristan and Isolde*, or cross the Channel without singing a note, or – Did you hear anything, Mr Mackenzie? You look as if you heard something.'

'That barking – I wondered if it could be Agnes.'

'No, it's Willoughby – my pug, you know,' said Clara. 'He always barks at the wind. Doesn't he, Mother?'

'Yes, dear. He barks too much. You should teach him not to be so worldly-minded. Or you could roast a small chicken. One hour at a time is quite enough for any reasonable person. I don't believe in anticipating; people only damage themselves by pinning their faith to the future. There was that woman who fell off a horse. "Between the saddle and the ground, she mercy sought, she mercy found." If she'd had more time, ten to one she'd have muddled it. Yes, Henry? Are you looking for something?'

'I'm looking for my dictionary of quotations. Come here, Elinor. You always quote that wrong. Come here, and see for yourself.'

Having got his wife into a corner, Mr Finch whispered, 'Can't you find anything to talk about except time and road accidents? She's over half an hour late, and of course he's worried.' Clearing his throat, he remarked, for general consumption, 'If you were a married man,

Mackenzie, you'd know there are two things women can't do. They can't get a quotation right and they are never punctual. Have a cigar.'

'But Agnes is usually very punctual,' said Mr Mackenzie. 'I don't think I'll embark on a cigar.'

'Why don't you and Henry play a game of chess?' Mrs Finch suggested. 'You could finish it on postcards, if need be. Or by telephone, if it suddenly got impassioned.'

'Telephone. I forgot that. Of course, if anything should go wrong, Agnes would ring up.'

'Of course she would,' Mrs Finch said. 'I daresay she's doing it at this moment, and explaining it all to the grocer because they've given her the wrong number. I expect that's why Willoughby is still barking. He always begins to bark before the telephone rings. But second sight is as easy as winking to animals. My aunt had a poodle, and on All Souls' Eve he used to go up to the attic, where she kept my uncle's remains – his belongings, I mean, for the rest of him had withered in the family vault years before – and there he'd scratch at my uncle's hatbox and moan under his breath, with every tuft standing bolt upright. It showed a generous disposition, for Uncle Cornelius loathed dogs and wouldn't allow one in the house. Bees, too. Did you know that bees won't go near a murderer?'

'No, I can't say that I did,' Mr Mackenzie said, somewhat absently. 'Do you know, I think I *do* hear – '

Casting an expressive glance at Mr Finch, Mrs Finch swept on. 'Perhaps you've never kept bees. Uncle Cornelius was an O'Kelly – he had banshee blood – and whenever he fell ill, the servants left the house in a body, because they were afraid of hearing the death howl. As it happened, he didn't die in Ireland but at a hotel, and in perfect health. The night before, my aunt kept on hearing bursts of very odd music, and at last she woke up Uncle Cornelius and said to him, "Wolverhampton is a strange town. Why do they choose this hour of the night to hold a choir practice on the roof?" He couldn't hear a thing! So she knew what was coming. Have you any interesting family ghosts, Mr Mackenzie, besides that bloodstained old gentleman in Edinburgh?'

'Mackenzie the Persecutor belonged to a different branch, I'm glad to say.'

'I'm delighted to hear it. You see, Henry, there was no need to make faces at me, after all. He's a different Mackenzie.'

'It is a cadet branch,' said Mr Mackenzie, warming to the theme. 'The youngest son of Ian Mackenzie of Tram married a Christian Hackbucket. That would be about 1490. The Hackbuckets –' He broke off. 'I can't help thinking I hear a voice.'

'It's the wind,' said Mrs Finch. 'Do go on about Miss Hackbucket.'

'It seems to be saying *"Edward! Edward!"* My name is Edward.'

'A north wind would say anything, Mr Mackenzie. You should hear the sort of thing it says at the equinox. Cordelia, darling, just switch on the light. Hell is murky . . . Won't it go on? I suppose the wind has blown a branch across the cable again.'

'It's in the garden, and it is saying Edward!' exclaimed Mr Mackenzie. 'Excuse me, but –' He hurried to the window but returned, saying, 'There's no one in sight.'

'I daresay it was some electricians come about the cable, and now they have gone round the corner of the house. One of them must have been called Edward. Coincidences often happen like that. Now that you've mentioned Hackbucket, ten to one I shall see a Hackbucket in *The Times* tomorrow – a new one, in the Births,' said Mrs Finch, resolutely combatting Mr Mackenzie's tendency toward Celtic brooding. 'Some people like to believe they are part of a cosmic plan, but I consider that's tame. I much prefer to think of them bounding about the universe like unreclaimed unicorns, always a pleasure to meet and never hounded into categories. Why do people want everything explained and pinned down and accounted for? I hate salted tails!'

Mr Mackenzie continued to brood.

'This room's getting insufferably cold,' said Mr Finch, and threw more wood on the fire. 'Move up your chair, Mackenzie. You're shivering.'

Mr Mackenzie obeyed, remarking that it seemed to have got much colder all of a sudden.

'It usually does toward sundown,' said his host.

A rush of cold air had, in fact, entered the library, because the door at the far end of the room had been slowly opened. A woman stood on the threshold. She was tall and gaunt, and water dripped from the hem of her long, colourless garment. But as they all sat facing the fire, no one had noticed her entry, and in the howling of the gale and the crackling of fresh oak logs her annunciatory coughs went unheard.

Clara remarked helpfully that ghosts chill the air.

'Stuff and nonsense! Cyanide of potassium!' exclaimed Mrs Finch. 'Don't you remember that young man from Cambridge who met a ghost and chemically analyzed it?'

The gaunt woman now advanced into the room, leaving a trail of puddles on the carpeted floor.

'I don't know if it's ever struck you, Mackenzie,' said Mr Finch, 'that if a conversation goes on long enough, it always leads to apparitions.'

Before Mrs Finch could postpone this unseasonable ripening, Cordelia, who for some weeks past had been trying to release her father from an inferiority complex, said urgently, 'Father, do tell your ghost story about the feet!'

Exposed to the draught from the door, Mr Mackenzie stirred uneasily.

Mr Finch exerted himself to entertain. 'When my godfather, Henry Monk, was a young man, he went fishing in Wales with his cousin Alfred, and they put up at an inn where they had to share a four-poster bed. Henry woke up in the middle of the night and said to Alfred, "I wish you'd keep your feet to yourself. They're as cold as ice." Alfred said, "So are yours." After a while, Henry said, "This is beyond a joke. That's the third time you've kicked me." Alfred said that on the contrary Henry had been kicking him. They disputed for some time, and the upshot of it was that they found that though there were only two of them in the bed, there were three pairs of feet. It gave them a very tasty turn.'

During this story, the gaunt woman stood waiting behind Mr Mackenzie's chair. As Mr Finch reached for another log, she tapped Mr Mackenzie on the ear. 'Edward! Edward, I've come for you!' she said.

Mr Mackenzie uttered a low howl and stumbled to his feet.

'Sit down, Mr Mackenzie! Sit down at once, and finish your coffee. Whatever it is, don't let it put you in a flurry. It only encourages them.' Saying this, Mrs Finch looked at the intruder as though she were looking through her.

Glaring at Mrs Finch with reciprocal imperceptiveness, the gaunt woman repeated that she had come for Mr Mackenzie.

Mr Mackenzie, his teeth still chattering, introduced his sister-in-law, adding the tactless comment that she had come at last.

'At last?' she retorted. 'As it happens, I've been here for some time. When I found that no one answered the bell I decided it must be out of order, so I walked round the house trying to make myself heard. By that time the rain was coming through my mackintosh, so I thought there was nothing for it but to walk in. I'm sure I hate asking you to tear yourself away, Edward, but if we are to get to town before midnight . . .'

The image of a modest, self-effacing matron, Mrs Finch left the appropriate apologies and assurances to the head of the household. It was Mr Finch who offered refreshments, and briskly submitted when they were rejected. It was Mr Finch who voiced an unforeseen confidence that they would reach London in no time. It was Mr Finch who supervised the turning of the car while Mrs Finch took a rather wan farewell of Mr Mackenzie. As they re-entered the library, Mr Finch said with resignation, 'Well, I don't suppose we shall ever see him again. Even if he wanted to come back, he won't have a chance to. She'll kill him long before they get to London. I've never seen a woman so incapable of backing a car. Poor Mackenzie! It's a pity his last days on earth were so – Why, Elinor, is anything wrong with you?'

'Fatigue,' said Mrs Finch, busying herself with the bellows, 'Strain. Nervous exhaustion. I thought the poor wretch would never go.'

'Then why did you choose at the last moment to offer him more coffee and tell him not to be flurried? If anything, you seemed anxious to keep him.'

'Did I? I suppose I felt sorry for him. Such a blood-curdling sister-in-law – for a moment, she quite frightened me.'

I MET A LADY

Malice makes easy the most uncongenial attainments – especially if it be the uncultivated malice that grows brisk as a weed out of a situation – and uncultivated malice made Thomas Black an expert on the register book of every hotel where he stayed with Cosy. Cosy, who on these occasions shared his surname and his bedroom but was in fact Holloway, had an ardent, selfless, indefatigable passion for the truth; for running it down, and handing it on. She liked facts to be ascertained, nails to be hit on the head, speculations to be shot on the wing, ambiguities to be resolved and pigeonholed. So when she said, as she inevitably did, 'You know those people with the dachs? Well, they are called Johnson-Hobson and they come from Oswestry,' Thomas, fortified by his mastery of the register, would reply, 'Yes, I know. 122A, Eisteddfod Road. British.' And this, for reasons of uncultivated malice, would give him considerable pleasure. It pleased Cosy, too. To share the same interests is the surest foundation for a successful married life; and though there was no explicit understanding that a successful married life was to develop from going away for weekends with Thomas, Cosy had that end in view, or she would not have done it: she never did.

One cannot memorize whole pages during a passing glance at a bowl of sweet peas or a colour print of Old Brighton, and if Thomas had taken Cosy to large hotels her pursuit of truth would have scoured wider fields, and achieved more picturesque data – 'You know that man who ate three boiled eggs? Well he's been to Cannes, Hotel Splendide, and now he's left for Wolverhampton,' which in turn would have challenged Thomas's malice to less mechanically adequate reprisals. They might even have quarrelled, which would have made their relationship a great deal livelier and more amiable. But Thomas was indolent, and calcined with self-mistrust. During the twelvemonth in which he had been aware that Cosy's conversation lacked the unexpected (he had known her for just over a year), he had been content to regard her as a kind of beauteous punchball, except when he happened to remember that he loathed clever women; whereas for the last ten years he had been implacably averse to driving in traffic whenever his profession, which was mercantile and something to do with wool, did not oblige him to do so. Accordingly, the hotel where this story takes place was so small and unpretentious that although it was filled to capacity (as in England any small unpretentious hotel situated in scenery with claims to desolation is apt to be), a brief semblance of attention to a stuffed polecat was enough to arm Thomas against any new facts that Cosy might unearth, and when the old gentleman and the old lady and the rather handsome middle-aged woman who had arrived overnight came silently into the lounge to drink their after-lunch coffee he knew as certainly as though it were emblazoned on the Sunday papers they wrapped themselves up in that their home was in Kent. There they sat, with Mr and Mrs Wulstan Brough of Clitheroe on one side of them, with Mr and Mrs Desmond Powler, Miss Beryl Powler, and Dr Dennis Raymond, all Londoners, on the other. There they were, newcomers, who had moreover arrived after dinner and breakfasted in their rooms, but fraught with no more mystery than the brace of Cardiff Brisewolds by the window, than Major Bertram Cary, Berwick-upon-Tweed, than the clock on the mantlepiece, than the Grisewold Sealyham morosely grieving over an unattainable flea, than Cosy and himself, Mr and Mrs T. Black, Huddersfield.

'Don't scratch so, Jukebox,' said Mrs Grisewold in a mild voice that hadn't much conviction in it. Jukebox responded with a despairing yet resolute groan. Mrs Brough remarked in an undertone to Mr Brough that the wind had quite died down. Miss Powler looked about for an ashtray and Dr Raymond moved one into her reach. Mrs Finch, rustling over to another page of the *News of the World*, a periodical that W. B. Yeats had in his time commended, said, 'There's been another horrid murder by Teddy Bears.'

Her voice was no louder than any other voice that had been raised, but her diction was so uncommonly pure that it was as though the words had been etched in dry-point on the silence. The *Observer* which Mr Finch was holding up between himself and the universe quivered slightly. Cordelia Finch − Thomas had noted with approval her unhackneyed baptismal name – replied in tones of calm assent and with a diction almost as exquisite as her mother's that they were perpetually at it nowadays. That was all.

But Thomas, after a momentary airy dream of somehow detaching Mrs Finch from her Mr and Miss Finch and keeping her for ever entirely to himself, fell into an enthralled contemplation of how the Teddy Bears would go about it. Invulnerable, being stuffed with those peculiar vitals of wood-wool, with changeless smiles of black stitching on their jaws, their eyes round, merciless, bright with innocent vice, their large criminal ears distended, they advanced in a gang – he could see them at it – with curt stockish movements of their short stiff legs, their short stiff arms. They carried no weapons. They had no need of weapons, even if they had been fashioned to handle them; for the Teddy Bear's weapon is in the victim himself, is his total unsuspiciousness, his lifelong conviction that Teddy Bears are good animals, covered with honey-coloured plush and stuffed with a modern equivalent of Hearts of Oak. No one companioned from infancy by a Teddy Bear that went to bed with him and was there in the morning, its glassy golden regard reflecting the light of a new day on the nursery ceiling, would look for a sinister glint in those unwinking eyes, would expect anything from that sturdy furry frame except a rough blanket kiss, a reliable passive portability, a chunky goodness, jointed at thighs and shoulders, and with a meek head that could in course of time and loving experiment be twiddled back to front. Nine-tenths of the British race, more, possibly, reckoning in the very small cheap ones, would rely on the goodwill of Teddy Bears as they rely on the goodwill of the Royal Family – for even austere republicans who disapprove of the Royal Family never question the warmth of its regard for them. Trapped on the illusions of childhood, of all illusions the dearest and the most dogmatic, what possible chance would the victim have? Even when he saw the gang advancing on him with fixed gaze and felt-soled tread, he would expect no evil. He might feel surprise, he might pinch himself in an attempt to get out of a rather disparaging dream, but he would not feel alarm. And so, smiling on him with almost identical black cotton smiles and led, probably, by a bear who had lost one eye, they would close in round his ankles. For bears kill by hugging; and the horrid murders by Teddy Bears would begin with a mass hug, a constriction of arteries between foot and knee, until the victim lost his balance and, screaming wildly in a silly attempt to wake out of a dream that wasn't a dream, would fall to the ground. The rest would shortly be silence. Planting their felted feet on his mouth and nostrils, flailing him with short swinging blows, buffeting him with smiling jaws, the Teddy Bears would soon make their stealthy competent end of him. Then they would troop off to another horrid murder; for as the daughter said, they were perpetually at it nowadays.

After an interval of silence, no longer than was compatible with the introduction of a totally irrelevant topic, Mr Finch put down his *Observer* and said to his nonpareil,

'What would you like to do this afternoon, Elinor? Shall we go for a drive, or would you rather rest?'

'Rest? On a Sunday? I don't think one should rest on Sunday unless onc has donc something striking during the week. That reminds me – do you know what I was thinking about last night, Cordelia? The Creation. Haydn's first, because you were humming it, and then the other one. Do you know, I think it may be the explanation of something I have always found very puzzling – why one eats fish at the beginning of dinner and fruit at the end.'

'If we start now we shall be just in time for evensong at Durham Cathedral,' Mr Finch said.

Thomas saw his one and only love taken away by her husband. Her gait was as flawless as her diction, and just as the door was closing behind them, he heard her speak again, 'The soup is Chaos.' The Griswolds, the Broughs, the Powlers, were now simultaneously rising – as though they were a congregation – and stumbling and shuffling out into the fresh air of common day. Only Major Cary seemed faithful to the emptied shrine. But he had fallen asleep in it, long before the bears. Thomas turned politely to Cosy. Her eyes, her large soft brown eyes, were beaming with the light of deduction.

'You know, when she talked about Teddy Bears murdering people, what she meant was Teddy Boys. It did sound queer, didn't it? But I daresay at her age she didn't notice the difference. Teddy Boys. Teddy Bears. Teddy in both cases, you see. She made a mistake, that was all. They're called Finch, the unmarried one is called Cordelia. I know she's unmarried, she isn't even engaged. I looked at her finger. No engagement ring.'

Poor Cosy smiled as she glanced down at the permanent emerald pledge of his affections and the plain gold band she put on for these excursions. The emerald pledge would continue to be more or less permanent, he supposed, for it was a handsome ring; and before long, he confidently hoped, she would again find a use for the plain gold band. But this would be the last time she would wear it in his honour. Sooner or later the Priestess of Delphi cries aloud, and the doom is spoken. And when the smoke of the altar clears away one sees plainly that the doom is inevitable and that one consents to it with a pure heart.

After that, one goes away immediately. Besides, it would be low and dishonourable to subject the unsuspecting Cosy to any more invidious comparisons with Mr Finch's nonpareil.

'That dog will be bound to give us fleas if we stay here,' he said. 'Suppose we went on somewhere else, somewhere with more life in it. How long would it take you to pack?'

In less than half an hour, for she had learned all about packing from some woman's magazine, they had looked their last on the stuffed polecat, and set out for Harrogate. There, they finished the week-end, and there Thomas was everything that is kind, lascivious, and honourable to Cosy; for his mercantile calling had given him high notions of how to fulfil a contract and ensure that no bale of wool left his warehouse improperly parcelled or inadequately addressed. After the letter of farewell was written he even, to allay any feelings he might have wounded, spent a decorous three weeks travelling in Turkey, alone.

A WIDOW'S QUILT

'Emma loves museums,' said Helena, 'and I think it's good for her to look at things being still, for a change, instead of that incessant jiggety-jog of television. Not like us when we were young, Charlotte – though you were never so tied to the box as I was.'

'I hated watching people breathe.'

The sisters were visiting the American Museum at Claverton, in Somerset. It was Charlotte's first visit.

'Do you come here often?'

'Yes. It's an easy run from Bristol, and I enjoy buying fancy jams from their shop. Expensive. But traditional things are always expensive. And Henry likes them. You should take something back to Everard.'

'Remind me to.'

Emma was staring into a quiescent period parlour. 'That clock doesn't strike,' she said. 'Why doesn't it strike, Mummy? Hasn't it got an inside? Is it too old to be wound up?' Other visitors smiled, murmured, seemed inclined to enter into conversation. 'Now I want to see the blue dogs.'

They moved on into the quilt room. It was hung with pieced and appliqué quilts, brilliant as an assembly of macaws. Emma ran from one to another, identifying the blue dogs in an appliqué miscellany of rosebuds, hatchets, stars, kites, apples, horsemen, and shawled ladies encircling Abraham Lincoln in a stovepipe hat, quitting them for a geometrical pieced design of lilac and drab.

'Queen Charlotte's Crown – that's for you, Aunt Charlotte. And here's Fox and Geese.'

'Darling! Don't touch.'

One would always have to be being patient, thought Charlotte. On the whole she was glad she did not have a child. Her attention was caught by a quilt that stood out from the others, dominating their rich vivacity with a statement of dulled black on white. She moved toward it.

'That's a widow's quilt,' said Helena. 'Narrow, you see, for a single bed. I suppose you made one for yourself, when your husband died. Or your friends made it for you. Rather grisly.'

'I think it's a hideous quilt,' Emma said.

They descended to the shop, where Charlotte was reminded of the something she must take back to Everard, and chose horehound candies. Then Helena drove her to the station, and she made her platform thanks and farewells. 'I particularly enjoyed the quilts,' she said. 'One doesn't see enough blue dogs.'

But between Bath and London Charlotte sat in a dreamlike frenzy, planning the construction of her own black-and-white quilt. Built up from hexagons, and narrow, it would not be more than a winter's work, once she had assembled its materials: half a dozen exact geometrical hexagons; heavy paper, over which she would tack her patches; fine needles for the small stitches; a couple of sheets. The black would not be so easily found – that lustreless soot-black, dead-rook black. Perhaps she might find some second-hand weeds in the Chelsea fantasy boutiques. Or should she qualify the white unanimity of the sheets by using a variety of blacks already available? There were remains of the official blacking-out curtains drawn over the windows at home during the war, kept to come in useful, her mother had said, and still kept in the inherited piece box from which she had pulled fragments of chintz for the patchwork cushion cover started for Great-Aunt Emma but never completed. There was the black shawl bought at Avignon; some black taffeta; some sateen; quantities of black velvet. As she recalled these varieties of black, the design of her widow's quilt shaped itself to her mind's eye. In the centre, a doubled, even a trebled ring of black velvet hexagons massively enclosing the primal hexagon of white wedding-dress brocade. Extending to the four corners of the quilt, long black diagonals, the spaces between interspersed with star-spangled black hexagons not too close together, and for a border a funeral wreath of black hexagons conjoined.

Dizzied, she got out of the terminus because everyone else was doing so, and took a wasteful taxi to the usual address without realizing she was going home.

Next morning, as soon as Everard had tapped the barometer, put on the indicated topcoat, and left for his office (he was a partner in a firm that sold rare postage stamps), she chose the pair of sheets and went out to buy the fine needles, going on to F. Wilkens, Electrician and Household Repairs – for during the night it had occurred to her that the basic hexagons would be much more satisfactory if they were exact to measure and cut out of tin. F. Wilkens, oddly calling them templates, knew exactly what she meant, and would have them ready in half an hour. She spent the interval in the Health Food Shop, buying Everard's muesli, then collected the templates and went back to the flat in Perivale Mansions. By the time he returned she had assembled most of the double garland of black velvet round the wedding-dress brocade, folded it away in a pillowcase, and prepared supper.

That night her pleasure in the progress of the black velvet garland was soured by seeing it as so much done already. At this rate, the quilt would be snatched from her hands, no more to the purpose than a daisy chain Patch after patch would lessen her private entertainment; the last patch in the border of black hexagons would topple her over the edge to drown in the familiar tedium. She did not want to make another quilt, or any other kind of quilt. This was her only, her nonpareil, her one assertion of a life of her own. When Everard left for his office, she hardly dared take out the pillowcase. While stitching in the first white hexagons, she realized the extent of even a single-bed quilt. She need not despair for some time yet.

By midday it was raining steadily. The barometer's counsel of an umbrella was, as usual, justified. The sound of rain was agreeable to work to. It rained. She worked. Between two and three in the afternoon, finding herself extremely hungry, she ravaged the larder for an impromptu meal – unwontedly delicious, since she fed on the tinned delicacies.

The weekend jolted her out of her contentment. Two days of Everard at home she was inured to, but to waste two days without setting a stitch in the quilt was torment. She festered in idleness; she had never hated his company more. And it increased her exasperation that he should be unaware of it.

Yet as time went on, and the quilt enlarged, and weekends fell into the pattern of her existence as though they were recurring hexagons of an unassimilable material which she would presently unpick, her disposition changed; she was complacent, she was even benign. Strange, to think that Everard, whose demands and inroads had compelled her to such an abiding rancour that seeing the widow's quilt had given her a purpose in life, should have supplied this soothing influence. Meanwhile she went on with the quilt, never losing sight of its intimations and in the main preserving her original scheme – though the diagonal had to be revised: the single black line lacked emphasis, and had to be changed to a couple of lines hedging a band of white. This, in turn, involved a reconsideration of the corners. The solution had been found (there was exactly the right amount of the black shawl to supply its hexagons) when Christmas stared her in the face – and Everard. She could not securely hope that his seasonal influenza would keep him coughing in bed and out of her way; but she was on fire to get at the revised corners, and told herself that a little publicity would be the surest safeguard of the secrecy which was an essential ingredient in her pleasure. On Christmas Eve Everard came home to find her with the quilt on her knee. He glanced at it warily, as though it were something that might disagree with him. When it was there next day and the day after, he mentioned its presence.

'What's that, Charlotte – all those bits you're sewing together?'

She displayed it.

'How nicely you've done it. What's it for?'

'In time it will be a quilt.'

'Oh. So it's not finished yet.'

'No. Not yet.'

She stitched in another hexagon.

'Do you make it up as you go along?'

'I saw one like it in the American Museum.'

'In a museum. How interesting. Was that black and white too?'

'Yes. It's a traditional pattern. It's called a magpie quilt.'

'Magpie? Magpie? Oh, because it's black and white, I suppose. Quite imaginative.'

She stitched, Everard pondered.

'I wonder the United States Post Office doesn't use these old designs – now that they go in for so many commemorative stamps.'

She thought of the blue dogs, but refrained.

By the New Year Everard's cough was so insistent that he had to give up taking his temperature. She foresaw herself stitching her widow's quilt at his bedside. Instead, his partner brought a Puerto Rican violet for his opinion. Finding it spurious, Everard felt equal to going back to his office.

With the enlarging days the quilt gathered momentum. It outgrew the pillowcase and had to be folded away in a bedspread. Each morning it seemed to have grown in the night; each day it was more responsive, more compliant. The hexagons fitted into place as if drawn by a magnet. It had a rationality now, a character; the differing blacks superimposed a pattern of their own, as well-kept fields do with the various tints of their crops. She was so much at ease with it that she could let her thoughts stray as she worked – not so far us to make a mistake, though. She hated mistakes, even those she could unpick. But looking forward to the time when she would rightfully sleep under it, her mind made excursions to places where she might go as a quiet travelling widow. To Lincolnshire, perhaps, with its 'fields of barley and of rye' bordering the river – a sinuous, slow-flowing river with no conversation, effortlessly engulfing the chatter of Tennysonian brooks. Then, on the one hand, a quiet cross-country bus would show her Boston Stump outlined against the pale eastern sky, or, catching a train at Dukeries Junction Station, she would survey the Vale of Beauvoir.

Not since her marriage had she gone beyond the Home Counties, and these had only been visited at licensed holiday seasons: a dab of green at Easter, in August a smear of summer with Everard's cousins in Surrey. Meanwhile, she had travelled a great deal in theory, studying guidebooks and ordnance maps and railway guides, even a list of bus routes in East Anglia which had chanced her way. The row of Methuen's Little Guides in the bookcase on her side of the bed had assured her in detail of the existence of what imagination left visionary: churches (E. E., Perp., restored in 1870), the number of different species of bat in Essex, an almshouse or a gasworks, a disused bridge, a local industry, an extensive prospect of rolling country, a forgotten battlefield, a clay soil, a sandy loam, floodmarks, plantations of conifer, a canal. On the whole, it was the dullish Midlands she preferred; romantic extremities, like Cornwall, could come later.

She was stitching away at Everard's demise – every hexagon brought it a step nearer – when Helena, who was in London to visit her dressmaker, came on to Perivale Mansions. After a momentary gasp, Helena admired the quilt, now three-quarters done.

'And what are you going to stuff it with?'

'Stuff it?'

'It would have to be interlined and stitched through to the backing, you know. Otherwise it wouldn't be a quilt. The one you admired in the museum has harps outlined in stitching – I suppose she felt strongly about Ireland.' She talked on about New England quilting bees, and left before Everard was due to return.

There was nothing for it but to swallow the shock, be glad that the quilt could continue into summer, and decide on the stitched design which should complete it. Not harps, anyhow. A speedy crisscross would be about as much as she could manage. For with the added weight of the backing and the interlined padding, the quilt would be too heavy to handle comfortably, could become a drudgery – another marital obligation, almost another Everard.

She began to make mistakes, straying from the order of her design, choosing the black sateen when it should have been the fustier black of the curtain material. Twice she sewed in a hexagon back side uppermost. The thread tangled, slid out of the needle's eye. When she came to re-thread a needle, she had to make shot after shot at it, holding the needle with a grip of iron, poking the thread at it with a shaking hand. Her heart thumped. Her fingers swelled.

If I were sensible, she thought, I would take to my bed. But the voice of reason reminded her of Everard's disconsolate fidgeting, his dependence on her (Where do I find the toaster? Oh dear, the milk has boiled over again! What am I to mop it up with?) when she had rheumatic fever. She was not in a fit state to be an invalid. The widow's quilt, even if at the moment it was thwarting her intentions, was the more enlivening companion.

She was in the last corner now. It was mid-March, and the east wind was howling down the street like the harlot's curse, when the last of her misfortunes, the silliest and most derisive, tripped her: she had no more thread. She shook some of the ache out of her back, put on her thickest coat, eased her swollen hands into gloves, grimaced at the barometer, and went downstairs and out. It was as though the wind had whirled her out of herself. She was loose again, the solitary traveller, and back in Lincolnshire. She took the narrow road across the saltmarsh flats between her and the sea. They stretched on either hand, featureless, limitless. Nothing would gainsay their level till the enormous breakers reared up, one driven forward on another, and fell with a crash and a flump on the beach. The wind streamed through her; she fought it with every step, and was one with it. At the corner of Perivale Street and Sebastopol Terrace a burly holidaymaker off an advertisement was blown overhead, exclaiming, 'Skegness Is So Bracing!'

She had to struggle for breath before she could ask for thread and civilly agree with the shopwoman that the wind was quite savage, wasn't it. And, indeed, as she walked back she could hardly walk straight. The wind was still roaring in her ears when she stood in the hallway of Perivale Mansions, with the stairs in front of her – three flights, each of seventeen steps. She paused on the first landing. The roaring in her ears had changed and was now loud beats on a gong. Twice seventeen was twice seventeen. She mounted the second flight. The gong beat on, but irregularly – thunder to the flashes of lightning across her eyes. At the foot of the third flight she stumbled and fell. She saw her gloved hands clutch the air. A little paper bag fell from one of them. Two reels of thread escaped from it, rolled along the landing, and went tap-tapping down the stairs. Another of her misfortunes. Her lips tried to grin but had turned to lead. The wind had blown out all the lights, and down in the hallway the sea rose higher and higher. A seventh wave, a master wave, would surge up the stairs she had climbed so painfully, thrust its strength beneath her, carry her away like a wisp of seaweed. She was still vaguely alive when Everard almost tripped over her. He called 'Help! Help!' and blew the police whistle he always carried on his key ring.

'There was something wrong with her heart,' he said to Helena, who came next morning. 'It might have happened at any moment. You can imagine what a shock it was to me. I think I must move.' He had not much to say, but he talked incessantly. 'At first I thought she had been killed. You can imagine what I felt. There is so much violence about nowadays – no post office is safe. I never felt easy leaving her. But it was something wrong with her heart. She was everything to me, everything, my poor Charlotte. Where do you think I should go?'

Helena had picked up the quilt and began folding it.

'And there's that quilt. What should we do about it? It's not finished, you see. Poor Charlotte, so unfortunate! It's a magpie quilt.'

'Magpie?'

'Yes, because it's all black and white – like the birds, she said.'

'I see.'

'I can't very well take it with me. Yet it would be a pity to throw it away. Could you take charge of it, Helena? It would be a weight off my mind if you would. You'd know how to finish it, and I don't suppose it would take you very long. Not that there's any hurry now. And then you could keep it, to remember her by. I'm sure she'd like you to have it. It meant a great deal to her.'

THE MOTHER TONGUE

Of the three girls who set out that day Florka and Teresa, who were smart and quick, were to work in an orphanage. The third, Magda, was to be a servant on a farm.

'But you will meet on Sundays. Magda will come to Ludby by bus to attend mass, all that has been arranged,' said Miss Oliphant, speaking clearly and cheerfully. 'Then you will be able to talk Polish together, for you must not forget your own language. That will be nice, won't it, Magda?'

Miss Oliphant, who was on the staff of an Acclimatisation and Training Centre for Displaced Persons, felt strongly on the language question. Speaking the tongue that Shakespeare spake, she could not imagine herself divested of the English language. And though these sad superfluities from Europe might never need their native speech again they ought, she felt, to retain something of it – enough, at least, to pray in. She had read somewhere that the language in which one says one's prayers is one's true mother-tongue, and this had struck her as a profound truth, even though it might be slightly impaired by the Roman Catholic habit of poll-parroting in Latin.

'Will be nice,' Magda repeated.

In England, Magda had learned that much, everything has to be nice. For Florka and Teresa it would be nice to work in the kitchen of an orphanage. For her it would be nice to be the servant of a Mr and Mrs Garland on a farm. Dinners, stockings, a toothbrush of one's own, or a given lot in life, all must be nice; and being nice, must be gratefully accepted. In gratitude to Miss Oliphant for producing the nice buns to eat in the train, the three girls struggled to talk English throughout the journey, thereby obliging Miss Oliphant to fall back on the consoling reflection that the Poles are natural-born linguists – think of Joseph Conrad.

But a language is a thing which can only be possessed by those who possess it in common. Language is a dozen voices clinging to the rope of a litany. Language is a hundred voices clattering against each other in the market place. Language is the lamentation of thousands crying out in terror and anguish. Language is the uproar of millions, a rustle of questions sprouting thick as corn all over Europe, saying, *What now? When? Whither?* And presently language is a hundred voices clinging to the rope of a new speech, saying, *I-am-glad-to-see-you. Please-have-you-the-needle? Thank-you-very-much.* After the first days at the farm, days of slow questions and anxious listening, Magda discarded her English. Clean floors, washing on the line, food for hens and food for pigs, these were the things required of her, not conversation. She retreated into her native language as an animal goes back into the wood.

But behind the wood lies the forest, dusky, pathless, and unsignalized. Behind not speaking lies the unspoken. Presently Magda began to forget her native language too. When she encountered Florka and Teresa she could find nothing to say. They talked of cinemas, of boys, of the matron at the orphanage and the clothes that hung in her wardrobe. To Magda they said, 'Still on your farm?' and Magda said, 'Yes.'

By the end of the summer she had entered a limbo of almost no language at all. She was not unhappy. She worked hard and well, and was kindly treated. As the Garlands increasingly trusted her, they left her more and more to herself. 'A nice quiet steady girl,' said Mrs Garland to her husband, adding, 'You'd never think, to look at her, all the terrible things she's been through. But I expect she's forgotten them by now.' 'I don't know so much about that,' he replied. 'There was that night she woke up screaming.'

But the night when Magda woke up screaming had no successor. And no kind questionings could elicit whether she had felt a pain, or had a bad dream, or been frightened by the owls. 'All gone,' she had said – the words a child uses who has drunk syrup or medicine; and that was all they could get from her, or that she could voice to herself.

As a fish slides through the net and drops back into the water, Magda escaped from the mesh of words, vanished from conversations, evaded any thought that might engage her in the discomfort of language. When the accident happened to Leonard, her silence was so much a matter of course that no one thought her unfeeling because of it. Leonard, one of Mr Garland's labourers, fell off a rick and broke his back. This was a terrible thing. Leonard was a good worker, and the accident took place after Michaelmas, which is the hiring season, so it would be difficult to get another man to replace him. The ambulance came, Leonard was taken to the hospital in Ludby, and there he died.

His body was to be brought back to the village for burial. He was a bachelor, and his relations lived in the north, so it would be a poorly attended funeral. Mrs Garland was thinking of this when it occurred to her that Magda could be included in the attendance from the farm. This was almost like killing two birds with one stone; for it would add another mourner to the ceremony, and at the same time it would make an outing for Magda. There was that blue costume, too. For some time she had been meaning to give it to the girl, and this would be a good occasion to do so. It was a very dark blue, quite dark enough to be suitable wearing for one who was neither friend nor relation.

'Magda, today is Leonard's funeral.' Magda began to rub at a smear on the table-top.

'You remember Leonard?'

In Magda's mind there appeared a large stubble-field, and at the further side of it a man wearing brown trousers who whistled. Then the man went suddenly out of the field, for he was dead. She sighed. 'Yes, poor Leonard! We shall all miss him. Today is the funeral.'

'Fu-ne-ral.' Magda spoke the word as though she were picking up in three pieces something that Mrs Garland had let fall.

'Yes. His funeral, you know. His funeral.' Mrs Garland felt that she could not explain the word. For what is one to say? There is a service conducted by a clergyman, and then the body, concealed in a coffin, is lowered into a hole in the ground, and earth is spaded over it. But why should she explain? Poor Magda must understand death and burial, if ever a girl did.

Magda liked the blue costume, and seemed to enjoy the drive to church. She sat snuffing the air and looking out of the car like a dog. Only on the threshold of the church did Mrs Garland remember her undertaking that Magda should not be taken inside any place of Protestant worship. Having been brought so far she must be left, still like a dog, to wait outside. She brushed the lichen off the stone slab of an old tomb, and told the girl to sit there till she returned.

Overhead the sky was deeply blue. The October sun was like wine, and though no wind seemed to be blowing, from time to time a faint pencilling of air ran up the towering chestnut trees. An autumnal pomp and intensity dwelt on the scene, everything seemed larger, brighter, and slower than usual. Yet it was a working day like any other. From the unseen village came the ordinary noises, buckets rattling, an axe falling, someone learning to ride a motor bicycle, and in the field below the churchyard wall there were the footsteps of a working man.

Idleness lay too heavy in Magda's lap. She began to feel afraid, and glanced over her shoulder to see if a thundercloud had come up. The sky was cloudless. She got off the tomb and walked to the edge of the churchyard to discover what the man whose footsteps she heard was doing.

From the retaining wall she looked down on a reaped field dotted with fusty-looking black faggots. They were bean-shocks, that had been left there to decay while the corn harvest was got in. Now they were being gathered into heaps, preparatory to being burned. It was a piece of husbandry that Magda knew familiarly. She had done it herself, she needed to find no words for it. She watched the man coming towards her, lifting the bean-shocks with a long-handled two-tined fork. The churchyard was higher than the field, she stood above him and he did not see her. He was clearing the strip of field just under the wall, and the smell of the rotten haulms became stronger as he approached. He speared a faggot and lifted it into the air, and for a moment it was level with her nostrils, and she smelled the whole force of its blackening corruption before he tossed it away to lie in a heap with the others.

Dizzy with watching, and perturbed, she moved off, and began to walk through the churchyard, dimly admiring the marble headstones and the bouquets of white composition flowers under their glass domes.

Now, out from the church porch came the heretic priest holding a book and speaking in a loud sad voice. He spoke in English, not Latin. After him a coffin was carried, and after the coffin came the mourners. The procession moved round the shoulder of the church and went out of sight.

Against her will, she stole after it. Kneeling behind a headstone, and clinging with all her force to the hot rough curve of the stone, she watched. The coffin was supported on a couple of planks above the grave-pit, and bands of white webbing dangled from its sides, like streamers. Some wreaths of flowers were propped against a heap of raw earth nearby, and already the sun was wilting them. The mourners stood in a little group beside the grave, and at the grave's head stood the priest. She saw him raise his hand, and make the sign of the cross. Immediately the men holding the bands which went round the coffin tightened their hold. The coffin trembled, and seemed about to rise into the air. Another man knocked aside the planks, and the coffin went down into the grave, hurriedly, and slightly head-foremost.

It disappeared from sight, and little showers of dusty earth began to trickle from the wall of the grave.

The priest opened his lips to speak, and at the same moment Magda heard her own voice. Something had happened, something had broken, and she had found her speech. She ran to the graveside. Shouldering away the grave-diggers, beating back their spades with her hands, she threw herself down and began to lament. She sobbed and wailed and dug her nails into the ground, grovelling face-downward and filling her lamenting mouth with the taste of earth.

Her outcry was of no language.

Those who were there were shocked and embarrassed and at a loss. But no one was angry. They knew who she was, and her circumstances, and the vast tract of human misery from which she came, and the innumerable dead she bewailed, lying on the brink of a stranger's grave. They stood back, their faces red and puckered, their inoperative hands dangling. The priest began to pray. But he soon left off again. He had only words. When at last she ended her lamentation and looked up with a breathless half-grin on her smirched face, no one could think of a word to say. She stared round on them, as if interrogating their silence. And then, as no one spoke, she began to look relieved, and got up, dusting the earth from her blue skirt, all the while gazing down into the grave as though she were intently listening to a reply.

THE PROPER CIRCUMSTANCES

My grandfather, a most amiable clergyman of the Church of England, had a terrible record with horses. He never bought a horse till he was sure it was the horse he needed, but no sooner was the beast in the rectory stable than it developed glanders or bit my grandmother or trampled on a churchwarden or couldn't walk uphill. In a month or so my grandfather, sanguine as ever, would be buying another horse. My grandmother said it was destiny.

I have never had to buy a horse. Why I have my grandfather so much in mind just now is because of Mrs Moor and Evie, our evacuees. Mrs Moor, when I first saw her, was sitting on a piano in a Rest Centre, holding a mug of tea. Three things about her made me notice her among the rest: she was so very large, she looked so very mournful, and she was the only person in the room who wasn't talking. I paused in front of her, much as one might pause before some oversized basalt deity in the Egyptian gallery of the British Museum, and just because she was silent and I can never let well enough alone, I asked her what part of London she came from. She replied that she came from Herne Hill.

Actually, the words she sighed out were 'Urn Ill.' And if I had listened to the sound instead of the sense . . . But instead I began to think of Grace, my nurse when I was a little girl, who lived at Herne Hill after she married, and of the tea set I chose for her wedding present, with poppies and ears of corn rambling all over it, and of how much I had admired it, and also of how much dear Grace, if she were still alive and living at Herne Hill, would have disliked flying bombs. Meanwhile, I was asking Mrs Moor how she felt after such a long journey in an open bus.

'*I'm* all right,' she said. 'It's Evie that preys on my mind. Because of her valve.'

Following the direction of her gaze, I saw Evie, a tremendous blonde girl with a heavy jaw.

'Bronichal, too,' continued Mrs Moor. 'She's got a doctor's sirstifficket to say so, and he said to me, "Mrs Moor, you must get her out of London or I can't be answerable." So we packed up and come. Not that I know where we are, for I don't.'

To see so large a woman not knowing where she was seemed to me peculiarly sad, considerably sadder than if she had been a small woman in the same predicament. Though I saw many women as pitiable as Mrs Moor and many more prepossessing, during the remainder of an afternoon that I spent going from one Rest Centre to another with a disillusioned relieving officer, the thought of Mrs Moor weighing so heavily upon the soil of Dorset without knowing where she weighed obsessed me, and by evening I knew we must have her. Evie, too, of course.

It was at this point that my grandfather cropped up. My friend Valentine, who lives with me, having listened to my reasons for thinking the Moors just the sort of evacuees she and I needed, changed the subject by asking me if I had inherited my eyebrows or my eloquence from my grandfather, to which I replied that as far as I knew I did not resemble him in any way. But I could only give him a passing thought, for we had to reorganize the house in order to give the Moors two bedrooms and a sitting room and that 'access to water and cooking facilities' insisted on by billeting regulations – access to water and cooking facilities consisting in our case of removing the *Memoirs of Casanova* from the bathroom window sill and some cobwebs from the kitchen. We were still breathless with the task of finding suitable landscapes to cover the damp patches on the walls of the room that was to be the Moors' sitting room, and enough chairs with strong legs, when the Moors arrived. They were both much larger than I remembered. Even in the vasty halls of the Rest Centre, they were notably tall and big, but inside our house they seemed at least eight feet high. As majestic as a state funeral, they followed me round their new home. At intervals Mrs Moor said, 'That'll please Evie,' and Evie said nothing whatever unless Mrs Moor referred to Evie's sirstifficket. Then Evie said coldly, 'Certificate.'

At last, bowing their heads, they vanished into their sitting room, where tea was ready for them. Tea is supposed to make English people feel happier, and Mrs Moor had remarked that Evie felt hungry, not having fancied the dinner at the Rest Centre. But when I looked in half an hour later, Mrs Moor and Evie were sitting mute and impassive, contemplating two boiled eggs that seemed by comparison to them to be the eggs of humming-birds.

'Now, she can't fancy eggs,' explained Mrs Moor. 'Rather strange, isn't it?'

Duty called me away from analyzing this fascinating problem. When Valentine and I saw Mrs Moor again, she was alone and in much better spirits. Evie, she told us, had taken a hot bath and had been so revived by it that she had put her hair in curlers and gone to bed, where she was waiting for her mother to make her a cup of hot cocoa. Stirring briskly, Mrs Moor began to tell us something of her own sufferings through aerial warfare, matrimony, childbirth, nervous debility, and her best shoes. 'Sevens and half is what I take, with a wide fitting, but these having rubber soles, they should have been eights. And when they got me out I was insensible, and remained so for hours on end. You never saw such a ruin – the chimney vases from my bedroom on the kitchen mat, and the pillows the girl was sleeping on two gardens off, and the lino, all inlaid it was . . . Never been able to scrub since,' said Mrs Moor, looking at us firmly.

Hastily I explained that if any scrubbing got done in our house, it was done by us.

' . . on account of my rheumatism,' continued Mrs Moor, 'rising into my knees from my feet. Dr Wilson, he begged me to stay at the hospital after I come to, but naturally my first thought was Evie's valve and the shock it would be to her to hear of her mum being buried, and her nervous from a child, and no wonder – never having had a home of our own till the bomb blew us out of it. Eighteen long years we lived with my husband's mother, bombs raining down all around us. Night after night I'd go down on my hands and knees and pray out loud, "O Lord, will I never be left in peace?" But that was after we'd moved to Herne Hill. Then it got quiet again and we really began to enjoy ourselves a bit, being on our own at last. I often say to my husband, joking-like, "Funny thing, it took us eighteen years to get a home of our own." Have to be tactful about it, for he fair worshipped his mother, being a widow.'

'Was she in the house when it was bombed?' Valentine inquired. Mrs Moor nodded emphatically.

'Was she killed?' I asked.

'Not as much as scratched,' said Mrs Moor. 'But she died of it. Six weeks later she died. From the shock. Evie was called after her, poor child. Ah, I shall never forget that night with the incendiaries. Might have been burned in her bed but for sliding downstairs as white as a sheet and spraining her ankle. All the top of the house burned out before we as much as noticed it being so taken up with Evie. Two baskets and a canister they dropped in all, and I so heartbroken I never even went upstairs to look at it but slept for six weeks on the bare boards without as much as a blanket under me and losing my flesh daily till my own relations didn't know me. "Lil," my sister-in-law said, "whatever's become of you?" And I couldn't speak a word, but I took her out into the garden and showed her all those lovely young cabbages I was counting on, burned as black as a crisp. Not that I ever eat greens myself.'

Still stirring Evie's cocoa, Mrs Moor assumed a mystical demeanour. 'And then something came over me, and I packed a suitcase and walked right across the common and sat down in the bus shelter and said to myself, "I'll take a fivepenny ticket and end it all." But every time a bus came up, I seemed to see Evie. Perhaps you think it a bit strange?' We assured her that we thought it very natural.

'There's not a hair on my head,' said Mrs Moor, 'that isn't wrapped up in that girl.'

When, in my W.V.S. capacity, I have to cheer reluctant hostesses about receiving evacuees, I lay stress on the importance of arranging some sort of programme for their first few days. Day 1, a trip to the country town to register at the Food Office and choose a butcher. Day 2, stroll round the village: 'This is our church. This is our ironmonger. Good morning, Mrs Doe. This is Mrs Rowley from London.' Day 3, a visit to the doctor. Day 4, with any luck, is Sunday. If not: 'Perhaps you would like to do a little washing.' Under this treatment, talents and proclivities unfold and confidence is established. Naturally, I applied it to the Moors. Mrs Moor responded most flatteringly. Before the end of the week she had rearranged her furniture, launched into making jam, and found herself a part-time job at the paper mills. But with Evie the method was a total flop. Even the Day 3 visit to the doctor, on which I had pinned my best hopes, miscarried. Though he renewed her sirstifficket and gave her a tonic, it was clear that he did so merely in deference to that Hippocratic oath which forbids one doctor to overthrow immediately the verdict of another doctor, for he refused an application for extra milk and extra eggs, and said that what her valve needed was more exercise. All this I learned from Mrs Moor, when she had left off crying. Evie, with a brow like thunder and a jaw like murder, had dragged herself upstairs, panting, and gone to bed. 'Evie feels things so,' said Mrs Moor. 'Though she doesn't say much.'

I agreed that Evie was taciturn. I had heard her say. 'No' seven times, 'Don't mind if I do' twice, and 'Hullo' once. Otherwise, I had only heard her say 'Certificate'. Remarks addressed to Evie were answered by Mrs Moor, if Mrs Moor was present, otherwise not at all. Having agreed that Evie was taciturn, I went on to say that she probably felt bored in the country but that we might reasonably hope she'd be happier when she'd made some friends of her own age. Mopping her eyes, Mrs Moor said that Evie didn't like Americans. I said that we had some Royal Artillery, too, in the neighbourhood. Mrs Moor replied that Evie really thought of no one but a boy friend in India, and that might be why her appetite was so uncertain. One moment she'd want a thing and the next she wouldn't look at it. She'd been like that ever since she was a wee thing. Stung into speculation, I asked Mrs Moor if she had any pictures of Evie as a wee thing, and she produced a snapshot of a very small Mr Moor, peeping out from behind a monster in satin.

During the rest of the day, Evie was a veiled presence to us – a sense of something resentful in a bedroom. At intervals we heard Mrs Moor carrying things upstairs on trays, and at intervals we heard the bathroom toilet being savagely flushed, but even without this we should have been aware of Evie overhead, for she diffused a kind of atmospheric pressure which led me to tap the barometer whenever I passed it, though in vain. At evening there was a glimmer of hope. Evie's bedroom window opens, most romantically, above our small river, and Evie was observed leaning from the window, lost in girlish dreams, with one hand pillowing her cheek and the other gracefully dangling a tear-sopped handkerchief, while on the further bank stood an R.A. corporal, similarly lost in manly meditation – meditation about our chimney pot, apparently, though a moment's thought, as Valentine pointed out, must have shown that his mind was far from architecture or he would have been running for his life, since it was obvious that if Evie leaned out much farther her specific gravity would tilt the house on top of him.

On the morrow, Mrs Moor greeted us with the glad news that the post had brought no less than six letters for Evie, all from abroad, and that this would cheer Evie up when she saw them on her breakfast tray. She also mentioned that during the night one leg of her bed had gone through the floor. It was providential, really, for it might have been a leg of Evie's bed. Evie was such a light sleeper and if anthing *did* wake her, it took a hot meal to get her off again.

Musing on Evie's insomnia, and on the worldwide nature of the war, and on what a cheered-up Evie would look like, I went off to my work. Throughout that day I heard myself saying – I hoped persuasively – that one cannot expect evacuees to be angels from head to foot, that faults can be found on both sides, and that above all one must not drift into becoming prejudiced. I may have persuaded others, though I doubt it. Myself I could not persuade. It was clear to me that I had drifted into being prejudiced against Evie; otherwise, why should I feel such distaste at the prospect of seeing her cheered up and why the curmudgeonly conviction that a cheered-up Evie would croon?

But the only crooning about the house when I returned that evening was being done by a great quantity of wasps. I followed the wasps to the kitchen, where Mrs Moor was tying on jam covers and looking mournful. Evie, it seemed, was still upstairs in her bedroom (with appropriate trays), answering her letters. And tomorrow she'd have one of her headaches.

'Does Evie have bad headaches?' I asked.

'Awful,' said Mrs Moor, and though there was pride in her voice, there was also apprehension.

Tactfully I turned the conversation to air raids, and Mrs Moor was well away on an account of the flying bomb that wrecked the fish shop and how she could never forget the kindness of the Indian doctor who understood her sinking sensations and what she said to the lady in the Rest Centre who threw up all night – what else could you expect if you brought cold sausages all that way by open bus and never as much as offered to share them round? – and how the noise was for all the world like a giant that wasn't there riding a motor bike right over your head, not to say through it, when I became aware that there was a noise over our heads, too – a noise like a giantess who was weeping convulsively. Since Evie was above us, it was natural to connect this noise with her, but Mrs Moor went on talking and hospitality constrained me to go on listening until the convulsive weeping turned to a steady cascading and Mrs Moor broke off to exclaim, 'Don't say that girl's left the tap on!'

It was the house cistern pouring its contents through the overflow pipe onto the back porch. I turned off the water at the main and rang up Mr Bobbin, who is not really a plumber but does his best. Mr Bobbin came and borrowed a flashlamp and disappeared into the attic. Presently he reappeared with cowebs in his hair, saying that he couldn't positively account for it but that he had found some string in the cistern, which might have been the trouble. He had removed the string and, unless it was grit or something perished, he hoped we'd be all right now. Just as he was leaping on his bicycle, I said we'd turn on the water and see. The cistern filled and overflowed, so again I turned the water off, and again Mr Bobbin borrowed the flashlamp and a hammer and some wire and disappeared into the attic. After a while he came down and wandered about the house, peering wistfully into cupboards for stopcocks that might be at the bottom of the mischief, and turning faucets on and off. Then he named one or two plumbers in the country town who might have come out if it weren't wartime, said he would consult old Mr Bacon, who'd be as good as any of them if he weren't past work and getting a bit rusty, and promised to come again when he had time.

When Mr Bobbin, a busy man, has time and comes again, there will be some more things for him to look into. The door of the cupboard under the stairs has stuck immovably, plaster is dribbling from above the kitchen sink, the lintel of the back door has shifted several inches out of plumb and looks as though Samson had been at work on it, and something undiagnosable has happened to the larder screen, so the larder is now quite unbelievably full of bluebottles. Though we assure ourselves that all this may be caused by Mrs Moor going up and down stairs so often with trays for Evie, the theory – since Evie never sleeps on the roof – cannot account for the fall of soot in my bedroom or the flashes that come from the electric switch in the bathroom. Even if Mr Bobbin can deal with these ailments, we shall still have the magpies that are eating all the green peas and the swarms of clothes moths that have suddenly infested every room in the house.

Many years ago I read a book called *Wild Talents*, a book about vampires, werewolves, and poltergeists. All of us, so the author implied, are potentially one or another of these things. It is just a matter of circumstances being right for us to develop that way. The proper circumstances to develop poltergeistism include being adolescent, preferably female, far from home, dull-witted, oppressed, and resentful. Dull-witted girls who are far from home and don't like it can achieve quite remarkable feats of poltergeistism. Water will fall from a clear sky, fires break out on tea tables, flat-irons and buckets fly through the air, hornets swarm, crops wither, beds turn somersaults, mirrors leap from walls, and treacle climb out of jars, while the young lady who is doing it sits brooding in a corner, not stirring hand or foot.

I say nothing yet. It is unscientific to jump to conclusions. It is uncharitable to give way to prejudice. I will wait till flames spout from my teapot or a flat-iron bounds from its shelf and knocks me senseless before I conclude that circumstances have been right for Evie to develop her particular wild talent. I don't think I shall have long to wait. Unless Evie's sirstifficket is renewed, she will come under the Conscription of Labour (Female) Act and be called on to work. That, as Mrs Moor herself says, will be the Great Divide. And if I am not greatly mistaken, catching the eight-thirty train every morning will be just that ripening touch needed to develop Evie's talent to its fullest.

Meanwhile, to complicate things yet further, I am growing attached to Mrs Moor. She is like that horse of my grandfather's who was such a nice, goodhearted beast, nothing wrong with it at all until it broke its loosebox to matchwood and disabled the sexton. My grandfather said it was thunder in the air.

NARRATIVE OF EVENTS
PRECEDING THE
DEATH OF QUEEN ERMINE

The elfin Kingdom of Deuce, in the Pennines, extended over a deep, green hollow that lay, like a dropped jewel, amid the bleak hills which rose sharply around it, guarding its seclusion, but allowancing its daylight. Of these, Tut Hill, on the eastern boundary was the highest, and when it was known that mortals had discovered a lode of iron ore beneath it the news was included in the agenda of the quarterly meeting of the Regulating Committee, which dealt with innovations, nuisances, torts and breaches of decorum. It was unusual for the land Regulating Committee to concern itself with theories, but at this meeting the majority opinion that the iron ore being underground elfin life on the surface was not likely to be affected was countered by Sir Haggard, the Queen's nephew, who claimed that territorial rights extended downward – adding that if kingdoms lay on the surface like carpets they could as easily as carpets be rolled up. The thought of being rolled up like a carpet shook the peace of mind of the majority, who attacked Lord Haggard for entertaining such a subversive theory, let alone advocating it. He was asked, satirically, if territoriality also extended upward, and if he proposed to prosecute birds for trespass. Other voices called for his impeachment for a breach of decorum. A small minority, lovers of novelty, supported him. The debate became stormy. Other items on the agenda were ignored, no conclusion was reached and the meeting had to be adjourned.

The controversy lasted on for months. The ladies of the court joined in. They were strongly partisan, but at one in demanding that something should be done at once. Life became so uncourtly that Queen Ermine was compelled to use her royal prerogative. She wanted to knock their heads together but being a constitutional monarch she commanded that any decision must be postponed for a twelvemonth.

By now it was winter. The Yule log was borne into the hall; there was the customary hilarious Snapdragon party; the apple trees were wassailed and apple dumplings distributed to the grateful tenantry – a mingled yarn of mortals, half-casts and changelings. If they did not seem so grateful as usual, this was nothing out of the common: they seldom did. The working fairies spread rumours about what was going on at Tut Hill, but these could be discounted, for working fairies always keep up their spirits by believing the worst. It was not till the spring that Sir Haggard (whose wife's pet name for him was Cato) began to exhibit his profile and ostentatiously have no more to add.

For the wind still blew from the east, and to those who strolled out to enjoy the first primroses it carried wafts of a disagreeable smell and sounds of distant rumblings and clankings. At intervals, there were explosions – at which the majority party rejoiced, saying that the mortals had blown themselves up again, and would presently go away. When it became evident that they were not doing so, majority opinion took a philosophic turn. Tut Hill was on the outskirts of the kingdom, beyond commanding a view which everyone knew by heart it had no amenities, the goings on were underground, and, *pace* Sir Haggard, what the eye does not see the heart does not grieve over. In any case, the wind would soon change.

It changed. There was a long serene summer, with a memorably good mushroom crop. It would have been perfect, except for incursions of mortal children stealing wild strawberries in the Great Park. Working fairies were sent out to deter them by invisible pinchings, scratchings and hair-pullings. This was dirty work, but they obeyed their instructions cheerfully, and added improvements, such as driving the marauders into wasps' nests, jerking them off boughs into nettlebeds, alluring them to toadstools or gay wreaths of deadly nightshade. By the end of the summer the bag amounted to nine children poisoned and an unknown quantity deterred.

This was thought pretty good by the majority party. Sir Haggard said that no deterrent could have been more fatally misapplied, and quoted figures about the mortal fertility rate. Parents with children by the dozen would be positively grateful for anything that lightened their burden. Far from discouraging the mortals at Tut Hill, the policy of child-eradication would inevitably lead to every child under a useful age being driven into the Great Park to meet its end. By midwinter, when just as many children as before, and now accompanied by mothers, swarmed into the Great Park for firewood and the cold was too intense to ask the working fairies to encounter it, his profile became even more pronounced, his 'I told you so' silence quite intimidating.

There is no pastime so engrossing as being in the right, and when it is crowned by becoming unpopular no person of intellect can withstand its charms. Sir Haggard was one of the few people at court who had an intellect; even when he judged from a false premise, he was clear-headed and unafraid of what conclusions he might arrive at. His aunt, the Queen, who was afraid of his conclusions, but a great deal more afraid of his dauntlessness, did not consult him. She enjoyed seeing his opponents unhorsed, but naturally did not wish to be unhorsed herself. Nor did anyone else, though for less constitutional motives. This was unfortunate, for by now the kingdom of Deuce was at a pass that everyone deplored and no one would speak about.

The workings at Tut Hill had led to the discovery of a richer lode in the valley and a new pit had been sunk within the Great Park. Spoil tips defaced the meadows where fairies had danced mushrooms into rings, the glare of a smelting furnace outbid the moon, trees shed their leaves, smuts settled on every face, naked women were seen coming up to the surface like moles – all this, and the uncertainty as to where it would spread to next, the certainty that it would not go away, was extremely depressing.

It was also depressing, and inconvenient too, that tenantry, formerly so innocent and willing, were no longer reliable. Corrupted by the vicinity of wage-earning mortals they scamped their work, failed to pay their dues, quarrelled with the working fairies, and went gadding to Tut Hill or hung about the new pit-head. Some alleging rheumatism hired themselves to work underground, where the weather could not get at them. Others, too young to be rheumatic, said they wanted to see life. Others again, females, talked of the pleasures of society and a sound roof over their heads. The slopes of Tut Hill were soon terraced by rows of small dwellings, identically ugly, with dirty children spilling out over whitewashed doorsteps. A larger building was going up among them, ugly as the rest, so inspecting working fairies reported, but distinguished by a sort of pepper-castor on the roof. It did not appear to have any purpose.

Later its purpose became clear. At regular intervals of seven days, a bell jangled in the pepper castor, and the mortals could be observed leaving their houses and walking at a slow pace towards the new building. Men, women and children, they went in, and the door was closed on them.

By hovering round, the inspecting fairies were able to report that after a single voice harangued for some time, there was an outburst of howls and groans. When this ceased, the harangue took over. When the howlings and groanings followed by the solo harangues had gone on for a couple of hours or so, the door was opened and the mortals walked glumly away.

The majority party fastened on these reports with joy. Plainly, this regular happening under the pepper-castor was susceptible to only one interpretation. Every seventh day the wretched mortals, no better than slaves, were forced to attend a judicial review of their conduct. The solo voice harangued them on their negligences, inefficiencies, and lack of zeal. Then they were scourged till they howled and groaned. Again they were harangued, again they were scourged. After a final harangue and a final scourging, they were released, to limp and writhe their way home. No better than slaves, in the end they would take the slaves' revenge, would revolt, kill their taskmasters, break the machinery and leave in a body. So it was merely a question of waiting. Then the Regulating Committee could put things right again, plant more trees, bury the dead (the pits would proviue), have the spoil-tips barrowed elsewhere, and demolish the dwellings on Tut Hill; perhaps the scourging-house might be preserved as a memorial.

Ermine had a kind heart. Though the mortal children were thievish and noisy, she did not think they should be scourged for their parents' offences (their childish trebles were piercingly audible among the howls); for their sakes, too, she hoped the revolt would come speedily, to release and remove them. She summoned Sir Haggard, who so far had said nothing, and asked if he shared the common opinion. 'Granted the howls,' he replied, 'and they are indisputable – I want to hear them myself – the deduction is logical. I see no reason to disbelieve it.'

'Oh, I'm so glad!' exclaimed Ermine, forgetting that he disliked being interrupted.

'But mortals are not logical animals. It may be some time before they can be goaded into deducing, A, that they are slaves, B, that slaves ultimately revolt, and C, proceeding to implement the deduction: killing will be no trouble to them. But as we are sure of a happy ending, my dear Aunt, why wait for it in discomfort? Why not go away for a general holiday? Particularly as the water supply is now so fitful.'

The palace drew its water from a never-failing spring; but some mining operation had impaired its flow. There were strict economy measures and the working fairies were under orders to drink nothing but wine.

Not everyone was convinced of the rightness of Sir Haggard's suggestion; even the convinced were at odds where to go. To suit the older elfins it must be lively; to suit the younger, romantic. Some wanted sea air, others, lakes. Queen Ermine wanted to revisit her Consort's tomb at Leamington Spa, where he had died two centuries previously, recovering from his excesses. Sir Haggard showed no preferences. He went about looking secretive and gratified, with a black leather wallet under his arm and a slightly prancing gait.

Again it was autumn – a farewelling time of year – though no move to be gone had been attempted. Ermine was walking in the Royal Glade, looking her last at the vista of tall aspen poplars, interplanted with younger specimens. The Royal Glade was at the remotest end of the Great Park, its trees were still beautiful, the grass green and unsullied. 'How much longer,' she thought, listening to the continuous rustle of the lightly attached leaves that sounded as though raindrops were falling among them. How much longer? It was only by keeping her attention on the aspen poplars that she was unconscious of the noise from the pit-head. How much longer? Her melancholy was intercepted by Jessamy, the head-gardener, coming up to ask her where he should sow next year's broad beans. For a queen, she was knowledgeable about vegetables. They fell into conversation, and did not see the young man come into the Royal Glade.

He was short, five foot, perhaps, only a head taller than an elfin, but active and well-knit. He had a book in his hand, and read as he walked, pausing now and then to read aloud some passage that pleased him. Then a flush of excitement swept over his face as though the blood had leaped into his cheeks; and waned as quickly. With his hand on the turn of a page he looked round him with a sort of unrecognizing delight, then turned the page and read on. At last he closed the book, kissed it passionately and thrust it into his pocket. From the other pocket he pulled a stout cord, climbed nimbly up a young aspen, straddled along a bough, tied one end of the cord to it and a running knot at the other, fitted on the noose impatiently – for it stuck at his ears – and jumped.

The bough gave a pettish creak. Ermine and Jessamy turned at the sound. Jessamy took wing and flew to the tree, grasping his pruning knife, and muttering 'The young fool!' as though he would attack the trespasser. He slashed at the cord. The jerked bough was torn from the tree. Bough and young man fell to the ground together.

When Ermine ran up Jessamy spoke to her from his heart.

'Here's a fine piece of work, your Majesty. Why couldn't he choose an apple tree? Apple wood's too tough to break, he could have hung himself from an apple tree and harmed nobody. But the young fool must needs pick on an apsen – and the best bough of it. Look how the leaves are trembling!'

The leaves were trembling, but silently. She picked at the knot of the noose and broke her fingernails before she could loosen it. Jessamy went off to get tar for the tree's wound. For a moment, sight came back into the young man's eyes. In that moment he saw a beautiful lady, richly dressed, bending over him. Behind her stooped head he saw the tremor of her wings. It was true.

On one of her impulses, Ermine had the young man carried into the palace and put to bed in a dressing-room where she could keep an eye on him. Moschatel, her mother's old bower-woman, would nurse anything from a privy counsellor to a hound: she took a mortal in her stride. He was a dull patient, for he gave her no trouble; he could give her no thanks either, for the jolt of the slashed cord had broken his larynx. When Ermine came in with a bunch of grapes or a flask of Hungary water he stared at her as though he would fill his eyes. She did not know what to make of him, and did not stay long.

Others knew exactly what to make of him. Jessamy had summed him up as a young fool. Lovers of nature, grieving for the young tree which would never be the same again, called him a typical vandal. Lovers of retirement saw him as the ultimate trespasser from whom not even the privacy of the Royal Glade was safe. The librarian who had examined the book in the young man's pocket said he had no taste: the book was vilely printed and the poems sentimental trash. As for his attempted suicide, it was universally condemned. The mortal span was contemptibly brief, anyhow; to shorten it, mere exhibitionism. Moschatel had never seen such bunions, and displayed them to Ermine.

'I wish I hadn't seen them,' Ermine confided to Sir Haggard. 'Do you think that's why he tried to hang himself?'

'To take the weight off his feet? No, my dear aunt. I can tell you all about that young man. His feet wouldn't carry him fast enough. He was a clerk at Tut Hill. He stole money, tried to falsify the accounts, spilt ink on the page, and ran away.'

'But how do you know all this? Moschatel says he can't speak a word.' Sir Haggard said he had heard it from Simpson.

'Simpson?'

'Simpson. Since nobody else would stir a finger to defend your property, I made it my business to introduce myself to Simpson, the fellow at Tut Hill, and remind him that he owed you rent for subterranean rights, and way-leaves. And that if he did not pay immediately we would blow the whole thing skyhigh – which as owners we are entitled to do.'

'But could we?'

'No need to. You never saw anyone more taken aback.'

'And he will pay?'

'Better than that. I am now on the board of directors. His conscience is in my hands.'

'But do people really have consciences? I thought they were a figure of speech!'

'We have no need of them. We have reason. But they are part of the mortal apparatus, as tails are to cats – and as sensitive. I admit, it took me some time to make Simpson acknowledge his conscience. You have a nose, I said. It tells you when an egg is bad. If you do not heed its warning, if you eat the egg, the badness of the egg infects your conscience. Proceeding from the analogy of his nose, I got him to agree that he was liable to fall into error and make incorrect decisions; and that when he did so, his conscience suffered, and revenged itself on him. He admitted that worry gave him dyspepsia. From that moment, I was sure of him. By process of correct analysis, I convinced him that his conscience was exasperated by his inattention, that hell has no fury like a conscience spurned, that it needed to be calmed and reassured; and that as he had lost control over it, he must entrust its welfare to an expert, who would guide him into discretion and inoffensiveness. And suddenly, as one who sees the light of reason, he asked me to join the board of directors. The other directors, I may say are quite useless – mere materialists, fettered to effects, incapable of deriving effects from causes. They thought pills would cure his dyspepsia.'

'What do they think about you?'

'They assume that I am just another director. Naturally, I remain visible, keep my wings well furled, and wear a cloak.'

Thinking all this over, Ermine wondered how Sir Haggard had directed Mr Simpson's conscience about the young man. In any case, the young man was dying. Jessamy had claimed the corpse for the kitchen garden, where he was preparing a new rhubarb bed; it wouldn't make up for the tree but was better than nothing. She hated rhubarb, but consented.

No money had come in from Tut Hill. However, no one expected it. Sir Haggard scorned the Managing Committee. Ermine was his only confident, and sworn to secrecy.

'About those rents, Haggard. Are they any nearer?'

Sir Haggard explained that he was now entered on an extensive redirection of Mr Simpson's conscience, which was to be awakened to the undesirability of iron. If iron were desirable, the scheme of nature would have made it available, like water or herbage. It would not have to be dug out of the bowels of the earth, where the scheme of nature had wisely concealed it. Potatoes were in a different category. Reason buries them, reason knows where they lie and in due course digs them up; but in no case does it have to dig more than a foot below the surface, and never at random. Potatoes were demonstrably part of the scheme of nature; in some countries they form the staple diet of a population. Further, they have a secondary function as commodities and can be sold by the peck. Finally, they are labour-saving. The grower plants in spring, lifts in autumn, for the rest of the year he is free to enlarge his mind. Compare – Sir Haggard continued – the generous potato with iron. Unnaturally ripped from the depths where the scheme of nature has secreted it, even more unnatural – when dislodged by explosives, dragged through dark windings by women harnessed to trucks, it comes to the light of day unlicked as a bear cub, a confused lump which has to be smelted in a furnace. While all a potato needs is boiling, iron goes through a dozen processes, all of them noisy and laborious. And to what end? It can't be eaten, it is incapable of increase, its detritus smothers natural fertility.

'So you want him to grow potatoes?' said Ermine, again forgetting that he disliked being interrupted. 'They have pretty flowers – blue or lilac.'

'And grow them all over the Great Park with an easy conscience? No, dear aunt. My purpose is to make him dissatisfied with iron, then to repudiate it, then to go away.' Her interruption had disarranged him, and he went away himself.

She did not like being addressed as 'Dear Aunt'. But the fact remained, he was her nephew as well as her subject, she was consanguineously as well as constitutionally bound to see he didn't get into mischief. She sent a message to Lady Briony, announcing that she would visit her, without ceremony. Even if Briony, too, were sworn to secrecy, a little tact would unswear her.

'And how is Cato? As busy as ever?'

Lady Briony said Cato was busy as ever.

'And with the same interesting ideas? He can make the dullest subject quite enthralling. I envy you hearing so much of his conversation.'

Lady Briony's face grew red, and she stared at the carpet.

'Though I'm sometimes afraid he may overtax himself. Does he still talk in his sleep?'

'Yes, he still talks in his sleep. All night long. I don't know who he's talking to, but he's talking to somebody – arguing, cajoling, insisting, saying the same thing over and over again, wearing her down. I know it's a woman, some woman he's obsessed with. Of course, I don't mind. I've always said . . . But he has never been so frantic, so wrought up, before.'

'My dear Briony, I'm sure you're mistaken. You know how excited Cato gets when he's bent on something.'

'Yes. And she's what he's bent on now.' Lady Briony burst into tears.

'Come, come.'

'Some very stupid woman at that.'

'There, there.'

'I'm sure I wish him joy of her.'

'Briony, I can give you my word it's not a woman.'

'Then it's some boy! That's not much comfort.'

It was sufficient comfort for Lady Briony to dry her eyes and agree to Ermine's suggestion of a walk round the garden. The visit ended on a calm horticultural note.

Time went on. Rhubarb tart appeared on the menu. The plants grew splendidly, their stems were sturdy as walking-sticks and later in the year were made into rhubarb wine – for the water supply was still erratic. No rent money came from Tut Hill. Nothing was decided as to where the court should go when it left Deuce. The mine-workers had still to decide to revolt. The Managing Committee matured and perfected its plan for rehabilitation after the revolt had taken place. Rhubarb tart again appeared on the menu. Blackbirds and thrushes flocked to the Great Park, where they fed on the leftovers of picnic parties. At long last Jessamy's complaints precipitated Ermine into summoning her nephew.

'I don't wonder you are beginning to feel impatient. Simpson's mental progress would drive a tortoise to despair. But he's improving fast since I adopted a new method. I now combine strategy with reason. While I continue to work on his conscience with reason I appeal to his cupidity with strategy. I pointed out to him that the inherent property of iron is to sink. He saw the force of that quite readily – for him. Hidden underground by the scheme of nature, the inherent property persists. It goes on sinking. It can't do otherwise. Instead of rambling about horizontally, I said to him, follow it down, sink a perpendicular shaft. Persevere, I said. Blast your way. Think of that massy deposit awaiting you. My dear, he swelled like a bullfrog. It's really shocking, this mortal cupidity.'

'And will he find it?'

'That's neither here nor there. If he does he'll be so grateful, he'll eat off my hand. If he doesn't, he'll be so disheartened and out of pocket and probably bankrupt that his conscience will make mincemeat of him.'

The door slammed, the light footsteps trotted down the passage. Mr Simpson said, 'Now we can get back to business.' Mr Simpson had grown grey, his forehead was deeply wrinkled, he stooped, he was a shadow of his former self.

'Who is that queer little packet?' asked Mr Utterthwaite, the new partner.

'He's what you might call a habituee. You'll get used to him.'

'He seems to talk a lot.'

'It's more than seems. He does. Not that there's any real harm in him. The men in the works call him the Tut Hill Mascot. The fact of it is, he's not all there. Delusions, and so on. One of those people with only one foot in the real world. There was a time when he used to right startle me, he seemed so positive – especially for a man of his size. Well, as I was saying, last year's profits – '

'Good Lord, what's that?'

There was a loud explosion.

The two men rushed to the window. Down in the hollow a cloud of thick yellowish smoke was wallowing out of the ground, wave after wave of it. A jet of water leaped up, pierced it, rose above it, wavered in a rainbow, frayed into descent. The jet continued to rise, the cloud of smoke was tinged with a watery sheen. As the jet slowly weakened, the watery sheen was transferred to the ground. Little jets of water rose everywhere, puddles were spreading, running together, beginning to form a shallow lake. A man was leaning over the pit-head, shouting 'Jack! Jack! Jack!' Suddenly a hundred voices were shouting. The man who had called for Jack had roped himself and been lowered down the shaft. When they pulled him up, he was drenched to his shoulders, his teeth chattered, his eyes stared out of his muddied face. By then, it was almost dusk. The cry, 'We've got him up,' sent the women surging to the pit-head. The hope that in a moment had grown sky-high was snapped short. They sat down to endure, and to gain the support of being huddled together, less wretchedly themselves in a common misery. Rumours flitted among them: that the jet of water had carried men in the deep shaft up to the surface, safe and alive; that the water had come from an upper layer and that at the bottom of the shaft it was dry; of what had been foretold by tea leaves, seen in a dream. Mr Simpson had hot drinks and food distributed among them; the parson came and exhorted them to trust in God, led them in prayer and got them hymn-singing. Because he was praying out of doors, he struck them as comical.

All night the water rose slowly and imperturbably, and as it rose an icy air came from it. By the first light they saw a lake with trees dabbling their branches, submerged islands of bushes, floating planks, drowned rabbits, and a bobbing bucket. The dawn wind rippled its surface.

The explosion had knocked Sir Haggard senseless. He came to, lying in a puddle. It was an uncomfortable repose, but better than the exertion of moving. He lay, and tried to account for it, and postponed that for later, preferring to watch a tiny fountain that twirled up among the grasses, and a couple of ants who had fastened on a pupa and were trying to carry it off in opposite directions. The insect world is dominated by instinct, he thought, which is why one so seldom sees an insect in a state of repose. He shifted his position. He saw concentric rings of water gliding away from him and realized the puddle had swelled to a wide pond. He struggled to his feet, fanned his wings to dry them, and flew to the palace to see how the Regulating Committee was managing.

They were holding a special meeting on the first floor, and had decided that the Queen must leave in the Royal Barge; working fairies had floated it out of its shed and moored it by the palace steps. They had also decided that there was no cause for alarm. Ermine was sitting in constitutional silence. Sir Haggard said that for himself he intended to be vulgar and fly. He kissed his aunt's hand and left.

It was the last he saw of her.

By midnight the Royal Barge had broken from its mooring and was knocking hollowly against the first floor balcony. In little more than an hour's time, the embarkation was in train. The youngest member of the Regulating Committee jumped aboard, the barge was steadied, the Queen was assisted into it, the rest of the Committee followed. It was then realized that there were no oars. Working fairies were sent to find them. After some time of searching in the darkness they returned with one oar and a hay-rake. The Chairman seized the hay-rake and pushed off – so vigorously that he almost fell overboard, and would have done if his fellow-members had not caught hold of his legs.

The Royal Barge was purely an Object of Parade. In the course of its long career as a symbol its timbers had shrunk. The heavy load and the scramble to save the Chairman forced them apart. Water poured in. It filled and sank. Other members of the court who were escaping on an extemporized raft saw the loss of the Royal Barge with horror. In order to get a full view they lined the side of the raft; it tilted and discarded them. All the working fairies survived, and so did Sir Haggard's minority party.

The flood subsided, leaving a thick layer of mud, strewn with corpses and the haunt of bluebottles. Those who returned recognized a few features, reclaimed some possessions, and withdrew to wait for better days. Sir Haggard did not return. Lady Briony had relations at the Court of Pomace in Herefordshire; he went as a visitor, was pleased to see Briony taking a more extrovert interest in life, liked the climate, and stayed on. It was there that he wrote his treatise, *On the Advantages of a Presidential System*. A copy of this, with Jefferson's marginal annotations, was in the library at Monticello, but has since been lost sight of.

QUEEN MOUSIE

As Elfins do not believe in survival after death they feel no obligation to placate the dead by post-obit tributes: monuments, animal sacrifices, shaving the head, wearing crape arm-bands, etc. Funeral pomps are reserved for monarchs. In the Northern Kingdoms of Thule and Blokula, the dead queen is sunk in a crevasse. At Broceliande she is cremated with fireworks. At Elfhame in Scotland queens are buried in air.

Before Queen Tiphaine had stiffened, the orifices of her body were plugged with spices, her corpse was dressed in scarlet and closely stitched into a scarlet shroud. Round the scarlet chrysalis was clasped a silver harness to which a couple of long silver chains were attached. To complete the rite, the chrysalis, attended by the court, would be carried to a remote and ancient pinewood on the heath, pulleyed onto a strong bough, and left to hang in the silver chains. The new Queen would set it swinging, and ride back to the palace where a banquet was served – distinguished from other banquets by the mort-breads (small buns with currant eyes and sugared teeth to represent skulls) laid in every place.

But the hanging and the banquet had to be postponed. Tiphaine had not named her successor. Till this was determined, she was put by in a cellar.

There she lay for some time. The season was quellingly cold, a freezing mist hung over the heath, the larks kept cover. Not till they mounted and a sufficiency of them had been netted and brought down to the Castle could the ceremony of Divination be carried out, for which the Court office-holders, accompanied by pages carrying flambeaux and caged larks, descend to the depth of the castle, where there is a well. Here the larks, which have had little weights wired to their feet, are cast one by one into the well. The name of each lark's lady is pronounced as it strikes the water and the Horologer with a stop-watch measures how long it struggles in her cause. It was beyond living memory when last a divination had been carried out but the Archivist had looked it up and compiled a list of Court ladies eligible for the succession. When at last the wind changed, the skies cleared, the larks mounted in skirl of song and the lark-catchers flew after them, all was in readiness. The list was in alphabetical order. 'Finula!' said the Archivist. The lark struggled and sank. The Horologer noted down the time. 'Nimue!' The lark struggled and sank. 'Parisina!' The lark struggled, the Horologer's eyebrows rose in amazement, but eventually the bird went under. 'Who is this Parisina?' asked the Bursar. 'I've never set eyes on her.' 'You have, you know,' answered the Archivist. 'But everyone calls her Mousie,' – and he hastened to call the next name. The final name – which if this had been a race-meeting one would call the favourite's – was 'Yolandine!' The lark barely flapped a wing before it sank. After a hurried conference the diviners agreed that it must be disqualified.

Fortunately, there were two larks left over for a retrial. To encourage a happy result, the larger was chosen for Yolandine. It struggled and sank. The diviners watched with embarrassment the Mousie lark making a brisk fight for its life. It seemed hours before it finally yielded. They climbed the long cold stairway to the Throne Room where everyone was assembled. Making their way into the back row they knelt before an inconspicuous middle-aged fairy and said with chattering teeth, 'Hail, Queen Mousie, Queen of Elfhame!' – for in the consternation of the moment, none of them could remember her right name. Mousie held out a trembling hand to be kissed, said, 'I am not worthy to follow such a queen,' and fainted.

It was the correct phrase of acceptance; and the thought darted through every mind that Mousie had been nursing ambitions ridiculously beyond her deserts. However, the larks had decided; the chopfallen expressions of the divining party showed there could be no possible handky-panky about it. Elfhame must submit to a Queen Mousie (the name uttered in the first loyal salutation is unalterable) and be the laughing-stock of Elfindom. Meanwhile, Mousie had recovered from her faint and was asking the Court Functionaries to retain their posts and guide her inexperience.

Two hours later, the mort-breads were in the oven and the hanging procession had set out. Queen Tiphaine was hoisted to her last resting place. Queen Mousie on horseback delivered the firm push which started her swinging, the court choir sang the traditional farewell of 'Rockaby, Lady, on the tree-top' (it still survives in a mutilated form as a Scottish lullaby), the mourners turned about and Queen Mousie led them back to Elfhame, where she presided at the banquet.

The worst was yet before her. She had to be undressed by her Ladies of Honour and laid to sleep in an unfamiliar bed.

Mousie was the child of a well-pedigreed house which was always meritorious and never rewarded – the kind of family which in Spain is called a *casa agraviada*, a slighted house. She was named Parisina, a family name; but as she was small and quiet and had a sharp nose, she was affectionately called Mousie, and by the time her parents were dead and Mousie no longer a pet name, it stuck to her as a nickname. As a nickname it was spoken without affection, but tolerantly. As the name of a Queen, it was spoken derisively.

She was not without her well-wishers. The functionaries, once they had got over the shock, built hopes on her simplicity and her willingness to be advised. Elfhame could do with a tractable constitutional monarch after the years of Tiphaine's headstrong charm and glittering insolvency. It was part of that insolvency that she died without naming a successor; but they might yet be glad of it, when they had formed Queen Mousie a little more and polished her natural diffidence, and provided her with a suitable Consort – a good-looking one, to compensate for her insignificance; but not showy.

Other well-wishers, good-looking and some even showy, were bringing themselves to consider bettering Queen Mousie's lot by marrying her. She was not really ill-looking; it was just that she lacked bloom. Nothing bestows bloom like a husband. The Bursar took alarm. He had watched with tenderness the Elfhame finances reacting to Mousie's constitutional compliance with his advice. She, and they, must be preserved at all costs from the depredations of love. Being, most fortunately, a widower, he proposed himself as a Consort. Without a flutter, she refused him, adding that she would say nothing about it. Afterwards it occurred to her that she should have garnished the refusal a little. But her mind had been differently occupied. She had just found an anonymous letter in her glove, telling her that Lady Yolandine intended to poison her that evening. The poison would be smeared on the rim of a loving-cup, and would be instant. She had been expecting something of this sort; but as her mind was essentially practical she had not expected Yolandine to act before making sure of the succession. Perhaps she had already made sure of it with tampered larks? Perhaps the anonymous letter was only another ill-natured hoax? – there had been several. The one thing she could be sure of was the concert. She had an ear for pitch, but not for music.

Punctual to the moment, she made her inconsiderable entrance to the saloon, sat down, signed to the company to be seated, signed to the players to begin. She had foreseen that the concert would open with a display-piece by the chief harpist. She had not foreseen that the second harpist also would shake back her flowing locks and take part in it. They played a piece referring to the cuckoo. The chief harpist sounded the interval with a twang, the second harpist replied with the same interval, not so twangingly, since she represented a cuckoo at a distance. It was a beautiful May evening, warm and serene, and the real cuckoos were still at it, as they had been all day. The second harpist's cuckoos grew bolder, came nearer. In a climax of agreement, both harps twanged their interval in an approximate unison. A tremor of distress flickered over Queen Mousie's face, and Lady Yolandine, who till then had been watching her complacently, wondered if by any chance some fool had blabbed.

There were two more items, a melody with variations and fanfare for drums and trumpets, before the interval. During the fanfare, Mousie saw Yolandine's current admirer hand her a silver loving-cup.

The interval was attained, people began to talk and move about. She sat and waited, Yolandine approached, walking with unhurried elegance – she was celebrated for her beautiful gait. She rose like a wave from her curtsey and held out the silver cup. Her hand was so steady that the wine was still as water in a well.

'Queen Mousie, I crave a boon. Drink with me to our eternal friendship.' She tilted the cup to Mousie's lip. There was nothing for it. Mousie drank, her eyes fixed on Yolandine's lovely face. She saw it transfigured with a look of intense delight. So this was revenge! She would not die without knowing this bewitching bliss. She gave a sudden twitch to the cup. 'Now you must drink,' she said, and turned the side where she had drunk towards Yolandine. 'Strike up!' she cried to the drummers. The drums beat, and Yolandine drank.

They remained face to face, holding the cup between them, each expecting the other to fall dead. Neither staggered, swelled, turned blue; it must be a slower poison than it was supposed to be. The concert went on, and after the concert there was dancing. The morning birds were chirping when everyone went off to bed, laughing and limping. Mousie beckoned to Yolandine and drew her into a corner.

'When we meet in the morning, remind me I must tell the Purveyor to buy fresh spices. They've lost their virtue, they've been kept too long. But you must remind me. By tomorrow I shall have forgotten all about it. I suppose he had better renew the poisons, too.'

Yolandine remarked that there was no commercial poison to equal the Blue Death Cap. But now was not the season for it. Perhaps in the late summer they might slip out before sunrise one morning, pretend to be hags, and gather it together?

Foiled in their murderous intentions by a blunted weapon, they thought better of each other. Friendship was out of the question. They felt a kind of brazen affinity.

Secure, at any rate for the time being, against being poisoned by Yolandine and sought in marriage by the Bursar, Mousie plucked up her spirits and re-addressed herself to the duties of a sovereign. The spice and poison cupboards were restocked, the Elfhame pearls were restrung, the Court officials given new uniforms, several ageing changelings dismissed and a programme of gaieties devised: this included a tournament to take the suitors off her hands. While the fine weather lasted, she was ignored. The weather changed, the tournament was held in a downpour, the court returned to its customary gibing and caballing; wherever she turned, she was impaled on looks of hatred. It occurred to her that if they could be got to hate each other instead of her, life would be pleasanter, and she summoned the Archivist to attend her in the Muniment Room. There, in an odour of dust and decaying parchment, she insinuated that his care of the Elfhame archives was not properly appreciated: one would expect people to be interested in their own family trees at least. The Archivist was conscious that several pedigrees had been impaired by mice, and agreed that Elfins nowadays had little respect for their ancestors. Her Majesty's family was a distinguished exception. He raised a creaking lid on a quantity of neatly rolled documents, where a gold-leaf crown and the date of her accession had been added to her birth certificate. When the news got round that Mousie's parchments filled an iron chest there was a general desire to prove a greater antiquity and grander connections. While her subjects bragged, disputed, made allegations, fought duels in defence of great-great-grandmothers, claimed dazzling bar sinisters and imputed discreditable ones, Mousie lived a quiet unmolested life, calm as a fish in the pool under the waterfall, and had the stables set to rights.

By following this strategy while varying her tactics, she became an accomplished schemer. If her life was comfortless, it was not without interest. Her skill was covert, she got no praise for it; but she kept a critical eye on her progress and never allowed herself to jeopardise the inconspicuousness which destiny had endowed her with. Just as in the coat of the most splendid tabby cat there is always one patch of dull second-rate fur, only noticeable to the hand that strokes the animal, Mousie was the dull patch in the court life of Elfhame, but, as no one stroked her, unremarked. She never employed a spy: the anonymous letters and the pasquinades pinned on the backs of screens and hangings did as well.

Of late the anonymous letters had taunted her with physical malformation, and the pasquinades insisted on the aloofness of a Virgin Queen. She saw that this was the moment to open a campaign which she had already given some thought to. Calling a Council, at which she wore her crown – a thing she did not commonly do for she had headaches enough without that – she waived her sovereign right to choose a consort, and requested that a Committee, whose members should be chosen by acclaim, would decide for her. Choosing the Committee took some months and engaged strong feelings. At the first sitting, the Chosen quarrelled till sunrise. The sittings continued. The Unchosen took turns to listen at the keyhole and report progress. They caught the word 'lobster' spoken with energy, and taken up by other voices. Subsequent listeners overheard mention of brooms, and bedroom candlesticks. Finally a page was concealed in the committee room, who reported that the Chosen talked about food, curling-matches, gallantries of past days, scandal about Queen Tiphaine; and constantly asked one another if he remembered Old So-and-So. They talked very innocently, he said.

Meanwhile Tomason, the Court Shoemaker, who had been journeying about Europe for skins, presented a sealed and scented letter to Queen Mousie, together with a list of travelling expenses. When she had checked the expenses, she opened the letter. It expressed Count Wolf's ardent willingness to become her Consort.

A Consort was a part of a Queen's equipage. Since marry she must, she intended to startle Elfhame, by importing a Consort from Europe. During the previous reign when an embassy from Dreiviertelstein in Styria visited Elfhame, a Count Wolf had been one of the party. He had well-turned legs, a dashing figure, china-blue eyes – so much she remembered; and was – so she had gathered – impecunious. Now he was hers. Tomason had carried the letter to Queen Aigle asking for his hand, and brought back the reply. Tomason was a natural genius, couldn't read, thought only of shoeleather; so he was a safe agent.

She allowed the Committee to deliberate a little longer and watched the Unchosen working up a loyal resentment at being kept waiting to know her fate. One unexpected morning she put on her crown, summoned her court to attend her and went to the Committee room. Her Chamberlain knocked three times on the locked door. It was opened, she went in and everyone thronged in after her. To their delight the Unchosen heard her say that she could not in conscience take up any more of the Committee's valuable time; that she was deeply obliged to them for their exertions, which she would reward by granting life pensions; and that as a mark of her confidence she had come to tell them that her choice had settled upon Count Wolf of Dreiviertelstein. She swept a curtesy and withdrew.

For once, for the first time, she was universally popular. She had supplied a rousing topic for conversation, the Unchosen had got the news hot, the Chosen had got their life pensions.

The swiftest flyer in Elfhame was sent to summon Count Wolf, and from the height of triumph Mousie fell into a pit of self-torment. Suppose he didn't come? Suppose she had kept him waiting too long, and all those adjectives had withered and dropped off and he had closed with a better offer? Why had she been so shortsightedly prudent, why had she wasted so much time nursing public opinion? The work of years might be undone in a night; she would be back again where she started – no, lower than that, even! Then, she was despicable. Now, she would be ludicrous.

But she was smiling and gracious and showed no ungainly surprise at being popular; and the swiftest flyer came back with the date of Count Wolf's arrival.

She had been through such turmoils of anxiety that the image of Count Wolf had become somewhat blurred. He was impecunious, with blue eyes and well turned legs . . . When he arrived with a considerable retinue of cousins and no air of impecuniosity, she found that she had not remembered that his legs were bow-legs. But that, she remarked to Yolandine, was due to his horsemanship. The Dreiviertelstein nobility had a passion for riding. She did not want Yolandine to take against him.

Count Wolf's bow legs turned out to be positively advantageous. Male legs at Elfhame were long and straight. Their owners looked tolerantly at the waddling importee, a typical European, who had never played ice-hockey or a round of golf or run down a wild goat, and was so well fitted to be the consort of a Queen Mousie. As for his cousins, a good hard winter would see the end of them, as with cucumbers. Mousie also hoped to thin the ranks of the cousins. But this must wait till her plan for Count Wolf had come about. She owed Yolandine a debt of gratitude for not trying to poison her again; now she was in a position to repay it and please everyone concerned, not least her loyal court.

At suitable moments she directed her Consort's blue eyes toward Yolandine. He was slow to take the hint; but she persisted, as though she were teaching a child to walk; encouraging his first faltering steps, picking him up when he tumbled, re-directing him when he went astray. The smiling Yolandine watched, drew a little nearer, withdrew, held out an apple . . . Wolf's advance suddenly became tempestuous. He whirled Yolandine out of a cotillion, and while the last figure was being danced the music was drowned by a series of high-pitched warbles. It was Wolf yodelling.

Oddly enough, her loyal court took it upon themselves to be prudishly indignant. She ignored everything except the relief of being able to give an undistracted mind to the business of rule. There were expenses to recoup, schemes withering for lack of attention, the affair of the Chief Harpist to be wound up, a territorial dispute with the Northumbrian Kingdom of Catmere about some quite accidental sheep-stealing to be tapered into a trading agreement, the purveyor to be consulted about a harmless deterrent for the cousins. She drew a decent veil of composure over her contentment. Once or twice it struck her that Wolf was aiming sheeps' eyes in her direction, but she put it down to his short sight. She had not been rid of him for a tranquil ten days before he was back, telling her that his heart had never strayed, that Yolandine was cynical and painted up to the eyes, that a cosy togetherness with his busy little wife was all he asked. It was not quite all that he asked; but she could never feel sure of his infidelity again. However, the cousins went.

It was not long before there were other riders – mortals, riding without elegance, their mounts plastered with mud, their boots the derision of Tomason; but they rode with purpose, pausing on the summit of every knoll to scrutinize the surroundings, poking their swords into heather-clumps, spurring across the moor to wherever they saw a whaup rising or goats take to their heels. For this was the period remembered in mortal history as the Killing Times, when perukes and high head-dresses were the mode, and troops of dragoons were hunting down the schismatics, whom some called Saints. The changelings knew all about it, or said they did. At any rate, they knew enough to take sides. Some were for Law and Episcopacy, others for the Covenant. The notion of a God is an inherent fever in mortals. No mortal constitution can escape it, and though the changelings had lived in Elfhame since they were stolen out of their cradles they took to the Killing Times as if they had been brought up in Oxford or Geneva.

Inside the castle, changelings squabbled. Round about it, fully-developed mortals killed and plundered. They hacked down young plantations to get firewood, fouled the streams by throwing dead bodies into them, left excrement everywhere, hung prisoners from any tree tall enough to carry them, and made a common gallows of the pinewood where the Queens of Elfhame were buried in air.

Mousie had a just and accurate mind: though courtiers, Functionaries and the upper working fairies pursued her with complaints about the changelings, she hated the mortals outside more than she hated the mortals within, not only because she had no control over them but flatly and without qualification. She hated the killers, she hated the killed. All were vile, and made each other worse. She in her castle was safe from them. But the smooth grassy hill which roofed and walled it was a landmark. The dragoons used it as a gathering-place, grazed their horses on it, sheltered with its bulk between them and the weather; she was never free from a sense of their proximity. And as people make sure of a tumour by fingering the place, she listened for sound of them, watched for sight of them.

Her cabinet had a slot window, extended from a rabbit-earth, through which she could look down on the outer world. A noise called her to it. A dragoon was galloping past with an old woman strapped to his saddle-bow. She was screaming curses at him, he was laughing like a jack-ass.

Yolandine had come into the room and was standing beside her with an expression of pursed-up amusement. She bobbed a reverence, graceful and limber in all she did, and asked permission to speak. Mousie looked at her wall-clock and gave permission.

'I think it my duty to tell you,' Yolandine began, 'that since early this morning you have been graciously harbouring a distressed mortal – an enormous distressed mortal, practically a monster – who is out of his senses.'

'A dragoon?'

'No. One of the other lot. A Saint. Shall I continue?'

'Pray continue.'

'It seems the dragoons had been chasing him, but lost him in the dark. The changelings heard him boo-hooing in the castle ditch and hauled him in through the back door – a tight fit, but they managed it.'

'Where is he now?'

'Locked in the old granary with some straw and bone. He can't get out and no one can get in, for they've kept the key. I heard all this from my dear Dandiprat. I can't understand why you don't make use of your changelings. They're invaluable creatures.'

'And how many people have you told?'

'My dear Majesty, how can you suppose I would tell anyone before telling you? But it's bound to get out.'

The silver trumpets blew, and they went downstairs for the meal. A distant gusty clamour filled the air. People stood in groups listening and saying nothing. Yolandine bestowed here and there a reassuring *sotto voce*, 'Her Majesty's monster.'

Mousie did nothing about the monster in the old granary, so no one else could. He remained the perquisite and Helen of Troy of the changelings. They quarrelled furiously as to whether he should be turned out to Law and Episcopacy or preserved for the Covenant; meanwhile, they were united in pride of ownership. A guard sat outside the granary door. Twice a day it was unlocked, and bread and water hastily thrust in. Favoured members of the kitchen staff were allowed to come and listen to his roars and ravings, his screams of terror, his prayers, his chattering teeth. The changelings were prepared to withstand any one in authority, but no one in authority came. Approached by Dandiprat, they consented to a visit from Yolandine, who, all agreed, was a sweet lady. Unfortunately, the madman was not at his best that evening. He heaved great sighs, and wept, but that was the extent of the performance. However, she seemed pleased, and ordered a distribution of heather ale to strengthen them for the nightwatch. On the following night, when the madman had been silent for many hours and the fun seemed over, Queen Mousie, holding a lantern, came among them stilly as the moon, beckoned them to their feet and demanded the key. Keeping the key she went in and closed the door behind her.

It was quite true. He was an exceptionally large man, raw-boned and sinewy. His naked feet stuck out through the straw like rocks. He was awake, but did not stir at her entry, or blink when she shone her lantern on his high forehead and hollow cheeks. He was bald, except for a few grey hairs. Remembering what she had heard about his frenzy, his wolfish howls, the violence with which he fought an imagined enemy, remembering the gusty clamour which Yolandine had dismissed as 'Her Majesty's monster', she felt defrauded. She waited a little, playing her lantern light on the straw which tomorrow she would order to be renewed.

'I know that my Redeemer liveth.'

It was the voice of a good child repeating its lessons. He had turned his head and his small grey eyes, pale in their red rims and dark sockets, looked at her, looked at her shadow, looked at the wall, saw, and saw nothing. After a while, in the same gentle, confiding voice, he repeated, 'I know that my Redeemer liveth.'·

But it was to himself that he confided it.

She locked him in with himself and went away, taking the key. Clean straw, a better diet . . . So weakened and harmless, he must not be sent out into the world again. She would give the key to some responsible person who . . . No! He must be given his liberty, and his due death at the hands of his enemies. All night she lay awake, listening to his silence.

She could not match his crass mortal confidence; and did not want to. Her life, so wretchedly spent in scheming, counterfeiting, suspecting, placating and despising, was not susceptible of redemption. She had never been brave, only sometimes desperate; or honest, except as a personal relieving bitterness. Where he was mad, she was sensible. And in the moment between one straw's rustle and the rustle of another straw his madness had overthrown her.

She rose knowing she must be very busy that day. She would call no council, no helpers, consult with no one. Just as usual, she would continue her scheme, carry it out inconspicuously, end it successfully. First, she must take that roll of cloth from the coffer; then supply herself with the cord; and find some pretext for wanting two large flat-irons. Then she must arrange the banquet, and somehow find time to snatch a couple of hours' sleep before it. The banquet was the captain-jewel of her scheme: it was to be an explosion of lavishness and ostentation, held in Wolf's honour and a total surprise. It must celebrate some anniversary or other: there are always anniversaries to hand; it was not the right time of year for his birthday, but it might well be the anniversay of the day the embassy from Dreiviertelstein first brought him to Elfhame – she could not remember the date, but neither would he. There would be speeches, music, drinking of healths. Only the Bursar would remain sober – he had a poor stomach and toadied it. 'About that fellow in the old granary,' she would say. 'The noise and riot is insupportable. Please see to it that he is turned out tomorrow morning. Let him have a good meal, and send him packing.' At midnight she would make a gracious withdrawal and go on with her private life.

The banquet went on long after midnight, long after her ladies had taken off her crown and undressed her and were safe gone. She had found time during the day to cut out the dress and tack it together. Now she began sewing, pleased with her neat firm stitches, amused to remember the dressmaking lessons which had been part of her prudent upbringing as the daughter of a well-bred penurious family, and came in so unexpectedly handy to a Queen. The noise of carousing assured her that her plan was going just as she intended, but it was the silence of the previous night which dwelt in her mind. Listening to that hidden silence, she sewed on, smoothly and steadily, till the last stitch was taken, and the tackings pulled away. Smoothly and steadily, she wrote the letter which would lie alone and conspicuous on her desk, naming as her successor the Chamberlain's niece – a tall waxwork, with the best ceremonial appearance in Elfhame. With a steady hand, she tied staylaces to the flat-irons.

In the grey twilight she fastened on the scarlet dress, put the cord and the flat-irons in a bag and woke her page, telling him to saddle two riding-horses withoug rousing the grooms. While she waited, she flexed her wings – disuse had weakened them but they would serve her purpose – pulled on her gloves and had a last look at herself in the mirror. The scarlet dress was so striking that she omitted to look at its wearer.

They set out over the moor. The dragoons had shifted their hunt elsewhere, nothing molested the morning. With Elfhame behind her, the time before her seemed to Mousie as wide as a holiday. A thousand things flitted through her mind like a charm of goldfinches, things of the present, things of the past, a mound of raspberries in a cabbage-leaf, a silver locket, the hoarfrost tinselling a withered fern-frond, the smell of gingerbread, eating woodcock, the stream chafing a lip of ice, her first fan, the sun rising: all of them delightful and none of them her doing. Now she had nothing to do but to enjoy herself and ride on. The pinewood enlarged against the sky. The bright fragments of sound she heard were Tiphaine's silver chains, idly clanking. How silly she had been, not to demand a second mort-bread, when she was so hungry with the sharp morning!

A stink of corruption came from the dangling bodies. She must ride round the wood and choose a tree to the windward.

The page saw Queen Mousie, who was behaving so strangely, rein up her horse, snatch the bag she had given him, unfurl her wings and fly high into the tree. There she hovered, putting the cord round her neck, knotting its other end to the bough. She threw down the flat irons. 'When I drop,' she said, 'you are to fasten the weights to my feet. That will be all.' She made sure of the slip knot and the holding knot, closed her wings and fell. Out of some other existence she felt the weights tied to her feet, and heard him ride away, with her horse trotting after him. Faster and faster they went.

AN IMPROBABLE STORY

—

(Part of a letter from Lady Ulrica, Dame of Honour at the Elfin Court of Dreiviertelstein in Styria.)

Bad Nixenbach . . . The baths are not doing so much for me as they did last year but the company is resplendent. The latest arrivals are Count Bibski and Count Muffski – vast estates, and such diamonds! I asked them about the Kingdom of Tishk. They had never heard of it. So Tamarind was an imposter – as we all thought. As for his journey to England, *he was here*, bragging on about how he had flown the Volga. Of course I cut him dead. The moment Bibski and Muffski appeared, *he vanished*! (Don't tell the dear Queen.)

When Tamarind, a political exile from the Kingdom of Tishk in the Urals, quitted Dreiviertelstein he intended to go to England, where he would study political economy and *le phlegme anglais*. He had not expected to leave Dreiviertelstein so soon, or understood why he left under a cloud – a cloud which suddenly gathered when he choked on a chicken-bone and Queen Aigle became so excited; but his intention was firm and heartfelt. One of the factors in the revolution which exiled him was that political economy was not sufficiently studied in Tishk; and though he had always admired spontaneity, Queen Aigle's declaration of love while he was choking made him think there was something to be said for taciturnity and calm.

He had crossed the frontier and was lodging economically at a mortal inn near Augsburg when in his bedroom, insufficiently tidied after a previous occupant, he found a pamphlet titled *Grub's Exposition of the Limited: an Account of the Grubian Philosophy*. Tamarind had often wished to have time for philosophy. It was a wet evening; he had had supper; he began to read.

The pamphlet opened with an account of Grub's career. He was the ninth son of a respected pig-breeder in Westphalia. As the family needed no more useful sons it was decided to make a scholar of him, and he was deposited with the Remigian Brothers, a teaching order, whose Superior reported for six years running that Hans (his given name) showed application but could do better. On returning home, he went through a period of storm and stress, learned to swim and took to horse-racing. Rashly ambitious, he put his mount to a jump it was not accustomed to. It reared, he was thrown, the horse fell and rolled on him. When pitying hands dragged him from under the animal, it was found he had broken both legs. It was at this moment that he conceived his Theory of the Necessity of Limitations to the exposition of which he vowed the remainder of his days. Beginning with the At Hand (in his case the parlour of the family home) he established that without its enclosing walls a room cannot functionally be. Complying with the walls' necessary solidity, those who wish to leave or enter the room must do so by a door, which is in itself a compensatory limit to the solidity of the wall. Further analysis led him to his Laws of Property and Tenure: a field must have boundaries before it can exist as a field; it is also governed by the limiting factor of Time: at the owner's death, he can no longer own it. From this, Grub soared to the heavens. Stars and planets observe their limits, therefore do not collide: only comets spurn limitations and dash about through space regardless; the reprehensibility of this is admitted in the international consensus that comets upset the weather and bode no good.

When the paternal Grub died Hans Grub, consoled by this further demonstration of the Necessity of Limitations, took his legacy and left home; hence forward he devoted himself to enlarging, deepening, enriching and codifying the theory which had flashed on him while he was under the horse. A modest man, he thought only of pleasing himself; but by degrees his theory became known, and its all-embracing adequacy admitted. He was resorted to by troubled souls, and calmed them; he was questioned by searching minds, and silenced them; he was invited to give a course of lectures. Those who saw him limp unhurriedly onto the platform (for his legs had mended unsymmetrically and he still needed a crutch), who listened to his clear and ample statements, who marked his simple but decent garments and, above all, his air of cheerful self-sufficiency (*selbstgenugsamkeit*) were almost unanimously reminded of Socrates (Grub was not, however, married), compared him favourably with Descartes, and realized that fulfilment could only be found in accepting the Necessity of Limitations and not barking the spiritual shins (*geistliche Schienbein zu abrinden*) by trying to transcend the necessarily untranscendable.

The rest of the pamphlet had been torn away.

But Tamarind was already so convinced by Grub's reasoning that applying the Grubian method he saw the removal of the rest of the pamphlet as imposing a providential limit, since it obliged him to settle down with what he had got and make the most of it. Like a handful of concentrated manure, it only needed to be spread. His first impulse was to return to Tishk where, brought to realize the necessity of limits, the savage gentry, the simple blood-stained peasantry, would accommodate themselves to their respective lots and form a harmonious society. If he re-entered the Kingdom of Tishk, the upper party would have him beheaded as a political subverter, the peasantry would tear him in pieces as a traitor to their cause. Nothing would be bettered and he himself would be the worse. Besides, he was on his way to England. Meanwhile, he would visit Grub. Grub had visitors, the pamphlet said so. He would find out where Grub lived and sit at his feet. He must first buy a firmly tailored surtout to hide his wings: Grub might not take a fairy seriously. Next he must buy a German dictionary. He had picked up a good deal of German while travelling in Styria, but it was not philosophical German: several fine compound adverbs in the pamphlet had stumped him.

There was, for instance, that statement that Grub had altogether wholly removed himself from his birthplace. The act was made plain: but where to? Neither the inn people, the tailor or the bookseller could tell him where the great Grub lived. Remembering that the world knows nothing of its greatest men, Tamarind visited several universities – places, he judged, where unwordly men studied the recondite. The universities were economically advantageous, for the unworldly men left a great deal lying about, but the name of Grub was unknown among them. He remembered that no man is a prophet in his own country – and that the disagreeable Lady Ulrica had expatiated on the Elfin Spa of Bad Nixenbach, and the number of distinguished foreign hypochondriacs she had met there: one of these might have come from somewhere sufficiently remote to have heard of the great Grub. He flew to Bad Nixenbach, buttoned on his surtout, spruced himself up, and bought a ticket to the Pump Room. While sipping what appeared to be warmish cabbage-water he caught sight of Lady Ulrica, who was examining him through her lorgnettes. Markedly avoiding her, he conversed with other drinkers, telling them briefly of the complicated chain of events which led him to seek out Grub. Minions of fashion, they cared neither for liberty or philosophy and knew nothing about Grub. One, indeed, surmised he must be dead; but it turned out he was thinking of Euclid.

Bad Nixenbach's parasitic shopkeepers (many of whom were fairies) were equally unrewarding. He was shaking off the dust of a Delicatessen, where he had been foiled in an attempt on a smoked eel and enquired in vain for Grub, when a voice from the doorway said, 'Never heard of Grub? You'd deny the Lord Jesus. That's a Grub cheese on your counter. I'd know it anywhere by the smell.' The speaker was a middle-aged mortal with a shopping basket. Tamarind seized on her. 'You know Grub, Grub the philosopher? Where can I find him?' 'The Grub I know is Bertha Grub, I always get my cheese from her. She lives in Old Nixenbach – Magdalen Lane, on the yonder side of the town. You'll know her place by the goats. Or you'd find her in Market Square, Tuesdays and Fridays. But I don't know about a philosopher – unless you mean her old uncle with the game leg.'

'I do, I do!' said Tamarind passionately. 'How can I show my gratitude?' Rummaging in a pocket he found a cake of soap from the Gentlemen's Cloakroom at Bad Nixenbach, pressed it into her hand, and asked the way to Old Nixenbach.

It was a distance of six miles, by a winding road, mainly uphill. Respect obliged him to approach on foot. The profile of Old Nixenbach (two spires and a verdigrised copper dome) remained obdurately on the horizon. When at last it condescended to be nearer, and then suddenly so much nearer that the dome disappeared behind the town wall, he was too hot and tired to feel anything beyond a sad certainty that just as when he had alighted on the western bank of the Volga he was immediately arrested as a spy some such formality would blemish his arrival in Old Nixenbach. He entered unmolested under a frowning archway. Except for a few dogs no one showed the least interest in him, and the mentio.. of Magdalen Lane made people look supercilious, and believe it might be in the suburbs. It took him a long time, many enquiries, many wrong turns down narrow twisting streets darkened by tall houses, before he found his way to Magdalen Lane, which in the course of enquiring for it, he learned was called Cow Lane. Cow Lane exactly described it. He was wishing he had not wasted the cake of soap on that misdirecting ignorant woman with the shopping basket when he smelled a reviving odour of goats. He quickened his steps, snuffing the air, and was imagining himself saying to Grub that goats have many classical associations when the door of a shed opened and a solidly constructed woman came out with a milk pail in either hand.

'Are you Miss Grub?' She set down the pails. 'I don't usually sell cheese at this hour.' 'But may I visit your honoured uncle?' As an afterthought, he asked if he might carry the milk pails. She preceded him across a muddy paddock to a one-story cottage with a lean-to, opened the lean-to door, signed to him to put down the pails. 'There!' she said. 'This is where I make my cheeses.' Tamarind looked round politely. The walls were bare and newly whitewashed. There were wide earthenware pans holding very white milk, several skimmers, wooden bats, drainers and other things; lengths of coarse wet muslin hung from a line and dripped; there was a pervading smell of sour milk. Tamarind disliked cheese, but he tried to sound appreciative as he said, 'How interesting!', and allowed a decent interval before saying, 'And now may I see your honoured uncle?' She opened a partition door into a low-ceilinged room, whose walls were also bare, and also whitewashed, though not so recently. Grub sat before the fire in a cushioned armchair. He was old, he was smoking a pipe, his feet were on a hassock, and a spittoon was beside him. The woman went back to her cheese room, Tamarind gazed with veneration at Grub. After a time, he said, 'Forgive me if I intrude . . .' At the same moment Grub took out his pipe and said, 'Well?' His voice was loud and gusty, he was probably deaf. Tamarind began again. 'I have come . . .'

'Where from?'

'From the Urals.'

Though almost overwhelmed by the realization that he was addressing the great Grub, Tamarind sketched the circumstances which compelled his departure from Tishk, and recounted the events of the journey (modifying his crossing of the Volga by introducing a raft, and bowdlerizing Dreiviertelstein to a gipsy encampment, in order to avoid any mention of wings) which led him to the inn where The Exposition of the Limited burst on him like the summons of a trumpet; the subsequent fruitless searching of universities, the good, unlettered woman at the Delicatessen, the final ascent . . . he broke off, leaving the rest to the eloquence of silence.

'Foolish to come all that way.'

It was the authentic voice of the Exponent of the Limited! Trembling, Tamarind waited for more.

'Brought anything with you?'

Tamarind searched in his pockets and pulled out a bag of pear-drops and a jar of caviare.

'A tribute – a pilgrim's poor tribute . . .' He sensed it was not enough, searched another pocket, found a half bottle of schnapps.

'Little,' pronounced the authentic voice. 'Little and often.'

Drinking steadily, Grub finished the half bottle, smiled, and fell into the blameless sleep of old age. Tamarind put more wood on the fire. It blazed up, and showed the idyllic austerity of the room, its bare walls, low ceiling, tiled floor, its boxlike assertion of limits, its content of the sleeping philosopher. Grub snored commandingly; from behind the partition wall came sounds of slapping and squelching, bursts of vigorous colloquial song. This was how to end one's days! One's conclusions reached, one's conversation whittled to essentials, one's wisdom matured and compacted (as with cheese), one's fame resounding in the monosyllable, Grub: a simple pyramidal identity, with a niece.

Tamarind could hardly wait for his old age. Meanwhile, he looked round for something to sit on. There were two stools; one was ricketty, the other uncomfortable, so he sat on the floor. When the niece came in she saw her uncle sleeping in his armchair, as he did every night, and Tamarind asleep on the floor. She tied on her uncle's nightcap and after thought fetched a rug and a bolster for Tamarind. She then picked up the pear-drops, the caviare, and the emptied bottle, and carried them away.

Tamarind continued to sleep on the floor. He had become part of the

Grub household – not so much a guest, for he had not been invited, as a habit. Every morning he rolled the rug round the bolster, thus providing himself with something to sit on during the day. Every evening he re-adjusted them into a bed, and fell asleep, garnering recollections of the words of wisdom which had fallen from Grub's lips; or if none had happened to fall, then lulled by the silence of a conscience that had nothing to take exception to. The sufficingness of the rug and the bolster symbolized how right he had been in his convictions: his dislike of etiquette and formality, his trust in the simple goodheartedness of the poor and oppressed, his acceptance of the Limited.

Life with the Grubs was regulated by the goats. When Bertha had milked, and staked them in the paddock to graze, she came in to wash and comb her uncle. When she had washed and combed herself, they ate a breakfast of bread and milk. At breakfast Grub was conversational, talking about the weather and telling his dreams. They were the dreams of an untroubled mind; he had been eating doughnuts; his nightcap had turned into a bishop's mitre. Afterwards, he lit his pipe and meditated. After the first day, when it was caviare, the mid-day meal was cheese. Supper was curds and whey, eaten early because by sundown the goats had to be milked and put back in their shed. Goats were as good as a clock and don't need winding, was a favourite observation of Grub's. Grub delighted in proverbs and proverbial comparisons. When Bertha had settled him for the night she habitually asked if he was comfortable, to which he habitually replied, 'Happy as a maggot in a nut.' Tamarind admired the consistency with which the great Grub rejected worldly, even philosophic terms of speech: it was the Necessity of Limitations exemplified in an acceptance of a way of life. He practised the same acceptance of the actual in regard to Tamarind. After the first evening's enquiries and Tamarind's explanatory narrative he showed no curiosity about Tamarind's past till two mornings later, when taking out his pipe he asked, 'Did they roast hedgehogs?' Tamarind, who had forgotten how he had bowdlerized Dreiviertelstein into a gipsy encampment, was at a loss. 'Did they roast hedgehogs in clay jackets?' amplified Grub. Tamarind recovered his wits, said they did and that the hedgehogs tasted delicious (he had always understood it was so). Grub said, 'Ah!' and resumed his meditation. Clay jackets, thought Tamarind. Of course, a variety of limitation: it was remarkable how unflaggingly Grub dwelt on the limited. He wished he could go further into the subject. His knowledge of it had ended where the pages had been torn out of the pamphlet.

Fortunately, there was one way in which he could solidly express his veneration. One morning Bertha, unexpectedly early to be out of a wrapper with her hair up, told him he must get his own breakfast as she was taking her cheeses to the market. The cheeses, dozens of them, were heaped in a hand-barrow. He offered to wheel the barrow part of the way. He wheeled it the whole way, Bertha following in case a cheese should fall off. As they neared the market the sharp morning air grew lively with voices, smells of fish and cabbage, new bread and hot coffee. He parted from Bertha, put on invisibility and went in search of a breakfast. A fairy's invisibility covers whatever is in his possession. A glass of hot coffee disappeared from the stall and reappeared empty. Tamarind was insinuating himself towards a mound of doughnuts when he remembered that Grub had dreamed of doughnuts, and took two, one for the philosopher, one for himself. They were good plump doughnuts, so he took four more to share between them. So far, he had stolen as a child might. Now he applied himself seriously to his mission, considering what would be the best value, rejecting apple tarts because the pastry would crush, choosing the sturdiest sausages. The caviare had not been a success with Bertha (possibly cheese had blunted her palate) so he added some smoked sprats, and more pear-drops as a concession to her femininity. By now the shops were opening. The wine-shop provided three half bottles of schnapps.

He could feel his invisible pockets bulging, so he waited for a quiet moment in Cow Lane before he made himself apparent.

This was the first of many excursions. As a matter of prudence, he distributed his attentions among the stall-holders and patronized more than one wine-shop. His personal fastidiousness prevented him from making as free with the fish-stall as he would have wished: some crawfish from the Nixenbach left an unpleasant clamminess in his pocket, eels, though coiling very conveniently, were slimy. He thought to overcome this difficulty by thieving from a charitable establishment which sold baskets made by the blind. But invisibility does not absolutely include impalpability. The basket was angular, and roomy; adjacent mortal marketers complained of being dug in the ribs and improperly assaulted. Quarrels arose. He had to give up the basket, and use plaited straw carriers instead.

None of this flawed his pleasure. Till now, he had never been responsible for others. A well-wisher to society, he had forwarded no interests but his own, expending his talents, his luck, his ingenuity, in looking after himself: he had lived in exile all his life. Now he was one of a household, and responsible for its well-being. The charm of being depended on was a thing he had never experienced, never imagined. It far excelled any satisfaction that could be sucked from the gratitude of the benefited (he had seen instances of that sort of thing and how poorly it worked out). Gratitude is conditional. Dependence, such dependence as that of the Grubs, is calm, implicit, inexhaustible. As Grub so often remarked, still waters run deep. Indeed, the surface of the Grub dependence was so unrippled by expressions of gratitude that the metaphor of running water was inappropriate; a pond would be nearer the mark. They received whatever he brought them, swallowed it, and were sure of more. Their calm trust in him touched Tamarind to the heart. It made him pleased with himself, and confident he could do better and be even more pleased. By nourishing the great Grub he had reached the end of six months' ambition. He had sought, he had found, he filled the Exponent of the Limited. And it had all come about quite naturally, a state of things to be taken for granted – a state of things taken for granted in mystic India where the disciple (he understood) is *ipso facto* also the purveyor.

If he could help it, there should never be another disciple.

Time went sweetly on. The goats were milked morning and evening, all day Bertha was busy making cheese. Tamarind had suggested that as the household was now not so dependent on cheese, she might crumble some and scatter it for the birds. She refused, saying it was wasteful to feed wild creatures who could fend for themselves. She had a womanly attachment to economy. If Tamarind came back with some unusual profusion she commented on it, though without censure. She took a peculiar pleasure in remainders. 'Look at all that pickled salmon left over! I can't use it for soup, we must finish it at breakfast.' Grub put by the schnapps bottle. 'The within is best. I will finish it now.' He did so, gravely and exactly, as if reverencing what he was about to contain. The salmon renewed his thirst. He took up the bottle. There was not much left in it, and there was not another bottle in the house.

Next morning Tamarind went to get more. Neither of the wine-shops had yet opened, so to pass the time he went for a stroll. It took him to the street by which he had first entered Old Nixenbach. He remembered the cobbles, the square beyond, where the dogs had snuffed him, the cart-rank with the chalked tariff for using it; it even seemed to him that he remembered some of the horses. Everything from the cobblestones to the verdigrized dome at the end of the square was endeared to him by the recollection of how dejected he had been – and how near his happiness. A procession came down a side street and entered the square. It was a funeral procession. The hearse had gilded skulls on its four corners, the coachman wore a gold-laced cocked hat, the horses were plumed. Mutes accompanied the hearse, and some black-scarfed mourners followed it. A few onlookers were gathered to watch it pass. Tamarind turned to one of them, and asked whose funeral it was.

'It's Doctor Grubenius. He came to give lectures, and honoured us by dying here. If he had been a citizen, the procession would have been larger.' Tamarind sighed. The procession reminded him that Grub was an old man, and mortal. His sigh was noticed.

'You knew Doctor Grubenius?'

The coffin was being carried into the church. He shook his head.

'Grubenius the Pragmatist. His grasp of the real renovated Moral Philosophy. In brief . . .'

The onlooker repeated precisely what Tamarind had read in the pamphlet, and added what in the pamphlet had been torn away.

'You should read his treatise, *The Exposition of the Limited.* You would find it most interesting – revelatory.'

A hen whose head has been chopped off can still make a few steps. Tamarind said, 'Indeed,' and walked away. Grub-Grubenius was dead and about to be buried. Grub-Grub was sitting by the fire and waiting for his schnapps and the mid-day meal. Bertha was slapping cheese. They had done him no harm. They had taken him in, a stranger. He had slept at Grub's feet. They were a simple, trustful, good-hearted pair . . . And they could go hang!

A yell, compounded of disillusionment, fury, woe, exasperation, burst from him. It was answered by a whinny. He turned on the mimic. The horse looked at him with a mild expression. It was harnessed to a two-wheeled cart. He leaped into the cart, gathered up the reins, lashed the startled beast into a gallop. They vanished under the archway, the noise of clattering hoofs died out on the Bad Nixenbach road.

THE DUKE OF ORKNEY'S
LEONARDO

The child, a boy, was born with a caul. Such children, said the midwife, never drown. Lady Ulpha was cold to the midwife's assurances; the same end, she said, could be reached by never going near water. She was equally indifferent to the midwife's statement that children born with a caul keep an unblemished complexion to their dying day. Lady Ulpha had long prided herself on her unblemished decorum. The violent act of giving birth, the ignominy of howling and squirming in labour and being encouraged by a vulgar person to let herself go, had affronted her. Seeing that encouragements were unwelcome, the midwife did not mention that cauls are so potent against drowning that mortals making a sea voyage will pay a great price for one. The child was washed and laid in the cradle, and a nurse given charge of it. As for the caul, by some mysterious negotiation it got to Glasgow. There it was bought by the captain of a whaler and subsequently lost at sea.

Sir Huon and Lady Ulpha were fairies with a great deal of pedigree, pride to match it, and small means for its upkeep. On the ground that it does not do to make oneself cheap, they seldom appeared at the Court of Rings, a modest Elfin kingdom in Galloway, preferring to live on their own estate, small and boggy, and make a merit of it. When the boy was of an age to be launched into the world, it would be different.

He was still spoken of as The Boy, because he had been named after so many possible legacy leavers that no one could fix a name on him, except his nurse, who called him Bonny – a vulgar dialect term which would get him nowhere. He was the most beautiful child in the world, she said, and would grow into the handsomest elfin in all Scotland. Looking at her child more attentively, Lady Ulpha decided that though he was now an expense, he might become an asset.

His first recollection of his mother was of being lifted onto her high bed to have his nose pinched into a better shape, his ears flattened to the side of his head, and his eyebrows oiled. As time went on, other measures were imposed. He had to wear a bobbing straw hat to shield him from getting freckles, and was forbidden to hug his pet lamb in case he caught ticks. In winter a woollen veil was tied over his face. This was worse than the hat, for it blinded him to his finer pleasures: the snow crystal melted in his hand, the wind blew the feathers away before he had properly admired them. Baffled by the woollen grating over his eyes, he came indoors, where sight was no pleasure. The veil was pulled off and he was set to study an ungainly alphabet straddling across a dirty page.

It was in summer that he got a name of his own. A trout stream ran through the estate, and as he couldn't be drowned he was allowed to play in it, provided he kept his hat on. Sir Glamie, Chancellor of the Court of Rings and an ardent fly-fisher, had permission from Sir Huon – who knew he would otherwise poach – to fish there on Wednesdays, provided he threw back every alternate fish. Having scrupulously thrown back a small trout, Sir Glamie approached a pool where he knew there was a large one. A ripple travelled toward him, and another. He saw a straw hat, and advanced on the poacher. Under the hat was a naked boy, whose limbs trailed in the pool. The boy was not even poaching, merely wallowing, and scaring every trout within miles; but as Sir Glamie drew nearer he saw that the boy was winged. 'Are you young what's-his-name?' he asked. The boy said he thought so. Sir Glamie said he was old enough to know his name. The boy agreed, and added, 'It used to be Bonny.' Sir Glamie replied that Bonny was a girl's name, and wouldn't do. Overcome by the boy's remarkable beauty, he had a rush of benevolence, and casting round in his mind remembered the worms, small and smooth and white, that fishermen call gentles, and impale on the hook when the water is too cloudy to use a fly. 'I shall call you Gentle,' he declared. By force of association, he took a liking to the boy, extricated him from Lady Ulpha's clutches, and took him to Court, where he was made a pet of and called Gentil.

It was not the introduction his parents had intended: it was premature, since clothes had to be bought for him and he would outgrow them; it was also patronizing, and made their heir seem a nobody. But as none of the legacies they invoked had responded, they submitted, called him Gentil, made him learn his pedigree by heart, and loyally attended banquets.

Gentil was scarcely into his new clothes before he grew out of them. A fresh outfit was under consideration when the need for it was annulled: the Queen made him one of her pages, and a uniform went with the appointment. For the first time in his life he was aware of his beauty, and gazed at his image in the tailor's mirror as though it were a butterfly or a snow crystal – a snow crystal that would not melt. At intervals, he remembered to be grateful to his parents, but for whose providence he might still be admiring the veined underwater pebbles without noticing his reflected face. It needed no effort to be grateful to his new friends at Court: to the Queen, who stroked his cheek; to her ladies, who straightened his stockings; to his fellow-pages, who shared their toffees with him; to Sir Glamie, who chucked him under the chin with a fishy hand and asked what had become of the hat; to Lady Fenell, the Court Harpist, who sang for him

> I love all beauteous things,
> I seek and adore them

– an old-fashioned ditty composed for her by an admirer, which exactly expressed his own feelings. For he, too, was a beauty lover, and loved himself with an untroubled and unselfish love.

Fenell's voice had grown quavering with age – she had actually heard Ossian – but her fingers were as nimble as ever, her attack as brilliant, and young persons of quality came from all over Elfindom to learn her method. The latest of these was the Princess Lief, Queen Gruach's daughter from the Kingdom of Elfwick, in Caithness. She had the air of being assured of admiration, but there was nothing beautiful about her except the startling blue of her eyes: a glance that fell on one like a splash of ice-cold water. During the reception held to celebrate her arrival, the glance fell on Gentil. It seemed like a command. He came forward politely and asked if there was anything she wanted. After a long scrutiny, she said, 'Nothing,' and turned away. He felt snubbed. Not knowing which way to look, he caught sight of Sir Huon and Lady Ulpha, whose faces expressed profound gratification. He knew they did not love him, but he had not realized they hated him.

If it had not been for Lady Ulpha's decorum, she would have nudged Sir Huon in the ribs. All that night they sat up telling each other that Gentil's fortune was made. There could be no mistaking such love at first sight. Gentil would be off their hands, sure of his future, sure of his indestructible good looks, with nothing to do but ingratiate himself with Queen Gruach and live up to his pedigree. And, as the castle of Elfwick stood on the edge of a cliff, the caul would not be wasted. The caul might count as an asset and be included in the marriage settlement.

It was just as they foresaw. Lief compelled Lady Fenell into saying she had nothing more to teach her (the formula for dismissing unteachable pupils), assaulted Gentil into compliance, and bore him off to Elfwick, where, after a violent set-to with Queen Gruach, she had him proclaimed her Consort and made a Freeman of Elfwick.

The ceremony was interrupted by the news that a ship was in the bay. Every male fairy rushed to the cliff's edge. Narrowing his eyes against the wind, Gentil was just able to distinguish a dark shape tossing on the black-and-white expanse of sea. He was at a loss to make out what the others were saying, except that they were talking excitedly, for they spoke in soft mewing voices, like the voices of birds of prey. Gulls exploded out of the dusk, flying so close that their screams jabbed his hearing. They, too, sounded wild with excitement. The sea kept up a continuous hollow booming, a noise without shape or dimension, unless some larger wave charged the cliff like an angry bull. Then, for a moment, there seemed to be silence, and a tower of spray rose and hung on the air, hissed, and was gone. Ducking to avoid a gull, Gentil lost sight of the ship. When he saw it again, it was closer inland. He saw it stagger, and a wave overwhelm it, emerge, and be swallowed by a second wave. There was a general groan. A voice said something about no pickings. A flurry of snow hid everything. He heard the others consulting, their voices dubious and discouraged. They had begun to move away, when a shriller voice yowled, 'There she is, there she is.' They gathered again, peering into the snow flurry. When it cleared, the ship was plainly visible, much smaller and farther out to sea. Everyone turned away and went back to the castle, where the ceremony was resumed, glumly.

When he said to Lief that he was glad to see the ship still afloat, and hoped no one on her was drowned, she said, embracing him, that he would never be drowned – that was all she cared for. He learned that Elfwick had rights over everything that came ashore – wreck, cargo, crew: the east wind blew meat and drink into Elfwick mouths. Next day

she walked him along the cliffs, and showed him where the currents ran
– oily streaks on the sea's face. A ship caught in a certain current would
be carried, willy-nilly, onto a rock called the Elfwick Cow, which
pastured at the entrance to the beach, lying so temptingly in the gap
between the cliffs. She pointed to a swirl of water above the rock, and
said that at low tide the Cow wore a lace veil – the trickle of spray left by
each retreating wave. He clutched at his retreating hopes. 'But if a sailor
gets to shore alive –' 'Knocked on the head like a seal,' she said, 'caul or
no caul. Cauls have no power on land.' Seeing him shiver, she hurried
him lovingly indoors.

Her love was the worst of his misfortunes. He submitted to it with a
passive ill will, as he submitted to the inescapable noise of the sea, the
exploitation of a harshly bracing climate. Wishing he were dead, he
found himself at the mercy of a devouring healthiness, eating grossly,
sleeping like a log. 'You'll soon get into our Elfwick ways,' Queen
Gruach remarked, adding that the first winter was bound to be difficult
for anyone from the south. She disliked her son-in-law, but she was
trying to make the best of him. If Gentil had inherited his parents' eye
for the main chance, he could have adapted himself to his advantages,
and lived as thrivingly at Elfwick as he had lived at Rings – where
everyone liked him, and he loved himself, and was happy. At Elfwick, he
was loved by Lief, and was appalled.

The first winter lasted into mid-May, when the blackthorn hedges
struggled into bloom and a three-day snowstorm buried them. The
storm brought another ship to be battered to pieces on the Elfwick Cow.
This time, the cold spared her plunderers the trouble of dispatching the
crew. The ship was one of the Duke of Orkney's vessels, its cargo was
rich and festive: casks of wine and brandy, a case of lutes (too sodden to
be of any use), smoked hams (none the worse), bales of fine cloth. In a
strong packing case and wadded in depths of wool was an oval mirror.
Lief gave it to Gentil, saying that the frame – a wreath of carved ivory
roses, delicately tinted and entwined in blue glass ribbons – was almost
lovely enough to hold his face. She was in triumph at having snatched it
from Gruach, who had the right to it. He thanked her politely, glanced at
his reflection, saw with indifference that he was as beautiful as ever, and
commented that he was growing fat. The waiting woman who had

carried the mirror stood by with a blank face and a smiling heart. To see the arrogant Princess fawning on an upstart from Galloway was a shocking spectacle but also an ointment to old sores.

Baffled and eluded, Lief continued to love her bad bargain with the obsession of a bitch. She beset him with gifts, tried to impress him by brags, wooed him with bribes. She watched him with incessant hope, never lost patience with him, or with herself; she was so loyal she did not even privately make excuses for him. If anyone showed her a vestige of sympathy, she turned and rent him. This and quarrelling with her mother were the only satisfactions she could rely on.

At first, she hoped it was winter that made him cold. Summer came, and Gentil was cold still – cold like a sea mist and as ungraspable. If she had believed in witches, she would have believed he was under a spell; but Caithness was full of witches – mortals all, derided by rational elfins. He was healthy, could swim like a fish, leap like a grasshopper – and none of this was any good to him, for he was without initiative, and had to be wound up to pleasure like a toy. The only thing he did of his own accord was sneak out and be away all day. Sometimes he brought back mushrooms, neatly bagged in a handkerchief. Otherwise, he returned empty-handed and empty-headed, for if she asked him what he had seen, he replied, 'Nothing in particular.'

And it was true. He could no longer see anything in its particularity – not the sharp outline of a leaf, not the polish on a bird's plumage. It was as though the woollen veil had been tied over his face again, the woollen grating that had barred him from delight. He saw his old loves with a listless recognition. Another magpie. Another rainbow. More daisies. They were the same as they had been last summer and would be next summer and the summers after that.

It was another April, and Gentil, wandering through the fields, was conscious only that a cold wind was blowing, when he heard a whistling – too long-breathed for a thrush, too thoughtful for a blackbird. The whistler was a young man, a Caithness mortal. He was repairing a tumbled sheepfold. Each time he stooped to pick up a stone, a lappet of black hair slid forward and dangled over one eye. Gentil was accustomed to mortals, took them for granted, and never gave them a thought. At the sight of the young man he was suddenly pierced with delight. The lappet of hair, the light toss of the small head that shook it back, the strong body stooping so easily, the large, deft hands nestling the stones into place were as beautiful and fit and complete as the marvels he had seen in his childhood. Weakened by love, he sat down on the impoverished grass to watch.

He went back the next day, and the morning after that he got up early and was at the sheepfold in time to collect some suitably sized stones and lay them in a neat heap at the foot of the wall. Love is beyond reason, and when the young man took stones from the heap as though they had been there all the time, Gentil was overjoyed. Civility obliged him to attend the celebrations on Gruach's birthday, telling himself furiously that no one would notice if he was there or not. On the morrow, he woke with such a release into joy and confidence that he even dawdled on his way to the sheepfold. It was finished, the young man was gone. Gentil took to his wings and flew in wide circles, quartering the landscape. A flash of steel signalled him to where the young man was laying a hedge.

This task had none of the scholarly precision of mending a dry stone wall. It was a battle of opposing forces, the one armed with a billhook, the other armoured in thorns. It was an old hedge, standing as tall as its adversary; some of the main stems were thick as a wrist, and branched at all angles with intricate lesser growths. Here and there it was tufted with blossoms, for the sap was already running. The young man, working from left to right, chose the next stem to attack, seized it with his left hand, bent it back, and half severed it with a glancing blow of the billhook. The flowing sap darkened the wound; petals fell. Still holding the upper part of the stem, he pressed it down, and secured it in a plaited entanglement of side branches, lesser growths, and brambles. Then he lopped the whole into shapeliness with quick slashes of his billhook. The change from dealing with stone to dealing with living wood changed his expression: it was stern and critical – there was none of the contented calculation which had gone with rebuilding the sheepfold.

It changed Gentil too – from a worshipper to a partisan. He hovered above the hedge, watching each stroke, studying the young man's face – how he drew down his black eyebrows in a frown, bit his lip. Secure in his invisibility, Gentil hovered closer and closer. They were moving on from a completed length of hedge when a twig jerked up from the subdued bulk. 'Look! Here!' – the words were almost spoken when the young man saw the twig and slashed at it. The bright billhook caught Gentil in its sweep and lopped off half his ear. Feeling Gentil's blood stiffening on his hand, the young man licked the scratch he had got from a thorn and went on working. Another length of hedge had been laid before Gentil left off being sick, and crept away.

Several times he trustingly lay down to die. The trust was misplaced; the cold shock and loss of blood forced him to rise from the ground into the clasp of the sunny air and walk on. When he tried to fly, he found he could not: the loss of half an ear upset his balance. He walked on and on, vaguely taking his way back to Elfwick and wondering how he could put an end to his shamed existence. He could not drown, but he remembered a place where a ledge of rock lay at the foot of the cliff, and if he could get that far he could let himself drop and be dashed to pieces. But he must make a detour, so that no one from the castle would see him.

Lief, impelled by her bitch's instinct, was there before him, not knowing why but knowing she must be. In any case, it never came amiss to look seaward: there might be another ship. He went past without seeing her. She grabbed him. As they struggled on the cliff's edge, she saw the bloody stump of his ear but held him fast.

As time went on Lief sometimes wondered whether it would not have been better to let him have his way. But she had caught hold of him before she saw what had happened, and her will to keep him was stronger than her horror at his disfigurement. So she fought him to a finish, and marched him back to the castle.

The return from the cliff's edge was perhaps the worst thing she had to endure. There were no more people about than usual but it seemed to her that every Court elfin was there, gathering like blowflies to Gentil's raw wound, turning away in abhorrence. It was natural, she accepted it. Elfwick had never lost the energy of its origin as an isolated settlement, embattled against harsh natural conditions: cold and scarcity, wind and tempest. Its savagery was practical, its violence law-abiding. Though it had grown comfort-loving, it had never become infected with that most un-Elfin weakness, pity. She herself nursed Gentil through his long illness without a tremor of pity traversing her implacable concern. She risked her reason to save him, exactly as the wreckers risked their limbs to snatch back a cask from the undertow, and she recognized the rationality and loyal traditionalism of the public opinion she defied. The mildest expression of it was Gruach's. 'He must be sent back to Rings.' While he was thought to be past saving (for the stump festered and his face and neck swelled hideously) there was hope. But the swelling went down and Gruach visited the sickbed to remonstrate in a motherly way against Lief's devotion. 'I chose him. I shall save him,' said Lief.

'But have you considered the future? It's not as though you were saving a favourite hound. He is your Consort, remember. How can you appear with such an object beside you? How could you put up with the indignity, the scandal, of his mutilation?' Lief replied, 'You'll see.' She put a bold front on it, but at times she despaired, thinking that if Gentil once left her keeping, public opinion would soon do away with him.

As it happened, this problem did not arise. No one was more horrified by his deformity than Gentil himself. He refused to be seen, he would have no one but Lief come near him. If she had to make an appearance at Court, he insisted that she lock him in and keep the key between her breasts. She still did not know what had happened. When she questioned him he burst into tears. She did not ask him again, for by then she was as exhausted by his illness as he, and only wanted to sit still and say nothing. They sat together, hour after hour, saying nothing, she with her hands in her lap, he fingering his ear.

The oncome of winter was stormy; two profitable ships were driven onto the Cow, the castle resounded with boasts and banquetings. Then for months nothing happened. A deadly calm frost clamped the snow, waves crept to the strand and immediately froze, the gulls flew like scimitars through the still air. Gentil sat by the fire, fingering his wound.

The smell of spring was breathing through the opened casement when he suddenly raised his head, looked round the room and on Lief, and said passionately, 'Everything is so ugly, so ugly!' Casting about for something to please him, Lief remembered her mother's gold and silver beads, which the Duke of Orkney had thought to hang round a younger neck. Schooling herself to be daughterly and beguiling, she persuaded Gruach to unlock her treasure chest, questioned, admired, put on the gold and silver beads, and asked if she could borrow them. And though Lief had never shown the least interest in the Duke of Orkney's importations, except when she carried off the oval mirror, Gruach thought she might be returning to her right mind, and handed over the beads and some other trifles. Gentil tired of running the beads through his fingers; a jewelled bird trembling on a fine wire above a malachite leaf and a massive gold sunflower with a crystal eye were more durable pleasures. Later, he was spellbound by a branching spray of coral. At the first sight of the coral, which to Lief was nothing to marvel at, since there was no workmanship about it, he gave a cry of joy that seemed to light up the room.

But this, too, eventually went the way of the sunflower and the bird. And when she brought fresh rarities to replace it, he thanked her politely and ignored them. Except for sudden fits of rage, when he screamed at her, he was always polite. The fits of rage she rather welcomed; they promised something she could get to grips with. It never came. He sat by the fire; he sat by the window; the maimed ear had thickened into an accumulation of flaps, one fast to another, like the mushrooms, hard as leather, that grow on the trunks of ageing trees and are called Jew's-ears. A scar extended down his cheek. The rest of him was lovely and youthful as ever.

Nothing deflects the routine of a court custom. The Freemen of Elfwick had no particular obligations except to wear a badge and have precedence in drinking loyal toasts at banquets; but in times of emergency they were expected to rally and attend committee meetings. Gentil was now summoned to such a meeting. Naturally, he did not attend. The emergency was still in the future, but it was inevitable, and must be faced with measures of economy, tightening of belts, and finding alternative sources of supply. For the Duke of Orkney was mortal, and over sixty – an age at which mortals begin to fall to bits. His heir was a miserly ascetic, always keeping Lents; there would be no more casks of wine and brandy, no more of those delicious smoked hams, no more candied apricots from Provence, fine cloth from Flanders, spices to redeem home-killed mutton from the aroma of decay; the Cow would advance her horns to no purpose, the Elfwick standard of living would fall catastrophically. The meeting closed with a unanimous recommendation to make sure of the Duke of Orkney's next consignment.

It could be expected before the autumnal equinox. Spies were sent out for hearsay of it, watchers were stationed along the cliffs, where they lolled in the sun, chewing wild thyme. It had been an exceptionally early harvest; rye and oats were already in stooks, rustling in the wind. It was a lulling sound, but not so to the Court Purveyor. For it was a west wind, and though it was gentle it was steady. Of all the quarters the wind could blow from he prayed for any but the west. With a west wind keeping her well out to sea, the Duke's ship would be safe from those serviceable currents that nourished the Cow. Elfwick would get nothing.

Subduing his principles, consulting nobody, the Purveyor put on a respectable visibility and sought out the nearest coven of witches. They were throwing toads and toenails into a simmering cauldron; the smell was intolerable, but he got out his request, and at the same time got out a purse and clinked it. 'A wind from the east?' said the head witch. 'You should go to my sister in Lapland for that.' He answered that he was sure a Caithness witch could do as well or better. She threw in another toad and said he should have his will. Handing over the purse, he asked if there was anything else he could supply. A younger witch spoke up. 'A few cats . . . seven, maybe.' 'Alive?' 'Oh, aye.' He carried the hamper of squalling cats to the place they commanded, and fled in trust and terror.

The storm which impaled the Duke of Orkney's ship on the Elfwick Cow did so at a price. Hailstones battered down the stooks and froze the beehives. A month's washing was whirled away from the drying yard. Shutters were torn from their hinges, fruit trees were uprooted, pigs went mad, the kitchen chimney was struck by lightning, the Purveyor, clutching at his heart, fell dead. Lief stepped over him on her way out. The clamour of wind and voices, the reports of a superb cargo, of a cargo still at hazard, had been more than she could withstand. Settling Gentil with a picture book, she locked him in, put the key in her bosom, and ran to the cliff's edge. Bursts of spray made it difficult to see what was going on. She caught sight of a Negro, fighting his way to shore against the suck of the undertow. He was down, he was up again, still grasping an encumbering package. It was wrenched from him by the undertow; he turned back. When she could see him again, he had retrieved it. Curious to know what it was he guarded so jealously, she descended the path. By the time she reached the strand, he had been dispatched, and lay sprawled over his package – an oblong wooden box, latticed with strips of iron – as though he would still protect it. She tried to pull it from under him, but it was too heavy for her to shift. More and more plunder was being fetched ashore. She stood unnoticed in the jostle till one of the Freemen tripped over the Negro. He started at seeing Lief there, and panted out felicitations: never had the Cow done better for Elfwick. She told him that the Negro's box was hers, under the old law of Finders Keepers; he must call off one of the wreckers to carry it after her to the castle.

On the cliff's summit she stopped to look back. Twitches of lightning played incessantly over the sea. Remade by wind and tempest, she felt a lifetime away from Gentil; when the grunting porter asked what to do with the box, she had forgotten it existed.

Yet in the morning the box was the first thing in her mind. Gentil had a cat's pleasure in anything being unpacked: had a crate been large enough, he would have jumped in and curled up in it. The box was brought to her apartment, the castle's handyman called in. Practised in such duties, he made short work of it. The iron bands were eased and tapped off, screw after screw withdrawn. At intervals he remarked on the change in the weather. The wind had fallen as suddenly as it had come up, and when he had finished the box he would see to the shutters, and then the pigsties, which the pigs in their frenzy had torn through like cannonballs. This box, though, was a different matter. Made of solid mahogany, it would baffle the strongest pig in Scotland. He laid the screws aside and raised the lid. Whatever lay within was held in place by bands of strong twine and wrapped in fold on fold of waxed linen. The handyman cut the twine, bowed, and went away. Gentil came out of hiding. Kneeling by the box, Lief lifted the oblong shape and held it while Gentil unwound the interminable wrappings. The oblong turned into a frame, the frame held a padding of lamb's wool. Gentil folded the linen and smoothed it affectionately. Pulling away the lamb's wool, he was the first to see the picture.

It was the half-length portrait of a young man, full face and looking directly before him. Behind him was the landscape of a summer morning. Wreaths of morning mist, shining in the sun, wandered over it. Out of the mist rose sharp pinnacles of mountain, blue with distance yet with every rocky detail exactly delineated. A glittering river coiled through a perspective of bronzed marshes and meadows enclosed by trees planted in single file, each tree in its own territory of air. It was as though a moment before they had been stirring in a light wind which now had fallen. Everything lay in a trance of sunlight, distinct, unmoving, and completed. Only the young man, turning his back on this landscape, sat in shadow – the shadow of a cloud, perhaps, or of a canopy. He was not darkened by it; but it substantiated him, as though he and the landscape belonged to different realities. He sat easily erect, with his smooth, long-fingered young hands clasped like the hands of an old man round a stick. His hair hung in docile curls and ringlets, framing the oval of his face. He had grey eyes. In the shadow which substantiated him, they were bright as glass, and stared out of the canvas as though he were questioning what he saw, as smilingly indifferent to the answer as he was to the lovely landscape he had turned his back on.

Lief tired under the effort of holding up the picture. She propped it against a chair, and went round to kneel beside the kneeling Gentil and discover what it was he found so compelling. The likeness was inescapable: Gentil was gazing at himself in his youth, at the Gentil who had come forward and asked if there was anything she wanted; she had said, 'Nothing,' and nothing was what she had got. Tears started to her eyes and ran slowly down her cheeks. She shook her hand impatiently, as if to dismiss them. He turned and looked at her. The sun shone full on her face. He had never seen her cry. The glittering, sidling tears were beautiful, an extraneous beauty on an accustomed object. He shuffled nearer and stared more closely, entranced by the fine network of wrinkles round her eyes. She heard him give a little gasp of pleasure, saw him looking at her with delight, as long ago he had looked at an insect's wing, a yellow snail shell. Cautiously, as though she might fly away, he touched her cheek. She did nothing, said nothing, stretched the moment for as long as it could possibly last. They rose from their knees together and stood looking at the picture, each with an arm round the other's waist.

Love – romantic love, such as Lief had felt for Gentil, Gentil for the young man at the sheepfold – was not possible for them. In any case, elfins find such love burdensome and mistrust it. But they grew increasingly attached to each other's company, and being elfins and untrammelled by that petted plague of mortals, conscience, they never reproached or regretted, entered into explanations or lied. This state of things carried them contentedly through the winter. With the spring,

Gentil astonishingly proclaimed a wish to go out-of-doors, provided he went unseen. Slinking out after midnight, they listened to owls and lambs, smelled honeysuckle, and ate primroses chilled with dew.

After the sweetness of early morning it was painful to return to the stuffiness of the castle, its oppressive silence shaken by snores. Gentil planned stratagems for escaping into daylight: he could wear a sunbonnet; they could dig an underground passage. But the underground passage would only deliver him up to the common gaze, the sunbonnet expose him to a charge of transvestism – more abhorrent to Elfwick than any disfigurement, and certain to be more sternly dealt with. Seeing him again fingering his ear and staring at the morning landscape behind the young man in the painting, Lief racked her brains for some indoor expedient which might release him from those four walls. Build on an aviary? Add a turret? The answer swam into her mind, smooth as a fish. The court library! It was reputed to be a good one, famous for its books of travel. And was totally unvisited. She had heard that some of the books of travel were illustrated. Gentil enjoyed a picture book. The midsummer mornings which had curtailed their secret expeditions now showed a different face: no one would be about at those unfrequented hours of dawn.

No one was. The snores became a reassurance and even a blessing, since they could be timed to smother the squeaks of the library door. Gentil sat looking at the travel books and Lief sat listening to the birds and looking at Gentil. One morning, he gave a cry of delight, and beckoned her to come and see what he had found. It was a woodcut in a book about the Crusades – a battle scene with rearing horses and visored warriors. It was unlike Gentil to be so pleased with a battle scene, but he was certainly in a blaze of joy. He pointed to a warrior who was not visored, whose villainous dark face was muffled in a wimplelike drapery, whose eyes rolled from beneath a turban. 'That ... that ... that's what I need, that's what I must have!' She said it would be ready that same evening.

Having embraced Islam, Gentil found a new life stretching before him. Turbaned and wimpled, he appeared at Court, kissed the Queen's hand, sat among his fellow-Freemen, studied sea anemones. This was only an opening on wider ambitions. It seemed excessive to go to Mecca, and Lief did not wish to visit his parents. But they went to Aberdeen, travelling visibly and using the alias of Lord and Lady Bonny. From Aberdeen they took ship to Esbjerg and inspected the Northern capitals. As travellers do, they bought quaint local artifacts, patronized curiosity shops, attended auctions. One has to buy freely in order to discover the run of one's taste. They discovered that what they most liked was naturalistic paintings. They concentrated on the Dutch School, Lief buying seascapes, Gentil flower pieces, and by selling those which palled on them they made money to buy more. In course of time, they acquired a number of distinguished canvases, but never another Leonardo.